A HEART OF
GOLD

A HEART OF GOLD

STACY HENRIE

Mirror Press

Interior Design by Cora Johnson
Edited by Kelsey Down and Lisa Shepherd
Cover design by Stacy Henrie and Rachael Anderson
Cover Image Credit: Arcangel

Published by Mirror Press, LLC
ISBN: 978-1-952611-00-1

For Monique,

Whose support and validation will never be forgotten

PROLOGUE

Montana, August 1894

FROM HER PERCH on the front steps, seventeen-year-old Octavia Rutherford peered through the gloaming light toward the road that ran alongside the Double R Ranch—same as she had every night this week. Jess Lawman, their former ranch hand, had promised in his last letter that he would finally be returning. And so Tava kept watch for him.

Seven months without Jess had felt eternally long. Only the memory of the kiss they'd shared the night before Jess had left, and the letters they'd exchanged, had kept Tava from despairing that the man she loved might never come back.

Movement on the road made her suddenly snap to attention. Her heart thrummed faster, even before the horse and rider turned down the drive. Tava rushed to her feet, her gaze locked on the face beneath the man's wide-brimmed, flat-crowned hat. Even at this distance, she recognized the upward tilt of those masculine lips.

She nearly sprinted forward to greet Jess, but an unexpected shyness stopped her, freezing her in place as he dismounted beside the corral. Should she hug him? Kiss him? Tell him right away that her feelings for him had only grown stronger in his absence?

1

Tava had been fourteen when Jess had first come to work on the ranch, yet she'd been instantly enamored with the thin young man with blue-green eyes, an infectious grin, and an occasional bout of grumpiness. From the start, Jess had talked to her as if she were an adult. He also liked to listen to her sing and didn't seem to mind that she was different from the other girls her age. The young ladies at church and in town didn't often dress in masculine clothes, and none of them had been raised solely by a father since the age of eight.

More than three years had passed since Jess's arrival at the ranch, and the man before her hardly resembled the seventeen-year-old adolescent he'd once been. Ranch work had given him a strong physique and enhanced his already handsome face. Tava had changed too. She wasn't a gangling girl anymore, though she still preferred trousers or a sensible skirt to dresses. Thankfully, Jess didn't care what she wore. He had even called her beautiful the night before he'd left.

With his horse secured, Jess turned to face her, that familiar grin in place. "Hey there, songbird."

The nickname—one he'd come up with the first time he had overheard her singing to herself—dissolved her uncertainty. "Jess!" she cried, jumping off the porch.

Tava met him halfway across the yard and threw her arms around him, knocking his hat to the ground. Laughing, Jess easily caught her and swung her around.

"I missed you," he murmured in her ear before setting her back on her feet.

"I missed you too."

She kept her hands looped about his neck as she stared unabashedly at him, their eyes nearly level. She was tall for a girl, like her mother had been, which meant she and Jess were nearly the same height. Kissing him all those months ago hadn't proven to be difficult, not when they stood nose to nose.

Would Jess kiss her again? Tava had often pictured their reunion in her mind, and it had always included a fervent kiss. But they wouldn't be alone for much longer.

"In a few minutes, my pa and Oscar and Rita are going to notice you're back." She paused, her pulse racing anew at the bold words she planned to say. "Still, I think there's time to steal a welcoming kiss—if you want."

She'd expected her words to draw another smile from him, but Jess's mouth tipped downward instead. A pained expression creased the tanned features of his face.

"Tava . . ." He slowly unwound her arms and lowered them to her sides, though he kept a gentle grip on her wrists. "We're friends, me and you, the very best of friends. But that's all we can be."

"I—I don't understand." Tava studied him with growing confusion. "What about our letters?"

They'd written each other at least once a week for the past seven months. In almost every letter, they'd each confessed to thinking daily, if not hourly, about the other. And Jess had consistently closed each missive with *Yours always.*

Except for his last letter. At the end of that one, he'd simply signed his name. Tava had assumed it was because he'd been so intent on sharing the happy news of returning to the ranch—and to her—that it had slipped his mind to close in the usual way. But maybe the small change had signified something larger. Something she hadn't wanted to analyze until now.

Ignoring her nigglings of doubt, Tava had one more piece of evidence that would refute Jess's declaration to remain just friends. "What about our kiss the night before you left?" She hadn't dreamt that up any more than she had his letters, which she'd tucked inside a metal tin that held several of her late mother's things.

3

Jess visibly swallowed at the question, then glanced away. "That kiss probably shouldn't have happened. But I hated the thought of leaving you, and you looked so pretty with your cheeks all pink from the cold." The line of his shoulders tensed as he returned his gaze to hers. "That still doesn't excuse me from getting caught up in the moment, and for that, I'm sorry."

"It wasn't all you. I kissed you back, Jess," she countered, though her words held more plea than protest. Other than his initial greeting, nothing about their reunion had gone as she'd hoped it would.

The look in his blue-green eyes begged for her to understand. But understand what? His reaction to finally being home again made no sense to her.

"I won't say the kiss wasn't wonderful, 'cause it was." Jess released one of her hands and motioned to the gap between them. "But we have to keep this between us to friendship."

Tava pulled free of his grasp altogether. "Why?"

When he didn't answer right away, something cold and painful lodged around her heart. She'd been so certain his feelings for her had remained unchanged in his absence. Now she could see she'd been horribly mistaken.

"You know how much I respect and admire your pa. But Quinn isn't going to take kindly to discovering there might be more than friendship between me and his only daughter. Especially when that daughter is still young." Jess's tone sounded resigned, as if he'd already rehearsed this speech a dozen times to himself. "Besides, just because I've been here, every day, for the past three years doesn't mean there aren't better men in town when it comes time for you to start courting."

She glowered at him as anger swept away the pain inside her. At least it stung less than the hurt. "You haven't been here

4

every day for months. How do you know I haven't already received interest from some of the men in town?" In truth, she hadn't noticed any other man since meeting Jess, nor she did want to.

"I'd say they're lucky to have earned your interest and your trust." He had to know she was bluffing, but rather than call her out like he normally would, he'd chosen to compliment her instead.

The realization made his rejection smart even worse.

"So that's it then? You want to go back to being friends and nothing more." It was Tava's turn to swallow hard. "And that won't ever change . . ."

Jess visibly cringed, but that didn't stop him from nodding. "Yes, that's what I'm saying."

With a backward step, Tava widened the distance between them. She wanted to press him for the real answer behind him changing his mind—not the cracker-thin one about her being young or the more substantial one about her father. After all, her age hadn't bothered Jess seven months ago, and her pa could surely be persuaded, in time, to consider Jess as a potential suitor for her.

But any attempt to learn the truth would be futile. Jess could be every bit as stubborn as Tava herself, and that meant he wasn't going to relent his current stance. He was drawing a firm line between them. One that allowed for nothing but friendship, now or in the future.

"You're back, Jess!" The sudden appearance of her father now came as a relief rather than a bother. Rita, their housekeeper and cook, gave a happy cry as she and her husband, Oscar, followed Quinn into the yard.

Unshed tears clogged Tava's throat, but she refused to cry in front of everyone, especially Jess. She blinked rapidly and moved toward his horse. "I'll take of care of Bounder," she managed to choke out, "so you can head inside with the others."

"Tava, wait," Jess quietly entreated.

When she glanced at him, she saw her inner torment mirrored in his expression. The sight of it should have eased her heartbreak, but the sight of his regret cut her as deeply as his decision.

"Welcome home, Jess," she whispered. Then, after turning away, Tava led his horse toward the barn as her tears slipped silently down her cheeks.

1

"LETTER FOR YOU, Miss Rutherford."

Tava spun away from the board of advertisements she'd been perusing with little interest. Had she heard the man correctly? She'd come to the post office today more out of habit than any real expectation of receiving something. Ten months of silence could do that to a person's hopes, crushing them beneath a mountain of disappointment and worry.

"You're sure?" She tossed her dark-brown braid over her shoulder and gripped the counter with both hands.

The postmaster, Mr. Turnstill, chuckled in amusement, but his eyes shone with kindness. "Unless your name isn't Octavia Rutherford anymore, the envelope's addressed to none other but you."

"Yes . . ." Tava nodded, the wide brim of her flat-crowned hat tipping farther into view with the movement. "That's my name."

Mr. Turnstill smiled. "Then here you go."

She accepted the envelope, feeling as if she held one of the gold nuggets coming out of the Klondike River and its tributaries rather than ordinary paper. "Thank you."

His response was lost on her as Tava moved slowly toward the door. Her finger traced the faded handwriting. The familiarity of those strokes drew unexpected tears to her eyes. She pulled in a steadying breath to be rid of the moisture—she didn't need anyone in town seeing her snivel over a letter.

Standing halfway inside the post office door and halfway out, she examined the envelope. Its worn appearance made it look as if it had crawled out of the wilds of Northern Canada. Tava feared it would fall to pieces if she handled it too much. Carefully, she broke the only part of the seal still intact and gingerly withdrew the two sheets of paper tucked inside. She unfolded them, not yet fully believing what she held. Then she read the salutation.

My dearest Tava . . .

He'd written—at last! Pressing the letter to her shirt, Tava rushed out of the building, nearly colliding with two girls who stood on the sidewalk out front. They appeared to be several years shy of Tava's twenty-one, though both of them wore long skirts and coiffed hair. Her mother would have heartily approved of their feminine attire.

"I'm sorry," Tava murmured as she squeezed past them.

She didn't miss their looks of contempt when they noticed her masculine shirt and vest and the shorter hemline of her skirt. Not that she cared what they thought of her appearance. They weren't running a ranch in a father's absence. Though, truth be told, Tava had worn trousers or shorter skirts since the age of eight. The only exception was church on Sundays. That day she always donned a dress, in hopes of appeasing her childhood guilt over thwarting her mother's countless attempts to raise a proper young lady.

Feminine giggles followed after Tava, causing her cheeks to heat with self-consciousness. But when she glanced back at the girls, she discovered they weren't watching her. They were ogling her Jess, who was loading the wagon with the supplies they'd purchased earlier.

From beneath his hat, his light-brown hair could barely be seen. However, his handsome, tanned face and jaw were still visible. And his rolled shirtsleeves showed the muscles of his forearms, which flexed as he lifted a heavy crate into the wagon bed.

Tava wanted to roll her eyes at the girls' blatant interest. After all, it was only Jess. He'd been working at the Double R Ranch for the past seven years. But as much as Tava wanted to pretend she didn't understand why the pair had taken notice of Jess, she couldn't. She, too, had been smitten with him. There had even been a time when she was sure he felt the same.

But she'd been wrong.

Tava still stung with remembered pain and embarrassment at the memory of the night almost four years ago when Jess had changed his mind about them being sweethearts. And yet Tava had learned a valuable lesson. To view Jess as anything other than a friend would lead her straight back to having her heart broken again.

In the weeks following that night, she and Jess had both struggled to resume their former bond. Eventually they had. However, it had taken Tava much longer—months, even—to fully bury her feelings for him.

All of that was in the past. She and Jess were close friends—nothing more, nothing less—and had been for several years now. And if there were times when Tava needed distance from him in order to reaffirm that fact inside her head, the ranch provided enough space and work to achieve that.

"Jess, look," she called out, holding her letter aloft as she hurried toward the back of the wagon. "It's from my pa!"

Jess straightened so fast he nearly dropped the bag of flour he'd hefted. "Quinn finally wrote?" His blue-green eyes shone with as much elation and incredulity as Tava had felt inside the post office. "What did he say?"

"I don't know. I haven't read it yet."

He narrowed his gaze in mock exasperation before settling the flour sack in the wagon and reaching for the next one. "What are you waiting for, songbird? I'm as anxious as you to hear what he has to say."

"All right, all right. Don't get your dander up." She pretended to huff.

Jess thought the world of her father. And in spite of not saying much about the lack of letters from Quinn, Jess had seemed as concerned as Tava.

She began to read the missive aloud while Jess completed the task of loading their supplies. Once he finished, they both climbed onto their respective sides of the wagon seat.

Tava had insisted long ago that she didn't need anyone's help getting in or out of the wagon; she could manage on her own. At the time her father had shaken his head, clearly believing her stubbornness had reared its head again. Tava couldn't tell him the true reason for being adamant—that she didn't want to risk having Jess hold her hand to assist her, thereby confusing her already bruised heart.

Jess took up the reins and guided the horses down the street as Tava continued reading. The only other letter she'd received from her pa had arrived last August. In it, Quinn had described his journey by steamer from Seattle to Alaska. This second missive spoke of new places, ones mentioned in the newspapers that Oscar Poole, the ranch's bronco buster, religiously read: Dyea, the Chilkoot Pass, the Yukon River. Her pa described a mountain trail so steep he had to crawl on hands and knees, rapids that could tear a boat to splinters, and hundreds of fellow gold seekers anxious to reach the Klondike before winter set in.

4

"*I arrived in Dawson City ten days ago,*" Tava read toward the end of the letter. "*But I've taken ill and haven't yet been able to do much on my claim. Give my best to Jess, the Pooles, and everyone else on the ranch.*"

Regret sliced through her as Tava lowered the pages onto her lap. "He clearly hasn't received my last letter, telling him I had to let all of our ranch hands go."

"It's all right, Tava." Jess shot her a sympathetic look. "Your pa would have done the same thing if he'd still been here. You're doing your best to keep from losing the ranch altogether."

His reassurance soothed a little of her remorse. She'd hated having to say goodbye to their loyal ranch hands, but Tava hadn't been able to afford to pay them anymore.

The nationwide depression of '93 might be over, yet the mortgage her father had taken out prior to that still had to be paid. That was the reason Quinn had decided to go to the Klondike in the first place. He hoped to mine enough gold to pay off the bank and keep the ranch solvent.

"Is that the end of the letter?" Jess prodded.

Tava lifted the sheets of paper once more. "Almost." She found her place and resumed reading: "*Remember that I'm praying for you every night, my dear daughter, and look forward to the day we'll be reunited.* Then he ends with, *All my love, Pa.*"

She could almost hear those endearing words spoken in her father's voice rather than her own. Tears threatened once more. After all the waiting, to finally hear from him, to know he was all right . . . Through the sheen of moisture in her eyes, Tava caught sight of something scrawled in the bottom left-hand corner of the letter.

"There's a postscript." She blinked and brought the page closer to her face to read the smudged words. "It doesn't look like Pa's handwriting, though, and it's signed by someone named Nelly."

"Nelly? Hmm. What does she say?"

"'Your father asked me to mail this for him. He's very sick at present but has a strong will. I'm hopeful he'll revive soon.'"

The troubled look Jess threw her way squeezed at Tava's heart as much as the stranger's note. "What's the date on the letter?" Jess asked.

Tava glanced back at the first page. "The end of October."

"He's probably well by now."

She nodded agreement. "You're probably right." Still, Tava couldn't completely squelch the feeling of uneasiness that crept over her as she refolded the missive and tucked it back inside its fragile envelope.

Two letters in a sea of silence—it wasn't much to go on. How had things been for her father since October? Was he truly recovered from his illness? Had he written them another letter at Christmas time? The winters lasted longer in the Yukon, which would affect the mail. But if her father had been healthy enough to write, wouldn't that letter have made it out around the same time as the one she clutched between her fingers?

"We can come to town next week," Jess said, nudging her with his shoulder. "There'll likely be a whole stack of letters waiting for you by then."

Tava offered him a smile as she bumped him back. "Maybe so. At least we know he made it to Dawson City and staked a claim." She smoothed one of the creases on the envelope, but it wouldn't lie flat after she moved her hand away.

Since her mother's death, she and her father had never spent more than a few nights apart. Now nearly a year had come and gone since he'd left, and she missed him so much.

6

Outwardly, Tava hadn't changed much in that time. Her nose still sported the freckles she'd assumed she would outgrow. Her hair was about the same length too, since Rita had cut it last month. But there were things inside her that had changed. She'd learned to make hard decisions and to lead others in her pa's absence. Her love for the ranch had grown as well, along with the determination to keep it. Yet she found herself smiling and singing far less than she once had.

There were constants in her life that did bring her solace. The daily ranch work, Sunday church services, and the three people who would sit down to supper with her tonight, including Jess.

Tava shot a sideways glance in his direction. Had he noticed those girls in town coquettishly watching him? Tava had never seen him pay particular attention to any young ladies at church or heard him mention being sweet on a girl. At twenty-five years old, he was of an age to settle down, maybe even homestead a place of his own. However, other than a seven-month absence years ago, he'd chosen to remain at the Double R. Tava had half expected him to go with her father to the Klondike, but Jess had stayed behind.

Some days she wanted to ask what kept him at the ranch, year in and year out. Other days, she was content with not knowing the answer—she was simply grateful to have him around.

"Thinking about your pa?" Jess turned his head to look at her.

Tava blushed and lowered her gaze. If she confessed that Jess himself had been the real subject of her thoughts, he would likely think she fancied him again. And she didn't. Every now and then, though, there were moments when those old feelings attempted to flicker to life. Moments when Jess smiled at her or called her by her nickname or listened to her without judgment. Yet recalling his rejection usually helped to snuff those feelings right out again.

"I hope my father's all right," she replied, dodging Jess's question. "Not knowing for certain how he's doing is almost harder than having him gone."

Jess dipped his chin in a nod. "I agree."

"You miss him too, don't you?"

"Quinn has been more of a father to me than my own ever was." Jess stared hard at the road ahead. "When I first came to the ranch, I'd sometimes pretend that I'd always lived there. That your pa was mine too."

Jess rarely spoke about his life before coming to the Double R. For a moment, Tava peered wordlessly at him. "I guess we would have officially been brother and sister then."

"Officially?" Some unnamed emotion darkened the color of his eyes as he glanced her way, but Tava couldn't identify what it might be.

She fingered the envelope in her lap. "I've heard people at church commenting on how we act more or less like brother and sister."

"Have they?" His jaw tightened as he faced forward again.

Tava frowned. "Does that bother you?" Would he tell her that they couldn't act like siblings now? How that differed much from being the best of friends, she couldn't say.

Rather than answering, Jess changed the subject. "You still planning on taking over the kitchen when Rita visits her daughter next week?"

The Pooles' daughter had recently given birth to twins, and Rita had toyed with the idea of going to Idaho to help the family for a few weeks. Tava had encouraged her to go. The older woman had seemed a bit displaced with so few to cook for in the past month and a half.

"I don't mind making the meals," Tava said with a shrug.

Jess tossed her a teasing smile. "You haven't asked if Oscar and I will mind."

"Very funny." She elbowed him in the ribs. "I managed things in the kitchen before Rita and Oscar came to work for us when I was twelve."

"And remind me again where you learned to cook?"

Despite blushing a second time, Tava straightened on the wagon seat and pretended to peer down her nose at Jess. "Some from my mother, but mostly from my pa and our old roundup cook, Gimpy."

"Which is why you make the best beans and cornbread this side of the Rockies."

When she glared at him, he laughed all the harder. "I can make other things too. I baked that cake for your birthday the year you turned twenty-one."

"I remember," Jess murmured, his tone strangely somber.

They'd celebrated his birthday early, since that was the year Jess had decided to leave the ranch and see the world. His ambition hadn't lasted long. Seven months later, he'd returned to the Double R.

He'd never told her where he had gone during those months or what he'd been doing. From Tava's perspective, the only thing to come from his time away had been his decision that they remain friends.

"You and Oscar are welcome to take turns cooking too." The words held more lightheartedness than Tava felt, but she didn't want to dwell on the past any more than she already had today. "Your flapjacks aren't half bad."

To her relief, the gravity slipped from Jess's face. "Half bad? Rita herself taught me how to make those." He shifted the reins to one hand and used the other to tickle Tava in the side before she realized what was happening.

"No fair," she protested, squirming to the far edge of the seat. "I'm going to have to jump off." But she couldn't help laughing.

That is, until Jess caught her wrist as she tried to tickle him back.

"Admit my flapjacks are every bit as good as your beans." The intensity of his gaze and the low hum of his voice felt at odds with the playful challenge.

Tava swallowed hard, her pulse thudding erratically with sudden anticipation. But what did she hope would happen? It wasn't as if Jess would tug her close and kiss her. Whatever she read in his eyes and soft tone wasn't real—he was merely teasing her.

"All right." She tugged her hand free. "Your flapjacks are as good as my beans."

It took a moment, but Jess finally nodded. "Thank you."

"They don't compare with my cornbread, though."

His deep laugh washed over her, drawing another smile from Tava. "You're something else, songbird."

She knew right then what he was trying to do. Jess was hoping to bolster her flagging spirits by making her laugh, as he had countless times over the past seven years.

While she didn't like the chance reminders of what they might have shared if Jess hadn't insisted on staying friends, he was still here in her life. And, for Tava, there was comfort in that constant too.

Brother and sister? Hah!

Scowling, Jess plunged the pitchfork into the hay and tossed the feed more vigorously than usual into the nearby stall. If Tava—and those at church—thought he viewed her as a sister, then he'd earned himself congratulations for hiding his true feelings for her all these years. Yet rather than a sense of victory, he felt annoyed . . . and unexplainably tired.

In reality, he'd never stopped loving Tava. She was beautiful, caring, and strong. And she deserved someone with an unmuddied past, instead of someone still carrying around the weight of his mistakes. Mistakes Jess had quickly learned could easily be repeated away from the ranch.

Most days he kept his regard for Tava in check—he felt certain not even Quinn or the Pooles suspected his feelings for her. If his feelings did attempt to resurface, Jess knew how to snuff them with hard work. Still, there were times when his heart took over and he acted without thinking. Tickling Tava earlier had been such a moment. However, after seeing his own concern for her father in her worried demeanor, Jess had hoped to make her laugh.

When she had, the effect had been breathtaking. Her rich brown eyes had lit up, and errant strands of her hair had caressed the adorable freckles that still dotted her nose and cheeks.

He hadn't been able to stop himself from capturing her hand in his. Thankfully, Tava had slipped out of his grasp before he'd done something really foolish—like tuck her hair behind her ear or kiss the skin beneath her wrist. Either action would have revealed too much, leading to Tava finally calling him out on his own ruse about staying friends and nothing more.

Jess wiped his sleeve across his damp forehead. He'd volunteered to unload the wagon and see to the horses himself. His excuse for working alone had been easy enough to contrive; Rita and Oscar would want to hear the contents of Quinn's letter right away. Surprisingly, Tava hadn't argued and instead had thrown him a grateful smile that made his heart leap inside his chest before she hurried into the ranch house.

What would Quinn say if he knew his ranch foreman was still in love with his daughter? The man probably would have demanded Jess go with him to the Klondike, rather than leaving him behind with a charge to watch over Tava. On the other hand, Jess would never do anything to misplace Quinn's trust in him—a fact that he knew Tava's father understood and appreciated.

This same trust had kept Jess vacillating for some time on how to move forward. Part of him wanted to confess his real feelings to Tava and ask her father for permission to court her. The other part of him cautioned him to wait, for fear her pa, with all of his knowledge of Jess's past, would tell him no outright. Before Jess had come to a decision, Quinn had left for northern Canada.

Tonight was one of those times when he questioned himself for staying as long as he had at the Double R. When the pain of loving Tava, and knowing she might never be his, made him want to ride away forever. But Jess couldn't do it. This was the only place that had ever felt like a real home, with people who truly cared about him. The ranch represented safety too. A place where his old vices couldn't reach him.

When the barn door creaked open sometime later and Tava appeared, Jess had finished tending to the horses. "Did you save me some supper?" he asked in a light tone as he exited one of the stalls.

"Actually, none of us have eaten yet. That's why Rita sent me to get you. We were too busy talking about the letter." Tava held something in her hand, but it wasn't the envelope from earlier.

"What do you have there?"

She lifted a folded piece of paper. "When I pulled out the letter to read it to Rita and Oscar, I noticed this had been tucked down inside the envelope."

Jess shut the stall door. "What is it?"

"A note from my pa, I guess." She shrugged with nonchalance, though her gaze held curiosity as she said, "It's addressed to you, but I didn't read it."

Sure enough, his name had been written on the outside. Jess didn't think the handwriting looked like Quinn's. Had Tava noticed that as well?

"Thanks." He took the paper from her, their fingers brushing in the exchange.

In that moment, he was no longer holding a note from her father but the one Tava had written him the night before he'd left the ranch. She had acted uncharacteristically shy when she'd given it to him and as she waited for him to read the words.

The message wasn't long. In it, Tava had asked him not to forget her and to write as often as he could. Jess hadn't understood why she worried he might not remember her. After all, he'd admired her for as long as he had been on the ranch. But to ensure she didn't forget him either, he'd sealed her request with a kiss. Their first and last.

"I'll let you read the note in private," Tava said, yanking Jess back to the present. Her cheeks looked slightly pink as she fell back a step. Had she been recalling that long-ago night too? She turned toward the door, adding over her shoulder, "Come up to the house when you're done."

"I will."

Jess waited until she slipped outside, then he unfolded the note. He could tell at once it hadn't been written in Quinn's hand. Even before he read the scrawled words, a sense of foreboding churned inside his gut.

I'm dictating this to Nelly, the woman who's been caring for me. She's done a fine job, but I don't think I'm going to recover from this, Jess. I can't bear to tell Tava that myself, so I need you to convey this message for me. Keep looking after her—make sure the right man wins her heart in the end. And be sure she remembers that I love her. Don't forget what a fine man you've become. If Tava wants my personal effects, she can write to Nelly at her boardinghouse, listed below.

He spared only a cursory glance at the name of the boardinghouse, his mind emptying of it a second later. This couldn't be Quinn's final goodbye. Not like this, away from those who loved him and respected him, who wished to be like him.

Shock delivered a hard punch to his chest. Jess gulped in a breath of the pungent air. A wooden crate sat close by, giving him a place to rest his shaky legs.

He sank down and wiped his free hand across his bristled jaw. Moisture stung his eyes, and a lump of grief and concern constricted his throat. How was he going to break such news to Tava?

2

HE'D BEEN SO confident that Tava's father had already recovered from whatever illness had plagued him. Now Jess held the man's last wishes in his hand. If only he could disregard the awful words, but he knew Quinn too well. The man wouldn't have written him specifically—or dictated a note to someone else—if things weren't dire.

Had Quinn already succumbed? Or was he tentatively clinging to life at this very moment?

Jess hung his head in anguish and offered a prayerful petition for the man, that perhaps it wasn't too late. Then he slowly climbed to his feet. He refolded the note and moved woodenly out of the barn to the house. The smell of fried chicken and fresh biscuits met him at the kitchen doorway. As he entered the room, the sound of happy conversation enveloped him. He winced at the thought of destroying the cheerful mood.

Tava noticed his arrival first. "Oh good. We can eat . . ." Her voice trailed off as she studied his face, her smile changing to a confused frown. "Is something wrong?" she asked.

Oscar lowered his newspaper. "Is it the animals?"

"No. The animals are fine." Jess gave an awkward cough. "I . . . I do need to talk to Tava."

Rita exchanged a concerned look with her husband as she

set a dish on the table. Was it better for Jess to blurt out the news to all of them? Or tell Tava in private first?

She made the decision for him when she rose to her feet. "Why don't you two start eating? Jess and I will join you in a few minutes."

He led the way through the house and onto the front porch. Tava didn't speak until he shut the door behind them. "What's going on?" She folded her arms tightly against her blouse and vest as if cold, despite tonight's milder temperature. "Does it have something to do with your letter?"

Jess faced the porch railing, searching for a way to soften the blow of what he needed to tell her. But there was none.

"You're scaring me, Jess. What's wrong?"

He pushed out a heavy sigh, then turned to face her. "You need to read the note from your pa."

Tava bravely accepted the paper from him, though her fingers visibly trembled as she unfolded it. As she read it, he watched the color drain from her face, making her freckles stand out against her now pale skin.

"He can't be . . ." Tava shook her head. "He has to be better by now, just like we thought. Right?"

He wanted to agree, to assure her that everything was fine, but it would be a lie. And while he'd avoided telling Tava many things about his past, Jess had always strived to be honest with her.

"I don't know," he admitted at last. "Your pa might be better, but he might not be." His next words stuck to his tongue, but Jess forced them into the open. "I think it's best if we prepare—"

"Don't say it, Jess Lawmen." The note crumbled in her hand as Tava jabbed a finger into his chest. "Don't you dare say that my father might be—dead." The last part came out no more than a whisper, but it dowsed the fire from her

16

countenance. Tava lowered her arm to her side and dropped her chin.

Jess didn't hesitate or pause to question the wisdom of his reaction; he simply gathered her to him and held her in his arms. "I'm so sorry, songbird."

Her quiet sobs resounded painfully inside him, while her tears soaked into his shirt. Having Quinn gone for so long had been difficult for her, for all of them. But Jess had never imagined the man's absence could be permanent.

What would the future be like without Quinn in it? Even as that thought pressed itself upon his mind, the tiniest flicker of hope nudged him not to give up. Tava's father could still be alive, but there was only one way to know for certain.

As if she'd been pondering the same thing, Tava stepped out of his gentle grip and announced, "I'm going after him."

"Hold on a moment." The news had understandably upset her. However, venturing that far north by herself wasn't the answer to her grief and fear. "You have a ranch you're trying to save, remember? You'd be gone several months to make a journey like that, longer if you didn't start back before winter set in."

Tava narrowed her eyes at him as if he was her only obstacle. "I can't just stay here." She paced the porch, the planks rasping beneath her footfalls. "He might already be— gone. But what if he isn't? I have to try to reach him, even if it's only to say goodbye in person."

How could he argue with that? "What about the money you'd need to buy the required year's worth of food and the other necessary supplies?" They were barely holding on now—there was no extra cash. Jess had even gone without wages the last two months to try to stretch things a bit longer.

"I can sell our cattle to Mr. Healey, and that portion of south acreage that he wants."

The Rutherfords' nearest neighbor, Mr. Healey, had somehow escaped the financial difficulties that others in the area were still recovering from. The man had wanted to expand his cattle operation for years and had tried on more than one occasion to persuade Quinn to sell land to him.

"That would give you the money. But what about the ranch?"

Tava stopped pacing. "We'd still have the house, the barn, and enough land to start over once I get back. Besides, the ranch is as good as gone anyway if my pa isn't able to reap anything from his mining claim." She crossed her arms again, her expression showing more defeat than confidence as she continued. "Whether we lose this place or not, if my father is still alive, I can be there for him. He should have someone he knows by his side for however long he may have left."

"Then I'll go."

The offer fell from Jess's mouth before he'd fully considered it. But it made the most sense. Quinn would likely spit nails if Jess let Tava travel to the Klondike alone. He ought to be the one to go, even if the notion set his heart drumming with a nervous rhythm over what had happened the last time he left the ranch.

"You can't go." Tava shook her head. "You're needed here."

Jess gave her a dubious look. "If you sell off the cattle, there'll be little to keep one person occupied, let alone Oscar and me."

"Exactly. What would I do if I stay, besides fret and worry the whole time you're gone?"

"I don't know. But you can't make that trip on your own."

He wouldn't add the consequences of something happening to Tava to his already troubled conscience. If anyone was leaving, it should be him.

"That's not a decision for you to make," Tava countered in a fierce whisper, though the front door remained closed behind them. "I'm *your* boss, remember?"

Jess shrugged. "I could quit. Then I'd be free to go where I wish."

"Oooh!" She glared at him. "You are the most stubborn man."

"This, from a woman who's insisting on traveling several thousand miles alone."

He stepped toward the door, but Tava beat him to it, blocking his way inside the house. "I wouldn't be alone. There are plenty of gold seekers heading to the Klondike this year."

Jess fought a shudder at the thought of her in the company of hundreds of gold-hungry men. "I understand why you want to go, Tava. I do. But there are . . ." How to put it? She had so little knowledge of the world beyond the ranch. "There are—dangers—along the way, and I'm not merely talking about bad weather or losing your supplies."

Some of the rigidity faded from her posture. "I'm not as naïve as you think, and I can take care of myself. I've been helping my father run this ranch since I was a child."

"You weren't running the ranch on your own back then." Why couldn't she see the sense in her remaining behind while he went in her place?

Tava lifted her chin a notch. The familiar gesture signaled she wasn't going to back down any more than he planned to. "I'm going to the Klondike, Jess." The coolness of her tone contrasted with the determined light in her eyes. "So I guess the question you need to ask yourself is if you're coming too."

◆◆◆

She didn't wait for his response, because she'd didn't need one. Tava had offered the potential solution as a way to end their stalemate. Jess wasn't likely to give in to the idea of joining her. Turning on her heels, she opened the front door and strode through to the kitchen.

"Everything all right?" Rita had taken a seat at the table, but the housekeeper had sampled very little of her dinner.

The couple had always been more like family than employees to Tava and her father. As such, they had a right to know what had happened to Quinn—and what Tava planned to do about it.

"My father dictated a separate note to Jess," Tava explained. "That's what we were discussing just now."

Uncurling her fingers, she revealed the crumbled piece of paper. She flattened the wrinkles as best as she could. Footsteps from behind alerted her to Jess's presence.

"What does the note say?" Oscar asked.

Tava shot Jess a look over her shoulder. Some of the contents of the note were surely meant to be kept private, such as Quinn's praise for Jess and his request that Jess ensure the right man claimed Tava's heart. She didn't feel right about reading her pa's words verbatim to the older couple.

She passed the slip of paper to Jess, who accepted it with a nod of gratitude. He clearly hadn't wanted her to share it all either. "At the time, my father believed he wasn't going to recover from his illness. He . . ." Tava swallowed the hard lump that rose into her throat. "He even went so far as to say where I could send for his personal effects."

"Oh dear." Rita covered her mouth with her napkin, her eyes filling with visible tears. "Poor Mr. Quinn."

Oscar shook his head back and forth. "And here we were thinkin' all would be right by now."

"It still might be." Tava couldn't give up on the possibility that her pa might pull through. If she didn't hold tightly to that hope, however small, she wasn't sure she had the strength to keep going. She'd already lost one parent; she couldn't bear to lose another. "I intend to find out what happened to him."

Rita lowered her napkin to reveal a puzzled frown. "What do you mean, honey? You've already written plenty of letters."

"She's not talking about sending a letter this time," Jess interjected.

Tava ignored him as she squared her shoulders. "I'm going to the Klondike."

Her announcement produced twin expressions of shock on the Pooles' faces. "That's quite a journey," Oscar said when he recovered, his tone laced with hesitation.

"The two of you ought to eat." Rita motioned for Tava and Jess to sit. Two plates of food awaited their attention. "Plans are best made on a satisfied stomach."

Tava sat in the chair at the foot of the table, while Jess took his customary seat to her left. Her father's chair, at the table's head, remained respectfully vacant.

Oscar forked a bite. "What about the ranch? It'll take more than me and Jess to run things, especially with all the ranch hands gone."

"There will be less to oversee once I sell our cattle to Mr. Healey. He can buy that piece of land he wants as well." Momentary regret pinched at Tava's determination. Would her father forgive her for not keeping the ranch intact? There was still the real chance of losing it to the bank in the near future anyway. "That should give me enough money to buy supplies for the trip and hopefully tide the three of you over until I get back."

"I can stay as long as I need to in Idaho. That way there'd be one less mouth to feed for a time." Rita reached for her husband's hand. Oscar cupped his fingers around hers and offered a silent nod of acquiescence at her suggestion.

The tiny act of solidarity tugged at Tava's thinly veiled

emotions. She had a few memories of her mother and father's interactions, so most of what she'd observed about marriage had come from watching Rita and Oscar through the years. The two were supportive and complimentary of one another, and each enjoyed the other's company. It would be a sacrifice for them to be apart for weeks. Yet they would do it for Tava and her father.

"Make that two less mouths to feed," Jess said.

Oscar released his wife's hand and peered at Jess. "You're heading somewhere too?"

"I'm going with Tava."

She nearly dropped her fork. "You are?"

"Yep." He hardly paused in eating, as if he hadn't said anything out of the ordinary.

Tava frowned as he bent over his food. He couldn't be serious, could he? "There might not be enough money to purchase supplies for both of us, since I'll have to give some to the bank to buy the ranch more time."

That ought to be an end to his plan of coming along. But Jess's next declaration brought an end to that prospect.

"I have some money set aside if we come up short."

Oscar's weathered face still showed uncertainty. "Should I find another job while you're all gone?"

Tava hurried to swallow the morsel in her mouth. "You can if you wish, but I hope you'll stay." She didn't want him and Rita leaving the ranch for good. Having her pa gone had been difficult enough—she wouldn't choose to have more people she cared about disappear from her life. "If you could look after things until I'm back, I'd be very grateful. I'll make sure you have enough supplies to tide you over in the meantime. Maybe Mr. Healey would even hire you to help some on his ranch."

Few people understood horses and cattle as well as Oscar,

except for maybe Tava's father. But even he'd learned a great deal from the older man.

"That's an idea," Oscar said, rubbing his whiskered chin. "I promise to care for things here. Don't you worry about that, Tava. You go find your pa and settle whatever you need to up north."

"Thank you." Fresh tears threatened to spill over. Tava blinked them away and concentrated on finishing her supper.

Leaving would be a little easier, knowing Oscar would be watching over things in her absence. Still, she'd never ventured far from home; there had been no reason to. Now she'd be traveling thousands of miles away. She and Jess.

Tava eyed him over the rim of her cup as she took a drink. His demeanor radiated casual determination, but she wished she knew his thoughts. Why did he feel the need to join her? He'd never challenged her independence before. Her father had often teased her that Jess was likely the only man he knew, other than himself, who wasn't threatened by a strong woman.

Setting down her cup, she returned her attention to her plate. Jess likely had more knowledge of the world than she did. Did that account for why he was insisting he accompany her? A more troubling question shoved its way forward in her mind. If her father knew what she planned to do, would he side with Jess?

Apprehension stole the rest of her appetite. Of course Jess wanted to see for himself what had happened to her pa, and Tava didn't actually want to deny him that chance. However, traveling with him all the way to the Klondike wouldn't be wise. It was one thing to see him every day on the ranch, where work took up their time and focus. But spending almost every waking moment in his company, with no chores to act as a buffer? That sounded far more intimate, and that was the last thing she needed with regards to Jess.

On the other hand, Jess had witnessed how hard Tava had worked to preserve the ranch in her father's place. If they both told Quinn as much, then surely her pa would see that she hadn't failed him. Not like she had her mother.

That settled it. All Tava had to do was bide her time with Jess in order to reach her father.

Resolved once more, she directed her focus to the conversation still circling the table. "I can take the train with you as far as our daughter's," Rita was saying. "She'll be pleased I'm coming earlier than I planned."

"Earlier?" Tava repeated.

Jess sent her a puzzled look. "Don't you want to head out as soon as you wrap things up with Healey and the bank?"

"Right, yes. We'd love your company on the train, Rita." She straightened in her chair. "I'll ride over and talk to Mr. Healey first thing tomorrow."

The four of them discussed their plans until the supper dishes had all been washed and put away. The one topic they had avoided, Tava included, was the potential that the entire journey could end in heartbreak.

Too restless to head to bed, Tava slipped into the barn to brush her horse. Jess had performed the task earlier, but the repetitive movement never failed to soothe Tava's troubled mind. According to her pa, her mother had often done the same, purging her muddled thoughts while brushing her horse.

Tava's mother, Gwendolyn Sharpe, had come from a wealthy family in Helena and had embodied all of the qualities of a well-mannered, beautiful young woman. Then she'd met Quinn Rutherford, a cowboy who worked for her father, and fell in love. Nothing her parents said or threatened would change her mind about Quinn.

A short time later, Quinn proposed marriage and

Gwendolyn accepted. She was promptly cut off, socially and financially. Only in death did her parents acknowledge her existence once more. Their will stipulated that Gwendolyn receive a sizeable amount of money, though it was small when compared to the fortune her brother had inherited and spent before he preceded his sister in death.

Grateful for her inheritance, however small, Gwendolyn had used it to build a ranch house on the land she and Quinn had homesteaded. That structure, along with a larger barn, stood as present testaments to the place she'd wholeheartedly embraced as her home.

She had adopted ranch life and all that came with it, but she was also determined to raise her daughter to follow in her ladylike footsteps. However, Tava had balked at every turn. Dresses were too cumbersome for running around; sewing left her with sore fingers; and polite conversation made her sleepy. Her father's activities with the horses and cattle fascinated her, while her mother's activities bored her.

The one exception was singing together. Her mother had purchased a piano when Tava was five. Most evenings after that, they sat side by side on the bench, harmonizing their voices to every song Gwendolyn could play.

One night, Tava had overheard her parents talking. "She'll grow up as wild and free as a prairie chicken," her mother had lamented, "if I don't keep teaching her."

Her father's gentle answer followed. "I'm sorry she hasn't taken to embracing all that you want her to learn, darling. But she's bright and healthy and sings as much like an angel as her mama."

Tava hadn't bothered to listen any more. What she had heard was enough to send shame burning through her. After that night, she'd tried harder to be a lady and not complain when she had to stay indoors. But her mother had taken ill a few months later, and the lessons in being ladylike had come to an abrupt halt. Before any of them were truly ready, Gwendolyn was gone.

Lifting her free hand, Tava wiped at her wet cheeks. Her resolve to be a lady all those years ago had come too late—in that way, she'd failed her mother. She wouldn't fail her father too. If there was the smallest chance that he might be alive, she would do anything to see him again, to tell him how she'd tried to maintain the ranch in his absence.

She finished her task, feeling less soothed than she'd hoped. After putting away the brush, Tava exited the barn. She wasn't the only person still awake. Jess stood beside the corral fence, his arms resting on the top rail, his gaze toward the road. How many nights had she stood in that exact spot while he was gone, gazing up at the stars and wondering if he was also thinking of her at that exact moment?

Not wanting to disturb him, Tava moved toward the house. She'd nearly reached the porch when Jess spoke. "You're still fixed on going?"

"Yes." She turned to find him watching her. "And you?"

He nodded once.

"Do you think we're foolish for going?" Everything inside of her urged her to go after her father, but it would be weeks before they even reached him.

Jess shrugged. "Maybe." Tava flinched at his honesty, though she'd expected nothing less. "Still," he added as he took a step toward her, "we have to try."

His words echoed those beating within her heart, and they buoyed her sinking confidence. They might not like what they discovered in the Klondike, but at least they were both resolved about making the journey.

"I guess I ought to thank you for being willing to come," she half teased as she folded her arms.

His half smile was visible, even in the dim light. "Don't you mean insisting that I come?"

The slip of laughter from her lips felt as surprising as it did calming. "Whatever your methods, I don't plan on looking this gift mule in the mouth."

"Ha. You callin' me a mule, songbird?"

She offered a casual shrug of her own. "If the shoe fits, wear it."

"That's the kettle arguing with the pot," he grumbled good-naturedly.

The corners of her mouth rose a little higher. "Perhaps. But where we're headed, a pair of stubborn mules is likely just what we need to make it."

3

THREE DAYS LATER, everything had been squared away with Healey, the bank had been temporarily satisfied, and two train tickets to Seattle had been purchased. Before Oscar drove the three of them to the train station, Jess had one last thing to do.

After entering the barn, he went straight to Bounder's stall. The dark-brown gelding stuck its head over the door in greeting.

"Hey there, boy." Jess rubbed the horse's nose. "I'm leaving on a trip."

Bounder's ears flicked forward with interest, and he snuffled Jess's shirt.

"I know. You want to come too."

Jess swallowed the lump of regret that attempted to settle in his throat. Bounder had been his faithful companion for years. The last time Jess had left the ranch it had been on Bounder's back. There'd even been moments during those months away when he'd wondered if his horse was the only other creature on earth who didn't judge him for his struggles or mistakes.

Ironically, it was that mutual affection and loyalty, along with a number of lengthy letters from Quinn, that had finally led Jess to hope again—in God, in himself, and in his future.

"You have to stay here this time, boy," he told his horse.

29

There was no telling how rough the terrain up north might be, and Jess wouldn't risk the animal's health or life by bringing Bounder along. Besides, the horse would hate being cooped up inside a train and a steamboat.

Clearing his throat, Jess pulled a stale carrot he'd found in the root cellar from his pocket. "You mind Oscar now." He fed Bounder the treat, which the horse eagerly munched. "When I get back, you and me will go for a good long ride. All right?"

Bounder nudged him again as if agreeing.

"Take care, boy." Jess rubbed the horse's head a final time, then exited the barn.

He pressed his fingers into the corners of his slightly damp eyes and adjusted the brim of his hat. Across the yard, Oscar was saying his own goodbyes. The older man held his wife's face between his hands, their gazes locked affectionately. Jess imagined they wished to say their farewells here rather than at the train station.

Wanting to give them a few moments of privacy, he slowed his pace and glanced away. The tender scene on the porch stirred longing inside him—for family, for belonging, for someone who would peer at him with the same adoration that the couple shared. Would those things ever be his?

His thoughts drifted to the time he'd stood beside a different house, preparing to leave. He'd been fifteen then, and more than fed up with his father's verbal assaults and swinging fists. One night Jess had announced that he was striking out on his own in the morning. His pa had laughed, telling Jess that he'd never make it. He was too lazy and too sorry an excuse for a son to amount to anything.

Jess's own doubts had kept him wavering over his decision throughout the night—one minute determined to leave forever, and in the next, afraid his father might be right and he'd never see or accomplish anything beyond these four walls. But something deep inside him whispered that he needed to go. The same inner voice had protected and comforted him more times than Jess could count. His ma had once told him those whisperings came from God.

Early the next morning, before anyone woke, Jess had put on his clothes and shouldered his knapsack. Inside he carried a knife, a canteen, some flint, and a book his mother had given him the Christmas before.

A loaf of freshly made bread sat on the table beside a scrap of paper in the silent kitchen. *For Jess,* the note read. He added the bread to his pack and slipped out the door. When he got a few yards from the house, Jess turned back. No one stood waving goodbye from the doorway, though the curtains at the front window fluttered as if someone had moved them.

Sadness nearly drove him back inside. Then, remembering the seed of feeling from the night before, Jess hiked his bag higher onto his thin shoulder and headed toward the road. That was the last time he had seen his childhood home and his family.

"You ready to go, Jess?"

Oscar's question thankfully scattered the painful memories. Jess lifted his head to find the couple watching him. "I'm ready." He picked up his worn pack from off the ground, where he'd set it earlier, and swung it onto his shoulder. "Will you ride Bounder for me now and again, Oscar?"

"Be glad to." The older man stuck out his hand, and Jess clasped it firmly. "You take care of yourself, and Tava too."

Jess answered with a solemn nod. He would look after Tava, but it wouldn't be easy away from the ranch. Especially with how stubborn Tava could be regarding her ability to take care of herself.

As if his unspoken thoughts had summoned her, Tava

appeared in the doorway. She wasn't wearing her usual getup. Today she had on one of her church dresses, and her regular ranch hat was missing from her head. She'd fixed her dark-brown hair differently too, pulling half of it back instead of into a braid.

He'd always thought of her as beautiful, but attired in such a way, Tava was sure to attract more notice. Jess frowned at the possibility.

"Why are you glaring at me, Jess?" Tava propped her hands on her hips. She likely didn't realize that without her usual vest the action served to accentuate her nice waistline. "Did I forget something?"

He couldn't voice what he'd been thinking, so he settled for a question of his own. "How come you're all gussied up?"

Her lips thinned with annoyance or embarrassment—Jess couldn't tell. But it was Rita who answered.

"It was my doing." The older woman gripped the handle of her travel bag with gloved hands. "I told her a dress would be more fitting for the train ride."

Jess glanced down at his simple jacket, shirt, and pants. "Should I change into my Sunday suit?"

"No," Rita reassured him, "you look just fine."

Relieved to be free of the conversation and that he didn't need to change, Jess loaded their bags into the wagon. Oscar handed Rita onto the seat, then took up the reins and settled next to his wife. Not surprisingly, Tava climbed into the back of the wagon unassisted. Jess settled in the corner opposite her.

The wagon shuddered forward and rolled toward the road, causing a lurch of panic in Jess's stomach. He wouldn't be returning to the security of the ranch for some time. Instead he and Tava would be risking a trip into the big, wide world, with all its virtues and vices. Would the hardships ahead drive him to pick up his former habits? Ones he'd been free of for four years?

You ain't never gonna change, Jessup Lawmen.

His pa's familiar vitriol seeped into his thoughts, kicking up his fears even more. Jess sent a quick look in Tava's direction. What would she think if she ever discovered the sort of man he'd once been?

Once been.

He clung to those two words like a drowning man to a rope. It was Quinn who'd repeated them to him often, especially after Jess had come back to the ranch after his short hiatus.

Jess wasn't the same person he'd been back then—he didn't have to manage things in the old way. Nowadays he believed in himself, even if his own father hadn't. Quinn believed in him too. That reminder served as another reason to find Tava's father as soon as possible, and hope and pray they weren't too late when they did.

As he forced out a slow breath, his gaze landed on the valise next to Tava. Compared to his, her bag bulged with belongings.

"You have more dresses stuffed in there?"

"Hardly," she countered with a sniff. "I only brought one other." She glanced up at Rita, then lowered her voice. "Since I've never been on a train before, I wasn't sure what to wear. Rita suggested my Sunday dresses would be better than pants or one of my work skirts." She stared down at her gown as if seeing it for the first time. "I feel like a goose parading around in peacock feathers."

Jess couldn't help a chuckle at her analogy. "You look nice, songbird."

"You're just saying that."

"No, I mean it." Though she had no idea how much.

33

Tava didn't obsess about her appearance the way he'd heard some girls did. However, that also meant she didn't fully recognize her own beauty, inside and out, regardless of her attire.

She twisted to face him, her soft brown eyes full of confusion. For a moment, Jess wondered if she'd press him to make sure he truly wasn't teasing. But she picked up their earlier thread of conversation instead. "I packed my hat, some other clothes, and a handful of my father's books that he didn't take with him."

"Ah." Jess nodded with understanding.

Her father might be a ranch man through and through, but nearly every evening, Quinn sat in his favorite chair with a book in hand. Reading was something he and Jess both enjoyed. Unless, of course, Tava was singing at the piano. Then they all gathered around to listen or join in.

"I'm sure he'll appreciate having more to read." Jess offered her a smile, but Tava didn't return the gesture.

"It might not even matter," she said, glancing back at the ranch growing smaller in the distance. "He'll be glad for the books if he's still alive."

Jess felt sure it was the first time since she'd received Quinn's letter that Tava had voiced the dreadful prospect out loud. The anguish in her tone drew him forward. He breached the space between them and rested his hand over hers. It was another moment that had Jess teetering on the edge of their established friendship. But he told himself that right now Tava needed his confidence and comfort, whether born out of friendliness or something more.

"I'm not giving up hope, Tava."

She lifted her eyes to meet his, her expression a painful mix of expectation and doubt. "I can't either," she finally said. She slipped her fingers out from under his and grasped the edge of something she held in her other hand.

"What's that?" It didn't look like her ticket.

Tava lifted the folded paper. "It's my father's letter. I—I wanted to bring it so I wouldn't forget the name of the boardinghouse." She ran her thumb across the missive's wrinkled surface. "I also thought I could keep a running tally on the back to mark each day of travel. That way I can see our progress."

"I think that's a fine idea."

Her countenance lightened with his praise. "All we have to do is reach him in time and bring him home."

Jess managed a noncommittal nod. If he knew anything about life away from the ranch, it was that things rarely turned out so cut and dry, no matter what a person wanted.

Tava followed Rita up the train steps and into their assigned car, while Jess came behind them. Wariness had her clutching her father's letter tightly in one hand and her heavy valise in the other.

She'd tried to tell herself she had nothing to be nervous about—people rode on trains every day. Most of them had never ridden in a roundup, either, or faced down two thousand pounds' worth of ornery bovine. But the reassurances rang hollow as she took a seat beside the window.

To her relief, Rita sat beside her. With how wound up she felt inside, Tava didn't think she could sit shoulder to shoulder with Jess. Especially since some of her unsettledness had less to do with the train ride and more with Jess taking hold of her hand in the wagon.

"We'll be underway soon," Rita said, patting Tava's knee where she bounced it beneath her dress. The older woman clearly mistook her restless energy for eagerness over leaving the depot rather than over the ride itself.

As predicted, the train rolled forward a few minutes later. They handed over their tickets to a train employee, then Tava turned her attention to the window. The landscape whizzed past, a kaleidoscope of unfamiliar plains, farms, and hills. A glance over her shoulder revealed that Jess was watching the scenery too. He'd been quiet the rest of the wagon ride. Tava imagined that his thoughts also centered on her father and the journey ahead.

She had lost count of the number of prayers she'd offered on behalf of her pa—that, God willing, they would reach him in time and that all of them would be watched over. There had been that moment of doubt in the wagon, when the magnitude of what she needed to do had overwhelmed her. But Jess's comforting hand had pushed back at her reservations.

After a few minutes, her middle twisted with a new round of churning. Tava shut her eyes, but that only increased the roiling inside her. The motion of the train had to be the cause. Opening her eyes, she shot another peek in Jess's direction. She didn't think he'd ever been on a train either, but nothing seemed amiss with him.

Tava turned to Rita and kept her voice low to avoid being overheard. "I—I think the motion of the train is making me ill."

"You do look pale, honey," Rita said as she studied Tava's face. "Not to worry. I have something to remedy your queasiness." From her bag, the woman pulled a cookie tin. She opened the lid and passed the container to Tava. "They're my homemade gingersnaps."

After thanking her, Tava bit into one of the cookies. The sharp taste of ginger coated her tongue. She swallowed and took another nibble.

Three cookies later, Tava's queasiness had disappeared. By then, Rita had dozed off, her chin nearly resting on her bodice. Tava attempted to peruse one of her father's books, but she couldn't concentrate. She read over his letter instead, wishing she could garner from it the same solace she had initially—before the note to Jess had changed everything.

She glanced over her shoulder at Jess and found him sleeping too. His head rested against the window, his hat propped on his knee. She couldn't recall a time she'd been able to observe him unawares in such a way. Tava twisted farther around in her seat.

Unlike this morning, when Jess had been almost pensive, the furrows in his brow had relaxed with slumber. His jaw and chin remained currently free of the brown bristles that would reappear by evening. The slight tilt of his nose drew her attention next. She'd once asked about it. Jess had told her it was the result of a broken nose but hadn't elaborated on the details.

Even after all these years, so much about her best friend remained a mystery, though that wasn't from lack of trying on her part to figure him out. In the beginning of their friendship, Tava had often asked him about his life before coming to the ranch, but Jess had either evaded the questions or provided vague answers. It was as if he didn't wish to discuss anything to do with himself prior to his arrival at the Double R. So Tava had quit asking.

Jess's eyelids suddenly flew open. "Did you need something?"

"No." A blush burned her cheeks. "Just seeing if you were awake." She hurried to face forward, chiding herself for regarding him in the first place.

"What do you think of the train ride?"

She glanced at the tin on her lap. "It's been all right so far."

Had her father been bothered by the train's movement? What of the steamer they'd board in a few days? Would she be able to stomach that new experience? They'd left the ranch behind a few hours ago, but already Tava felt out of her element. Too bad looking after cattle and riding for hours in the saddle weren't skills needed to reach her father in the Klondike.

"Have you ever been on a boat?" she asked Jess.

"Nope."

She shifted to peer at him. "I thought maybe you had."

He shook his head, his gaze returning to the window. "I saw plenty of boats four years ago. Even considered boarding one but decided against it at the last minute."

"Why?" It couldn't have been fear that stopped him. Jess wasn't afraid of anything. "Wouldn't a boat ride have been the type of adventure you wished to find?"

Some unnamed emotion sketched new lines around his mouth. "I learned pretty quick that adventure isn't everything." He lifted his hat and fingered the brim. "I wasn't sure I'd find my way back if I set foot on that gangplank. As it was, I almost didn't."

"I . . . I didn't know that." She wanted to ask what he meant, but there wasn't time. Rita awoke, bringing an end to the semiprivate conversation. The older woman passed around the contents of a cold lunch, and the talk shifted to other topics as they ate.

However, Jess's admission wouldn't leave Tava's mind. What had happened to change his mind about seeing more of the world? A part of her wanted to know, to hear the things he'd kept guarded inside for so long. Yet what if she didn't like the answer?

Jess gaped in awe at the city as their hired driver navigated the wagon through the crowded streets. Tall buildings, wagons, and streams of people met Jess's wide-eyed gaze whichever direction he looked. He'd visited a few cities in his lifetime, but Seattle was the largest he'd seen. Its size left him feeling uncomfortably small. What had Quinn thought of this place? Jess wondered.

"This is the boardinghouse I recommended," the driver said, pulling the conveyance to a stop in front of a two-story brick structure.

Swallowing his discomfort, Jess paid the man and pulled his and Tava's luggage from the back of the wagon. "Thank you again."

"Hopefully it's not too expensive," Tava said, taking her bag and moving beside him up the walk.

He conceded with a nod. They'd need enough money to buy both of them a year's worth of food and other supplies. Any leftover cash they could save and use at other points along their journey.

Jess knocked on the boardinghouse door. After a moment, a middle-aged woman answered. "Hello." She smiled cheerfully at them. "May I help you?"

"We're in need of a place to stay the next two nights," he answered.

"I have a lovely room that was vacated this morning." The woman waved them inside. "You and your wife are sure to enjoy it."

Jess threw an awkward glance at Tava. "That sounds nice, ma'am. Only we're not married."

"You're not?" she said flatly. She looked them over, her smile vanishing. "Well then, you'll have to stay elsewhere." She drew her amble shoulders back. "I run a proper boardinghouse here."

In the tense silence that followed their dismissal, Jess tried to figure out the best way to correct the woman's erroneous assumptions. It was Tava who came to his rescue.

"That's wonderful to know your place is aboveboard, ma'am, because we'll be needing *two* rooms, if you have them."

"Two rooms?"

"Yes." Tava nodded. "One room for me." She pointed to herself, then at Jess. "And one for Mr. Lawmen. He's my friend and business partner. We're heading to the goldfields to find my father."

The woman's demeanor changed at once. "Oh, how nice. Two rooms it is." She waved in the direction of the stairs before leading them up to the second floor.

Jess indicated for Tava to proceed him. "I should have started with telling her we needed two rooms."

"It's all right."

Her lack of frustration soothed some of his lingering clumsiness at his mistake. "I'll be sure to ask differently next time."

Tava's brown eyes crinkled at the corners with hidden laughter. "Did you see how shocked she looked? Thinking some sort of romance must be brewing between us, and no chaperone?"

"Yeah." He offered a tight smile in response and trailed her up the stairs.

Would Tava herself be shocked to know his feelings for her ran closer to the romantic than to friendship? Could she ever go back to seeing him as more than a friend, as she once had?

Jess shook his head at the pointless questions. He was getting ahead of himself. They needed to learn what had happened to Quinn first. Then Jess could decide whether to finally give voice to his heart or whether to surrender his desire for a future with Tava once and for all.

4

FINDING AND PURCHASING a year's worth of food as well as camping supplies and warmer clothing took the better part of two days. By the end of it, Tava never wanted to step inside another store for the rest of her life.

Each night during dinner in the noisy dining room of the boardinghouse, she and Jess had checked off the items they'd purchased that day from their list of necessities. Their one extra acquisition had been some fresh eggs and a canvas case for packing the precious cargo.

The next morning they hired another wagon to cart all of their things to the docks, where they would catch the steamer bound for Dyea, Alaska, and the start of the Klondike Trail. They weren't the only people waiting to board. The cries of the milling crowd, the busy ship workers, and the gulls overhead created waves of sound that rose and fell and crested again.

Tava grasped her bag and stepped toward the forming line. "We have everything." They'd gone over each item last night, but Jess kept circling their pile of supplies.

Jess grunted. "I want to be sure we haven't forgotten something."

"We haven't, so let's get in line." She didn't want to miss climbing aboard. The sooner they were on the steamer, the sooner she'd truly feel on her way to reach her father.

Jess pulled his gaze away from the various boxes. "Why don't you wait in line? I'm going to double-check everything one last time."

"Fine." There was no point arguing with him—not when he had it in his head what he needed to do.

Tava moved to the end of the line, the hem of her dress swishing around her ankles. She'd debated whether to don pants once their train ride had ended but had decided against it. Her mother would have been appalled at the idea of her daughter walking around a city in ranch clothes. However, once they reached Dyea, Tava planned to trade her dresses for her sensible shirt and vest and a pair of the mackinaw trousers she'd purchased.

"How long have you and your husband been married?"

Lifting her chin, Tava discovered a woman with auburn hair and green eyes watching her. She appeared to be about nine or ten years older than Tava. Her dress, though not fancy, fit her trim figure well, and her coif had been artfully arranged beneath her hat.

"Do you mean me?" Tava asked.

The woman laughed lightly. "Yes. Is that your husband over there? I saw the two of you talking earlier."

Tava clamped her lips over a groan. How many more times would she or Jess have to correct people's false perceptions about them?

"I'm not married." Tava peered back at Jess. "He and I are just old friends."

"Ah, that would explain the familiarity between you."

For some reason those words drew a blush from Tava. "He's worked at our family ranch for seven years."

"Are you traveling to the Klondike together?"

Tava nodded. "We're going to find my father."

"Is he missing?" The woman's face revealed true concern.

"No, he's sick."

Tava switched her bag to her other hand. Most women ignored her, save for the elderly matrons at church who clucked their tongues at her for running the ranch alone and not yet being married. She wasn't sure what to make of this stranger's genuine interest. Yet something about the woman's kind expression nudged her to share more.

"I guess I should say he *was* sick. I don't know what's happened to him since he wrote his last letter." The uncertainty, which rarely left her alone, resurfaced with her admission.

The woman rested her hand on Tava's sleeve for a brief moment. "I'm so sorry. The unknown is the worst, isn't it?"

"Do you know someone in the Klondike?" Surely she must, with how accurately she'd guessed at Tava's feelings.

"I did." The woman gazed toward the water. "My husband passed away up there last year. His mining partner wants to sell their claim, but I told him that my son and I would like to see it first. I don't know if I'll wish to keep it or not, but I do want to see where my husband spent the last few months of his life."

If things didn't go as Tava hoped and prayed, she might be doing the same, viewing the places that had been a part of her father's final moments. "I'm sorry for your loss. That must be so hard." She noticed a boy of seven or eight sitting on a box nearby, staring down at the planks of the dock. His hair held a hint of red. "Is that your son?" She motioned in his direction.

"Yes, that's Felix." The woman studied her son, then returned her attention to Tava. "My name is Carolyn Hall, by the way."

Tava shook Carolyn's hand. "I'm Tava Rutherford, and my friend is Jess Lawmen."

"A pleasure to meet you." Carolyn smiled. "You have a lovely and unique name."

Tava returned her smile. "Thank you. My mother was an accomplished singer, so naturally she decided to name her only daughter a variation of the word *octave*. My full name is Octavia, but everyone calls me Tava."

"Or songbird," Jess said as he approached her.

"Songbird?" Carolyn repeated. "I like that. Do you sing as well, Tava?"

"I do, but I'm not as talented as my mother."

Jess nudged her with his shoulder. "She's being modest. Her singing is incredible."

"Spoken like a true admirer," Carolyn mused, glancing at each of them in turn.

Another blush blossomed on Tava's cheeks. Without looking directly at Jess, she introduced him to Carolyn. "This is Carolyn Hall. Her son, Felix, is sitting over there."

"A pleasure to meet you, Mrs. Hall." He removed his hat and shared a friendly handshake with Carolyn.

"It's nice to meet you too, Mr. Lawmen."

"Jess suits me just fine."

Carolyn dipped her chin. "Very well. Then, please, call me Carolyn." Jess inquired if she was heading to the Klondike, and Carolyn repeated the somber tale about her husband. When she finished, she called to her son, "Felix, come meet two of our fellow travelers."

The boy rose slowly to his feet and walked over. "This," his mother said, "is Miss Tava Rutherford and Mr. Jess Lawmen."

Felix nodded. "Hello."

"Have you been on a boat before?" Jess asked him.

"Sure." Felix shrugged. "We took a boat to get here."

Carolyn ran her hand over the boy's hair. "We live in San Francisco."

"Well, this is a first for me," Jess admitted. "Any tips for a non-sailor like myself?"

The boy's melancholy eased a little at the question. "My ma says that seeing the boat up close can help." He looked to Carolyn for permission.

"Go on. I'll wait here."

Jess fell into step with Felix, and they moved toward the waiting steamer.

"Is your friend always that considerate of children?"

"He—uh . . ." Tava frowned, uncertain what to say. She didn't know the answer.

There were no children on the ranch, and though there were youngsters at church, Tava couldn't recall if Jess usually took the time to talk kindly to them or not. He'd once confessed to being the oldest in his family, but he hadn't shared how many younger siblings he had.

"He has a way of talking with anyone that makes them feel as if their opinion matters." It wasn't a direct response, but it was the truth nonetheless.

Carolyn glanced at Tava. "That's a nice quality."

"It is," she agreed.

Her new acquaintance seemed to expect Tava to elaborate, but she had nothing more to add. Helping others, children or adults, feel important was one of Jess's many qualities. Someday this one in particular would be a blessing to his future wife and children. Only Tava wouldn't be around to witness it, since Jess would surely leave the ranch for good once he married.

The thought of him—and possibly her father—gone from the Double R filled her with sorrow. She gripped her bag against her waist, thinking of her pa's letter tucked safely inside. There were already three tick marks on the back. Tonight she would add a fourth. That was as far into the future as she dared look right now. One day, one mark, at a time until she reached her father's side.

———————◆◆———————

From his spot at the deck railing, Jess fixed his eyes on the distant shore, which was thickly covered with pine trees. The action helped lessen the queasiness in his stomach. How ironic that he hadn't been affected by the train's movements but that being aboard the rocking boat was another matter entirely.

The sickness had come on gradually. Jess hadn't even noticed it when he and Felix had stood along the rail earlier, waving goodbye to those on the docks as the steamboat pulled away. After making plans for Tava to share a cabin with the Halls, the two women had joined them. The talk among the adults had centered on the journey ahead, and Carolyn had asked if she and her son might travel with Jess and Tava. They'd both been quick to agree.

Jess was relieved to know Tava would have another woman along as a companion. Hopefully that would put a stop to the reactions they'd received thus far at being unmarried and unchaperoned and traveling together.

Once they'd left Seattle behind, Jess had gone belowdecks to find a berth and had met two of his cabinmates. One was an eighteen-year-old young man from California named Archibald Gilbert, though he preferred to be called Archie. With his light-blond hair, pale skin, and light-blue eyes, he reminded Jess of a snow hare that been caught out in the open in the middle of summer.

The other fellow was Eugene Abbott, a longtime miner from Texas. He'd been wandering around Alaska the previous year when he'd heard about the Klondike strike. Eugene had hightailed it to Dawson at once and managed to secure a profitable claim off another fellow who'd had his fill of the mining life. The old-timer had been "outside" for a month now, but he was heading back.

After the introductions, Jess became acutely aware that the pitching of the steamer was more pronounced inside the cabins. He'd hastily returned to the top deck, where he'd been ever since. Not only did his position at the steamer's bow provide much-needed air and less movement, but the scenery was incredible too. Towering trees ended at rocky shores, and birds soared over the waves. The air against Jess's face felt cool and smelled of salt and portending rain.

"Sure is pretty." Archie joined him at the railing.

Jess nodded with ready agreement. "I've never seen the ocean before." He'd intended to—just as he'd intended to travel on a boat before now. Unfortunately, his buried pain and former habits had thwarted his well-meaning plans.

"I've lived near the ocean my whole life." Archie matched Jess's stance, resting his elbows on the rail and leaning into the wind. "I guess I've gotten used to it. But this feels different. It's wilder up here."

"You have family back in California?"

"My parents."

The younger man's tone hinted more at bitterness than familial affection—something Jess could identify with himself. "How do they feel about you heading to the Klondike?"

"They're not happy," Archie admitted, "especially since I'm their only child." His shoulders drooped as he continued. "My father is afraid I'll be killed. Then he will have no one to take over as chairman of his bank someday. But he did agree to finance my trip. My mother, on the other hand, begged me not to go at all. Neither of them believes I have what it takes to reach Dawson in one piece."

Jess could relate. His own pa had never believed he would

accomplish much either. However, his ma hadn't begged him to stay, as Archie's had, when Jess had announced his intentions to leave home. She hadn't voiced her opinion one way or the other. It had only been her eyes that revealed to Jess her inner conflict. He'd wondered back then if she actually wanted him to stay. Yet she'd done nothing to stop him when the time came.

Looking back, Jess felt immense gratitude that she'd let him go. If she hadn't, he would have stayed for her and his siblings, however detrimental that decision would have been to himself. Staying would have also meant not growing and changing in the ways he had.

Archie pushed out a weary sigh. "I guess they have reason to worry."

Jess cut a glance at him. "What do you mean?"

"I was sick a lot as a child, and as a result, I don't have the stamina that a lot of others my age do." He shrugged, his gaze lowering to the water. "It's not as if I'm afraid of hard work or danger. But I do wonder if my parents may be right."

The young man's lack of confidence stirred old memories as well as compassion inside Jess. Archie's uncertainty reminded him of his own from years ago. "You're here, aren't you?" he pointed out. "On your way to the Klondike? That's a big first step if you ask me."

"You're right." Archie straightened. "I made it here. And I'm going to prove to them that I'm more than some rich, pampered son. I'm strong too."

His determination drew a smile from Jess. "That's the spirit." They both returned their focus to the ocean and the landscape for a minute or two. "You heading to Dawson through Dyea or Skagway?" If Archie was also headed to the Klondike by way of Dyea, then maybe the young man would want to join Jess and Tava's growing party.

"I'm going to try my luck via Dyea and the Chilkoot Pass."

"Gonna need more than luck, boy." Eugene came to stand beside them. "It took me nearly a month to cart my supplies, one fifty-pound pack at a time, over the mountain and down to Lake Lindemann. Then you gotta build yourself a boat, which takes a few weeks. Even after that, you still have over five hundred miles of water to navigate 'fore reachin' Dawson."

One look at the old miner's weather-beaten face told Jess that Eugene wasn't exaggerating the extent of the journey. But he and Tava couldn't afford to spend an entire month shuttling their things up and over the pass—they needed to reach Quinn as quickly as possible. Particularly if they were going to be stalled at Lake Lindemann for several weeks while they constructed a boat.

"Is it better to go by way of Skagway and the Dead Horse Trail, then?" Jess asked the miner.

Eugene shook his head. "Naw. That way's troublesome too. I'd stick to the Chilkoot, but I'd hire me some natives to carry your things from Dyea to Sheep Camp and then over the pass to Lake Lindemann. You can get from Dyea to the lake in two days that way."

The suggestion seemed worth considering and was a far better option than making the same trek over the pass again and again. He and Tava could probably pool what money they had left to hire help. "Is that what you plan to do, Eugene?"

"No, not me." The old man chuckled, deepening the crinkled lines around his eyes. "I've done my time on the pass. I'm going the all-water route—the rich man's route—and the only way outside, lessen' you go by dogsled." He grinned, revealing several blackened teeth. "You run the risk of the river freezing before you make it to Dawson, but . . ." Eugene paused to thump a gnarled finger against his chest. "This ticker of mine deserves a bit of a rest after hauling these ancient bones up and over the mountain and in and out of mine shafts."

Jess spied Tava and the Halls emerging onto the deck and waved them over. He introduced them to Eugene and Archie. The miner removed his battered hat and nodded politely at Carolyn and Tava. "A pleasure, ma'am, miss."

Archie shook hands with Felix and the women, but Jess noticed the young man held Tava's hand longer than necessary. Even after letting go, Archie continued to assess Tava with an appraising look in his light-blue eyes. Irritation tightened Jess's jaw.

No doubt, Tava was beautiful, but that didn't mean she'd have any interest in someone who had barely crossed the threshold from adolescence to manhood. Jess narrowed his eyes. Maybe it wasn't such a good idea to invite Archie to tag along. After all, this journey wasn't some parlor social call; they were braving the trail ahead to find Tava's father.

"Gilbert?" Carolyn said. "That name sounds familiar. Are you related to Lionel Gilbert of San Francisco? My husband worked as clerk in his bank before deciding to go to the Klondike."

Archie pulled his gaze away from Tava and cleared his throat. "That would be my father."

"Oh? Really?" Carolyn's eyes widened in surprise. "I remember reading in the newspaper that Lionel's son was headed to the goldfields."

"Yes, well, hopefully the paper's readers will be cheering me on," Archie murmured, "even if my parents aren't."

The sour admission met with silence from the rest of them. Jess figured the others were no more sure how to respond than he was. After a moment, Eugene excused himself, then Felix asked his mother if he could explore the ship.

"Why don't we go together?" Carolyn scooped up her son's hand, and the two walked away.

Throwing an embarrassed glance in Tava's direction, Archie shoved his hands into his pockets and faced the ocean again. Tava raised her eyebrows in silent question at Jess, but he could only shrug. She stepped up to the railing, a few feet down from Archie.

Jess scrubbed his hand through his wind-tousled hair, debating whether he ought to get involved in helping the troubled young man. They could let Archie make his way to the Klondike by himself—it wasn't a bad option, considering how keen the young man seemed toward Tava. However, the truth was that Archie had no one. Jess didn't have to go back too far in his memory to recall being in a similar position before Quinn had taken him in. Perhaps their group of four could offer Archie some of the support and encouragement he clearly wanted.

Would Tava agree to adding a fifth member to their party? Jess moved to stand next to her at the rail. "Do you think we ought to invite him to come with us and the Halls?" he asked in a low voice.

"He does seem a bit lost, doesn't he?" Tava peered over at Archie and pressed her lips together in a way that meant she was mulling over the idea. After a few seconds, she looked at Jess. "If he wants to join us, I'd be fine with having him along."

"That's my thought too." They both walked over to Archie. "The four of us are also taking the Chilkoot Pass," Jess explained, "and we'd be happy to have you in our group. If that's agreeable to you."

Archie spun to face them. "You mean that?"

"We do," Tava said with a kind smile.

Jess loved that smile. Tava had worn it the first time Quinn had introduced her to Jess. He'd had a hard time believing the friendly gesture had truly been meant for him.

The young man stuck out his hand to Jess. "Thank you." Archie grinned as they solidified the arrangement with a handshake. "It's going be a real pleasure traveling with you." While he likely meant the group at large, his gaze remained on Tava.

Swallowing a grunt of regret, he lowered his arm to his side. Traveling with Archie might not prove to be pleasant for all of them, especially Jess. But if he could offer the young man even a fraction of the help Quinn had given him through the years, then maybe having Archie join them would prove to be worth it in the end.

5

GRIPPING THE HANDRAIL, Tava navigated the stairs to the top deck of the steamer. In her other hand, she held Rita's cookie tin. Overhead the stars attempted to shine through the scattered clouds that dotted the night sky. These same stars gleamed over the ranch and her father, and for a moment, she felt less far away from both.

The deck wasn't devoid of other passengers. Some had chosen to spread their blankets and themselves on the floor rather than sleep in the cramped quarters below. Nearly everyone appeared to be asleep, except for the lone figure at the ship's bow. Even in the dim light, Tava recognized Jess.

He'd eaten little at dinner, and the color of his face had nearly resembled Archie's pale one. Tava had wondered if the rocking of the boat affected him, but there hadn't been a private moment between them to confirm her suspicion. Thankfully the steamer's movements didn't bother her the way the train had, but she'd saved some of the gingersnaps just in case. She hoped the cookies would prove helpful to Jess too.

Tava maneuvered her way around the sleeping forms and approached Jess. He must have seen her coming, because he turned before she reached his place at the railing.

"Is everything all right?"

She nodded. "I couldn't sleep." She'd been thinking

about her pa and how far she still had to go to make it to his side. Rather than continue to lie there awake, she'd slipped back into her dress and coat and had decided to see if Jess was still on deck.

"That makes two of us." Jess flicked a glance in the direction of the stairs. "Just remember, once we're on land, it's not wise to wander around by yourself after dark."

Tava stiffened at his warning. They might be far from home, but she wasn't a fool. If she hadn't seen Jess on deck, she would have returned to her cabin.

"I'm not by myself. There's a deck full of people." She waved her free hand at the sleeping passengers. "But I didn't come up here to argue with you. I wanted to give you these."

Jess accepted the tin she extended toward him. "Are these Rita's gingersnaps?"

"They're left over from the other day." She watched as he opened the lid and peered inside. "I noticed you didn't eat much at dinner and wondered if you were feeling seasick. I thought the cookies might help."

An awkwardness she hadn't felt around him in years seeped through her. Would Jess think her offer stemmed from something more than compassion? It didn't, did it? She pulled her coat more tightly around her in the chill air and fell back a step.

"Thank you," Jess said, disrupting the uneasy silence between them. "But wouldn't you like to have the rest?" She'd told him the other day about feeling sick on the train.

The concern behind his question warmed her in a way his words of caution hadn't. "Actually, I haven't felt that sick on the boat."

"So you struggle with trains, and I struggle with ships?"

His teasing coaxed a smile from her, but she felt a prick of guilt at drawing pleasure from it. Was it right to feel even momentarily happy when she had no idea what had happened to her father?

Jess selected a gingersnap and took a bite. "These may help by the taste alone," he announced after he'd swallowed.

Reluctant to return below with just her thoughts as present company, Tava moved to stand beside him at the rail. "After tonight's dinner, I will never take Rita's cooking for granted."

"That meal definitely left something to be desired. Makes your beans and cornbread sound like manna from heaven."

She jostled him in the side with her elbow, grateful for their familiar banter in this place of new experiences and unknowns. "We'll be eating a fair amount of my beans between Dyea and Dawson. You may change your mind about how good they are by the time we reach my father."

"Not a chance." The words resonated with surprising gravity. Tava lifted her chin and found Jess studying her, his eyes nearly ebony in the shadows. "Your cooking will always be my favorite."

She gave a snort of disbelief, certain he was jesting again. "Why is that?"

"Because whatever you cook, it's always done with great love for the people you care about."

Tava swallowed, unsure how to respond. If any other man had voiced something that sweet to her, she might have accused him of flirting. But this was Jess, her best friend, who wanted nothing more than friendship from her.

"I . . ." She searched for something else to talk about. "I think it was nice that you suggested having Archie travel with us. He seems happy to be part of the group."

Jess finished his cookie. "That's because he likes you."

"No, he doesn't." Tava shook her head. "He treated me and Carolyn with polite interest."

Jess's answering chuckle lacked genuine cheer. "Believe me, Tava, he likes you."

For some reason, his assertion bothered her. Maybe because Archie struck her as rather young in his attitude and perspective. Or maybe because she didn't want or welcome Jess's opinions on matters of the heart, regardless of what her pa had said in his note.

"He hung on your every word during dinner," Jess added, "and I saw the way he watches you too."

Now he was simply making up stories. "He didn't watch me any differently than the rest of you."

Jess shrugged and stared at something over her shoulder. "I know what I saw. Archie watched you tonight like a man watches a beautiful woman he hopes will eventually notice him."

It took work for her to keep her jaw from dropping. The last time Jess had referred to her as beautiful had been four years ago, on the night they'd kissed. To know he still viewed her in that way produced a confusing mix of emotions inside her. Perhaps her stomach wasn't as calm as she'd thought.

"Archie is nice," she finally managed to say. "But he doesn't seem the sort of person who can see much beyond his own wants and ambitions." That had been apparent to Tava during dinner, when the young man had answered questions posed to him but hadn't bothered to ask any of the rest of them.

Jess bit into another cookie. "Noticing others is an important trait to you."

"Among other things."

"Such as?" He finished eating the gingersnap and closed the lid on the tin.

Tava rubbed a finger against the damp railing. How had the conversation taken such a strange turn? "Well, I would say diligence, a sense of humor, strong faith, and honesty."

She glanced his way, but she could only see his profile now. "All good traits," Jess muttered, but there was an edge to his voice.

"Regardless, I'm not here to find a potential beau." Tava folded her arms tightly against her coat. "It doesn't matter who comes along showing interest in me. You and I are here to find my pa."

His expression seemed almost sad as he nodded, though Tava wasn't sure what had elicited his remorse. "Thank you for the cookies. They're helping already."

"You're welcome." She stepped away from the railing. "I should probably try to get some sleep."

"Good night, Tava."

"Night."

Turning, she blinked back the unexpected moisture in her eyes to see where to walk. She was glad the cookies had helped, but from now on, she'd avoid talking with Jess about suitors or their admirable qualities. Perhaps he was only trying to fulfill her father's wish about the right man winning her heart. Yet why her pa had solicited Jess's aid in such a matter, she couldn't begin to understand.

Quinn still didn't know that Tava had once hoped Jess would become her suitor. But those dreams had ultimately shriveled up like a creek in a drought.

The memory of that loss would overwhelm her if she let it, especially as she faced the prospect of possibly losing her father. She had to keep her focus on reaching Dawson. Everything else would have to wait.

With that resolve, Tava didn't look back as she headed down the stairs to her cabin.

Jess stared down at the tin in his hands. He'd been happy

to see Tava, even if he didn't condone the idea of her moving about the boat alone after dark. Then when she'd offered him the gingersnaps . . . It wasn't the first time he had been on the receiving end of her compassion. However, tonight she'd given him something she might still have need of in the future—all because she'd noticed his need.

Could there be anything more endearing or attractive? If she hadn't already stolen his heart, he'd have fallen for her right then.

He hadn't meant to bring up Archie's interest in her or ask what traits Tava admired in a person. The latter wasn't a topic they'd ever discussed, and his curiosity had been piqued. At least until she'd mentioned honesty.

While Jess strived to embody the other qualities Tava had mentioned, he couldn't call himself completely honest. Not when he'd held back from telling her everything about his past and the real reason behind his request to remain friends. Even now, he still feared losing her respect and friendship if she ever learned of his mistakes.

And he'd choose to be friends with Tava over not having her in his life at all.

He was relieved to learn she wasn't interested in Archie or in accepting any other potential suitor who might cross her path on this trip. That gave him the advantage in hopefully winning her over after they found Quinn. But what if Tava's father didn't approve of Jess's intentions? Could he really go back to the ranch with them? There would be no other obstacles to Tava meeting and finding a beau at that point. And if his annoyance at Archie's interest in Tava was any indication, Jess didn't want to stick around while some other man courted the woman he loved.

On the other hand, what would he do if Quinn didn't survive? If Jess claimed Tava's heart after that, would he be able to live with the guilt of never knowing if his deceased father-in-law would have given them his blessing?

He shut his eyes against the conflict stirring inside him. The way ahead appeared as murky as the dark water he'd been staring at earlier.

The feel of the cookie tin against his palms nudged his consciousness. Opening his eyes, Jess ran his fingers over the etched surface. He could temper his irritation toward Archie, for his own sake, and continue to act as friendly as usual toward Tava. In time he'd hopefully know what to do.

Jess turned away from the rail. But as he found a spot to sleep, he couldn't help wishing that everything in life could be solved as easily as eating Rita's remarkable cookies.

The sharp movement of the steamer sent Tava's stomach lurching into her throat. Each jerky turn of the vessel meant they'd escaped dashing into the rocks and islands that made this section of sea difficult to navigate. However, the reminder brought Tava little comfort.

What if they were shipwrecked before they reached Dyea? Surviving such a disaster would require her and Jess to return to Seattle to replenish their supplies, and they didn't have sufficient funds to purchase two new outfits for the trip. What would become of her father then?

Please, watch over us, Lord, Tava silently pled as the boat pitched again. *Bless our captain and crew and all the passengers. Guide us safely to our destination.*

"Not the smoothest mode of travel, is it?" Carolyn sat on the bottom bunk of the opposite berth, her knitting needles steadily clicking in her hands.

Tava shook her head. "Makes me glad we aren't going the all-water route."

"Me too." Carolyn glanced at the door. "I hope Felix is all right."

Her son had complained of being stuck inside the cabin with nothing to do. When Jess had knocked on their door a short time later and asked if anyone wanted to wait out the boat's lurching on the top deck, Felix had jumped at the chance.

"Jess will watch out for him," Tava reassured the boy's mother.

Carolyn bobbed her head in a nod. "You're right. He's been very kind to us, and I'm grateful."

Her words had Tava recalling what she'd told Jess their first night on the steamer—about how she appreciated people who noticed others. She hadn't realized it at the time, but she prized that trait because it was one that Jess possessed in spades. He noticed those who were discouraged or hurting or victorious in some task. Or at least that's what he'd always done for her. Now his watchful care included the Halls and Archie. His actions were admirable, but she had to be careful not to admire him as anything more than a friend.

"You look deep in thought," Carolyn said, "which is a real talent given all this tossing about."

Tava quit staring at the floorboards. She'd been so consumed with her thoughts she'd forgotten the movement of the steamer for a few brief seconds. "I'd try knitting, but I'm hopeless when it comes to wielding a needle."

Carolyn's answering chuckle eased some of Tava's agitation over the fate of the steamer. "I like to knit when there's nothing more I can do to fix a situation. At the very least ..." She lifted what looked to be the beginnings of a sweater. "I end up with something to show for all of my fretting."

"If you don't mind my asking, how did you manage all those months with your husband away?"

Her friend shrugged. "A lot of prayer and a lot of time spent creating sweaters and scarves." Carolyn paused in her work. "It's hard, I know. I rarely heard from him, and sometimes my letters didn't reach him."

Tava wondered again if her letters detailing the tough decisions she'd had to make for the ranch had made it to the Klondike yet. Or would her father find out the situation when she and Jess relayed the story to him in person?

"I feel like I've traveled so far already, but there's still such a long way to go."

Carolyn examined her handiwork. "Of course, you're anxious to get to Dawson." Apparently satisfied with her progress, she resumed her knitting. "Jess seems just as anxious. It sounds as if he holds your father in high regard."

"He does." Tava pushed her shoes out from beneath her hem. "My pa respects Jess too. He's always treated all of our employees as family."

She sensed Carolyn's gaze on her. "What about you? Do you think of Jess as family?"

Heat sprouted on Tava's cheeks as she lifted her head. "I'm not sure what you mean."

"Is Jess like a brother to you?"

How easily it would be to answer yes. Tava could even taste the word on her tongue. Yet she couldn't bring herself to say it out loud. Doing so would be a lie, to God and to herself.

But did she dare tell Carolyn the truth? She'd never confided to anyone her feelings for Jess.

Tava moistened her dry lips. "Jess has been a part of the ranch for a long time, and my best friend for all those years." She grasped each of her elbows as if that would keep her past longings at bay. "There was a time when I thought he and I might mean more to each other, but nothing came of it."

"I'm sorry, Tava. Unrequited love is never easy."

"I wouldn't call it love," she countered with a false laugh. Rationalizing that what she'd felt for Jess four years ago had been merely a girl's infatuation helped his rejection hurt less.

Carolyn pinned her with a meaningful look. "Are you sure?" Her tone was gentle. "If I'd been in your shoes, and a handsome, solicitous young man looked at me the way Jess looks at you, I would have fallen in love too."

"The way Jess looks at me . . ." Tava frowned. While he might have once looked at her with tenderness, that had changed in an instant. He certainly didn't look at her that way now. Her friend was mistaken.

The room felt suddenly too warm, the walls pressing too close. Tava needed space to breathe. "I think I'll see if it's less rocky upstairs." She held on to the upper berth to get her feet underneath her.

Carolyn's expression became instantly apologetic. "Forgive me if I've been presumptuous."

"No, it's fine. I just need—"

The door opened, and Felix entered, looking disappointed. "The captain told us we had to go belowdecks."

So much for escape. Tava suppressed a frustrated sigh. She dropped back onto the edge of the bunk as Jess and Archie appeared in the doorway behind Felix. After her conversation with Carolyn, Tava blushed at seeing Jess again. She scooted back against the wall to avoid him noticing her flushed cheeks.

"Did the captain say how long we need to wait below?" Carolyn asked the men.

Jess shook his head. "It's raining now. Maybe till it clears."

The steamer pulled hard to one side, and all of them reached out to steady themselves the best they could. From what Tava could see, Jess's face reflected the same sickly hue it had their first day on board.

When the vessel righted itself, Felix scrambled onto the bed beside his mother. "Will the ship be all right?"

"I believe so." Carolyn put an arm around her son. "Would you like me to read to you to pass the time?"

"No."

Carolyn exchanged a glance with Tava. It was one thing to manage their own concerns about the boat. How could they help assuage Felix's worries too?

"What if we sing?" The suggestion tumbled from Tava's mouth at nearly the same instant the idea entered her head. "That's what my pa likes to do whenever he's feeling sad or worried."

Had there been anyone to offer him music these past few months? A desire to be at his side at this very moment filled her with a keen ache. Tava pressed her hand against her collarbone to ease it and cleared her throat of the emotion lodged there.

"Do you know any fun songs?" Felix asked, his tone dubious.

She nodded, relieved she didn't have to muster her way through a serious piece right now. "What about 'My Bonnie Lies over the Ocean'? That's a fitting number for today." Tava began, and the rest of the group, including Felix, joined in on the chorus. They warbled through one number after another. And the longer they kept at it, the more Tava's melancholy and fear melted away.

Sometime later, she noticed Felix's eyes drooping with drowsiness. The boy shifted to rest his head against his mother's leg. Tava suggested a slower number. One by one the adults let their voices fade away until she sang alone.

"That was beautiful," Carolyn said when Tava finished.

Archie jumped in with compliments as well. But it was Jess's opinion she most wanted to know. Tava moved away from the wall to get a better look at him. His gaze met hers, and he gave her an approving nod. It was what she would have expected from someone who'd heard her sing for years. So why did she feel less than satisfied with his response?

"It seems the ship has stopped rocking about," Carolyn declared with a relieved smile. She set aside her knitting and brushed a lock of Felix's hair off his forehead.

Eager to flee the room and her own jumbled thoughts, Tava rose to her feet. "I'm going to see if we're allowed on deck now."

"I'll join you." Archie opened the door for her.

She'd hoped for some time to herself, but she didn't want to be rude and refuse his company either. "That would be nice."

Tava had to pass by Jess to exit the room, but she kept her face trained forward to dodge having to look at him directly. But as her feet neared the threshold, she heard him say quietly, "Well done, songbird."

Surprised, she stole a peek at him. His blue-green eyes regarded her with no teasing in their depths. This time longing, regret, and admiration filled his steady gaze. The sight of it left her breathless. Carolyn's words from earlier repeated through her mind—*the way Jess looks at you.* Could this be what her friend meant?

Confusion tumbled through her. "Thank you," she muttered as she hurried out the door.

She chided herself as she followed Archie up the stairway. Clearly she'd let Carolyn's assumptions go to her head. Things with Jess remained unchanged, and for good reason. Yet as Tava emerged onto the top deck and drew in a full breath of damp air, she couldn't help wishing, for one moment, that things between her and Jess could change—for the better.

6

THE RELIEF JESS felt at finally disembarking at Dyea quickly faded to consternation when their group faced the chaos of the wharves. Men moved among the small mountains of equipment—all of it haphazardly dumped on shore with no thought to who owned what. The human noise of shouts, curses, and arguments set his ears to ringing. The others stilled beside him, each one gaping at the confusion.

Jess scrubbed his fingers down his face. It was going to take a fair amount of time to separate out every piece of his and Tava's outfits, as well as assist the Halls, and maybe even Archie, in locating theirs.

"Where are our things?" Tava asked, her voice full of dismay.

Jess waved a mocking hand at the scene before them. "Somewhere in all of this."

"How are we going to find it all?" Her hands settled at her waist. Today she wore a shirt, vest, and pants rather than a dress. Her regular ranch hat sat atop her braided hair.

Looking around for an empty bit of ground, Jess motioned to a spot he spied off to one side. "Why don't you wait over there with Felix while Carolyn and I look for her things?" He turned to Carolyn, who gripped her son's hand firmly in her own. "Is that agreeable with you?"

"Yes, thank you, Jess."

"When we finish," he told Tava, "I'll search for our belongings."

"But I can help now," she protested. She glanced down at Felix before adding, "Felix too. We'll be done much faster if we all help."

Jess bit back an annoyed sigh. He didn't blame Tava for wanting to hurry. They were finally on land again, and that much closer to Quinn. But this wasn't the time or place for her to assert her usual independence. Not with so many men around who might not think twice about shoving a woman out of the way in their haste.

"I know you're capable of helping, but I'm asking you to let me handle this." He hoped he sounded more patient than he felt. "Everyone here is as desperate to gather their things and get to town as we are. And if anything goes missing, you'll have to turn right around and take the next steamer back to the States. Tempers are running hot and short right now."

The words had barely left his mouth when a sharp cry rose above the din of the crowd. Two men a short distance away started brawling, fists flying between them. Tava's eyes widened as she took in the spectacle.

"See what I mean."

She huffed a breath of displeasure, but she didn't press the issue any further. "I suppose."

"I'm going to get started," Archie announced before entering the fray.

Jess led the rest of them to the waiting place he'd indicated earlier. "We'll bring everything to this spot."

Nodding, Carolyn transferred her hold of Felix over to Tava.

"Why don't you count all the barrels you can see?" Tava said, crouching beside Felix. "I'll count the boxes, and we'll see who reaches the highest number."

Felix smiled. "All right."

Satisfied the two of them would stay away from the melee, Jess followed Carolyn as she hunted for her belongings. Each time she found something, she would point it out and Jess would carry it over to Felix and Tava. Soon he had a large stack of the Halls' things piled together. Knowing he still had his and Tava's goods to locate, he didn't slacken his pace.

He'd set down yet another box when Tava suddenly charged past him, declaring over her shoulder, "I'll be right back."

"Where are you going?" Uneasiness shot through him as he straightened. "Tava?" he called when she didn't answer.

She spun back, a well-known glint of stubbornness in her brown eyes. "Someone stole our crate of eggs, and I'm going to get it back."

"What? Wait!"

Rather than listen, she rushed into the horde of people and possessions. Jess ground his teeth together as he dashed after her. She was going to land herself—and likely him—in a heap of trouble.

No sooner had the thought crossed his mind than he watched Tava approach a Goliath of a man and tap him on his beefy shoulder.

Alarm pumped through Jess, and he quickened his steps to reach her before something happened.

The man wheeled on Tava. "What do you want?" he demanded. His hardened expression didn't lessen in the least, even when he realized it was a woman standing before him. He towered a good six inches or more over Tava's head.

Her face visibly paled as she tipped her hat back to peer up at him, but her chin lifted in a determined tilt. "You, sir, have our crate of eggs. And . . ." She wet her lips. "I'd like it back. Please."

The stranger's eyes narrowed. "Are you accusing me—"

"What she meant," Jess said in a placating tone as he squeezed between them, "is that the crate you're holding *might* be ours."

"No, that isn't what I meant." He could feel Tava's glare boring into his back. "I know that crate is ours. I packed it myself, and I don't want to lose it."

Jess whirled to face her, his hands clenched at his sides. He'd also recognized the crate as theirs, but this wasn't the way to get it back. Anger at her obstinance and her disregard for the tense situation gobbled up his alarm. He would protect her, even if it was from her own folly.

"Go back and wait at our spot, Tava."

"But . . ." She glanced past him at the stranger, her brow furrowing with uncertainty for the first time since racing after the man.

He took her arm gently but firmly in his grasp and led her back the way she'd come. "I'll take care of this, but I need you to stay put."

Her hesitation drained away, transforming into frustration of her own. "Fine." She pulled her arm free. "I'm going."

After turning, Jess caught sight of the stranger's hat dancing above the crowd and headed after it. He would attempt to rectify the situation, as promised, but he was more likely to receive a fist in his face than recover anything.

"Sorry to bother you a second time," he said, jogging alongside the man.

The stranger stopped and scowled at him as if Jess were merely some pesky gnat. "You again."

"Uh, yes." Jess attempted an apologetic smile. "Is it possible those eggs might not belong to you?"

The man clenched the crate tighter against his barrel-sized chest. "I bought this same amount."

Removing his hat, Jess ran his hand through his hair, thinking fast. "Do you remember if your crate had a large knot in the back-right corner? Because ours did."

The other fellow released his hold on the box long enough to sneak a look at the corner.

"Is it there?" Jess asked, despite already knowing the answer. He'd seen the unique mark earlier.

"Might be." The stranger gave a noncommittal shrug.

Jess tamped down the urge to yank the box away and be done with it. He was wasting time. But if he pressed the stranger any further, he'd likely end up nursing a bloodied lip with nothing to show for it.

"What do you say we split the batch?" He put his hat back on. "I'll take a dozen, and you take a dozen."

"I'm still out half the eggs."

Jess reached into his pocket and pulled a bill from his pocket. "What about five dollars for my share?" It was ridiculous to pay for something he owned outright, but he was more than ready to end the tense exchange and return to the business of collecting their supplies.

"All right," the stranger conceded.

He went to reach for the money, but Jess held it out of the way. "My half first."

Growling beneath his breath, the man set down the crate and removed one of the canvas cases. He set it to the side, then held out his meaty hand for the cash.

Jess plunked it into his palm, hoisted the case, and headed back toward the others. All four of them watched his approach.

"What happened?" Tava asked.

He placed the eggs on top of a box. "We came to an agreement. He got half, and we got half." He figured he didn't need to share the part about also having to pay five dollars, since it was his own money.

"All of those eggs were ours."

"I know that, and you know that, but I wasn't going to convince him of that fact."

Tava folded her arms. "I could've recovered the whole crate if you hadn't jumped in."

"Really?" Jess matched her stance. "Would that have been before or after he pushed you out of the way?" The hold he'd had on his mounting irritation was slipping. "You could have been seriously hurt, and no amount of food is worth that."

Why couldn't she understand that? He was only trying to look out for her in this place so far from the ranch.

Her glower increased. "It may have been a risk, but I was willing to try in order to keep what was rightfully ours."

"Well, not me. That wasn't a risk I was willing to take— not when it involved you."

He hadn't meant to voice the latter. The admission ran too close to the truth of how he felt about her. Would she, or the others, realize that? Jess flicked a glance to where Archie and Carolyn had stepped aside, busily checking and rechecking their piles and clearly trying not to overhear the heated conversation. Felix had gone back to counting barrels and didn't appear to be paying anyone much heed.

"The rest of us aren't helpless, Jess," Tava said, lowering her volume. "We're capable of doing things on our own."

Her impassioned words told him that she hadn't under-stood his slip of the tongue. He felt partial relief, yet he also wondered if it would be better to simply lay bare his feelings instead of guarding them so tightly.

"That's not what I'm saying, but I am glad I was there to intervene."

"Like you did four years ago?" Her eyes widened in a way that suggested she hadn't meant to bring up that night. The words had merely slipped out, just as his had a moment ago.

They had never discussed the evening he'd returned to the ranch, and Jess had hoped to keep it that way. But now that Tava had brought it out in the open, he couldn't ignore it. He swallowed hard to bring moisture to his dry throat. "How did I intervene back then?"

"You made a decision about us, but you did it all on your own." The pain of her expression perfectly mirrored the one from that night. "You didn't bother to ask me what I thought or what I wanted."

Fresh regret knifed through him. He had known he'd hurt her with his decision, however necessary it had been. However, until this instant, he hadn't realized her ache hadn't completely healed.

"I'm sorry, Tava."

What more could he say? He hadn't discussed his decision with her because he feared he wouldn't be able to go through with it if he did. By deciding on his own, he'd hoped to protect her and ensure she found happiness with someone worthy of being with a woman as extraordinary as she.

"It hardly matters now." Tava raised her chin, signaling an end to the discussion. "I'll wait here while you find the rest of our things."

Her dismissal hurt, but he had other things to do than dwell on it. "Is that all of your belongings?" he asked, turning to Carolyn.

"I believe so. Thank you for your help." She gave him a tight smile, which he wasn't able to return.

Jess pointed a thumb over his shoulder. "I suppose I'll keep at it then."

He walked away, barely aware of Archie trailing after him with an offer to help. Perhaps he shouldn't have stopped Tava. Or maybe he should have let the stranger go unchecked. Either way, the thought of fresh eggs no longer held any appeal for him.

———————◆◆◆———————

At last all of the equipment had been collected and everything accounted for. Jess volunteered to secure a wagon in order to move their things away from the chaos of the wharves and to find a place to make camp for the night. Archie would stay with Tava and the Halls until Jess returned.

The town of Dyea boasted a number of permanent structures jammed along its narrow streets, including false front hotels and saloons. Jess marched right past the latter. He hadn't set foot in a saloon in four years—he had no plans or desire to do so now.

Searching for a campsite took longer than expected, but he eventually located a place for their group among the maze of other tents. He then had to visit four different hotels before he finally obtained a recommendation for an available wagon driver.

"Murray ain't cheap, and he don't move fast, but he'll see that all your things make it in one piece," the clerk assured Jess. "You can find him at the saloon next door."

Jess thanked the man, but back outside, he hesitated. He didn't want to go in the saloon. Still, the more time he spent tracking down someone with a wagon, the longer the rest of the group had to wait at the wharves—and that was no place for women or children.

Making up his mind, he set his jaw and stepped with purpose through the saloon door. The raucous talk and laughter crashed over him like a wave, and with it, old memories. His pace faltered, but Jess locked his gaze on the bartender at the counter and forced his feet to move across the room.

"I'm looking for a driver by the name of Murray."

The bartender inclined his head toward Jess's left. "Thin fellow in the corner there."

"Much obliged." Jess wound his way through the crowded tables until he reached the corner one. "Are you Murray?"

The older man glanced up, his bloodshot eyes blinking as if trying to get Jess's face in focus. "You needin' a driver?"

"We do. There's five of us, so we'll need you to make several trips."

With a sluggish nod, Murray lifted his mug in the air. "I aim to finish this first." He took a drink, then peered at Jess again. "You want a pint?"

"No." His answer came out sharper than he'd planned. Jess tempered it with, "I'm fine, thank you."

"You sure?" The driver bent forward, his brow creased with doubt. "You look like you could use one. 'Specially before you head to the pass."

At the moment, the mountains were the least of Jess's concerns. The group was counting on him, and Tava still acted angry with him. Not that she didn't have good reason. He'd hurt her, however unintentionally, in the past, and he had upset her at the wharves earlier.

The thought resurrected a painful throb inside his chest—one Jess hadn't felt in ages. His father's voice echoed in his head, increasing the thrumming tension inside him.

You think you're all high and mighty with your book learnin'? That you're smarter than your own pa? Well, you're nothing, Jess. Them wild dreams of yours are for other people. Better, smarter people. And that ain't you.

"Hey, mister?" Murray said. "You all right?"

Jess stared at the mug in the driver's hand. A few swallows would dull the pain. It would drive his pa's remarks from his thoughts and numb his regret over Tava.

But he couldn't do it.

He wouldn't go back on the vow he'd made to God, to himself, and to Quinn. Never again would Jess deaden his pain. The ache and the remembering would ultimately pass if he let them.

And his father's words of loathing? Jess had come to understand that they weren't actually about him at all. They'd been aimed at him, yes, but they had been a reflection of his pa's private fears and unfulfilled ambitions.

"I'll wait for you outside," he told Murray.

Jess headed toward the door, his gaze straight ahead. Out on the street, he sucked in a gulp of air. *Thank you, Lord.*

He didn't know what other trouble, hazards, or discord the days ahead might bring him or those in his care, but he'd passed his first test away from the safety of the ranch. And knowing that, he hoped to face whatever came with greater confidence.

Their temporary campsite became its own hive of activity once their supplies had been unloaded, and Tava welcomed the chance to focus on something other than her argument with Jess. At the recommendation of the old miner they'd met on the steamer, the group could save time if they divided all of their things into fifty- or hundred-pound portions during their stay at Dyea. So that's what they would do.

While the men set up two tents, Tava and Carolyn, with help from Felix, worked at sorting the supplies into the more manageable weight groups. Though without a scale, much of what they did was guesswork. The myriad of smaller piles would then be repacked into canvas bags to make them easier to carry. All of their flour had to be poured into new sacks as well, then placed inside ones made of heavier canvas to protect against water.

Jess and Archie soon joined them, making the tasks go faster. Still, by the time they were finished, Tava felt sore from all the bending and straightening.

"Should we set up one of the travel stoves and start on supper?" Carolyn asked as she stretched her back.

Archie mopped at his forehead with his sleeve. "What if we ate at one of the hotels instead? My treat."

"You sure?" Jess exited the men's tent after placing the last of their bags inside it.

The young man nodded and plunked his hat on his head. "I'm too hungry to wait."

"Me too," Felix announced. The boy had spent the last quarter of an hour trying to coax a gray-and-white husky away from its spot in front of a nearby tent. But the dog refused to move.

If Archie was willing to pay, then Tava would gladly forego working over a warm stove this evening. "That's very generous of you, Archie."

The young man grinned in a way that made her suspect he'd taken her appreciation to mean something more. "Let's go."

"Will our things be all right?" Tava directed the question at Jess.

He studied the tents. "They might be, but I'd hate to have anything stolen while we're gone. Why don't the four of you go? I'll find something to eat here."

Tava considered protesting—she didn't like the thought of Jess missing out on a warm meal. Yet she also knew he wasn't likely to change his mind about being the one to stay back. "We'll bring you some bread from the hotel if we can."

His gaze jumped to hers, as if her offer surprised him.

The possibility sent a ripple of guilt through her. Her frustration over what had happened between them at the wharves hadn't completely waned, but she wasn't so angry that she wouldn't try to bring him something better to eat than some plums or evaporated fruit.

"If that works, I'd appreciate it." His tone rang with sincerity, though Tava sensed a cautiousness to it as well. He wasn't any surer than she was on where they stood with each other at present.

Archie took the lead, and Tava and the Halls followed him. The noise of the town, which had dulled in her ears while she'd worked, swelled to a crescendo as Tava moved along the street. It was a dissonant symphony of beasts and humans. And the excessive, continual cursing from the latter shocked her. She'd always taken her father's rules against coarse words for granted, but now she felt grateful for those directives, ones she'd continued to uphold in his absence.

As the four of them stepped onto the raised boardwalk in front of one of the hotels, a fight erupted in front of the saloon next door. Men jostled forward to get a better view at the brawl, forcing Tava to scramble out of the way. But Carolyn wasn't fast enough. Someone shoved her, breaking her handhold on her son and sending her tumbling backward into the street. She landed on her backside in the dirt.

"Ma?" Felix called down to her.

Tava knelt next to him. "Are you all right, Carolyn?"

Her friend tipped her head in a shaky nod. "I—I'm fine."

"Let me help you." Archie moved down the nearest set of stairs and offered Carolyn his hand.

She allowed him to help her up, then brushed off the back of her dress. "Well, that was unexpected."

"Are you hurt?" Tava asked when Carolyn had regained her footing on the boardwalk.

"Only a bit of my pride." She clasped Felix's hand again. "Shall we try this one more time?" she said good-naturedly.

They entered the hotel and were ushered into the dining room, but Tava's thoughts were less on their surroundings and more on what had happened to her friend. Carolyn hadn't even provoked the man who'd pushed her, yet she'd been momentarily hurt anyway.

Might Tava have experienced something far worse than a smarting backside if Jess hadn't jumped into the confrontation with the man over the stolen eggs? Possibly. And if that was true, then perhaps she'd overreacted toward Jess's caution. She shouldn't have brought up the past with him either.

Remorse spilled through her. She needed to apologize to him for her part in their disagreement—and soon. Then they could go back to being friends.

She hardly tasted her food in her restlessness to return to camp and make things right with Jess. But she did remember to bring him some of the sourdough bread they'd been served. Back at the tents, they found Jess guarding their things from his seat on an empty crate.

"Your bread." Tava handed him the paper-wrapped slices.

He smiled as he took the package from her. "Thank you."

"What should we do for the rest of the evening?" Archie asked.

Carolyn yawned. "I think we'll try to get some sleep." She ruffled Felix's hair. "We have a long hike tomorrow."

"But I'm not sleepy, Ma." Felix's protest ended with his own yawn that made the rest of them laugh.

Tava wasn't ready to turn in yet. She needed to make amends with Jess first.

"I'll be along soon," she said to Carolyn.

After bidding the rest of them good night, the Halls disappeared inside their tent.

"Well, I'm not heading to bed yet." Archie nudged Jess's crate with the toe of his boot. "Want to come explore the town with me, Jess?"

He shook his head and removed a slice of bread from the paper. "I'll pass."

"Come on," the young man persisted. "I want to see more of Dyea."

Jess took a bite. "You've seen it."

"Won't you at least share a drink with me?"

Jess's jaw visibly tightened. "Nope."

Tava shifted her weight from one foot to the other. She felt awkward listening in on the uncomfortable conversation between the two men. But she needed to talk to Jess before she headed to bed

"You're no fun," Archie said with a frown. "I just want to experience some adventure while I can."

"Sorry to disappoint." Jess finished his first slice and started on the second. "If I were you, I'd get some sleep. We're going to have all the adventuring we need crossing the pass."

The young man's scowl intensified. "I'm my own man, and I'll do as I please."

"You're right." Jess crumpled the paper as he stood. "I'd still advise against it, but you're free to do what you want."

Archie jutted out his chin. "I plan to. Like Tava said earlier, the rest of us are capable too. You don't know what's best for all of us."

She winced at hearing her own words repeated. "I shouldn't have—"

"You do what you wish, Archie," Jess said, pocketing his hands.

"I will." Nodding farewell to Tava, the young man stalked

away, muttering something about people interfering in his life.

Tava watched him go. "I hope he'll be all right." She didn't condone Archie's obstinance, but neither did she know what it was like to live with an overbearing father who lacked faith in his child's abilities.

"I'll wait up a while for him." Jess turned to look at Tava. "Did you enjoy supper?"

"It was good, but I wish you could have eaten with us."

He shrugged. "I didn't mind staying here. Though I am grateful for the bread."

A long pause followed his statement, then they both spoke at once. "I need to say—"

"About earlier—"

They chuckled before Jess waved at her to continue. "You first."

"All right." Tava focused on the tent canvas beside his shoulder. "That wasn't right of Archie to repeat what I said at the wharves. It wasn't right of me to say what I did, either." She met his gaze straight on as she continued. "I'm sorry I got so mad at you. You were only trying to help, and I see that now."

"Help or not," Jess replied, "I didn't respond well to your arguments, and for that I apologize." He blew out his breath as if he'd been holding it ever since their row. "I had no idea what that man would do when you confronted him, and frankly it scared the tar out of me."

Tava laughed softly. "He sort of scared me too."

"Really?" The corners of Jess's mouth quirked up. "You didn't show it."

"I had no idea he was so large until I was standing under his nose."

"I felt the same."

His blue-green eyes no longer reflected the tension they had throughout the afternoon and evening. The sight filled Tava with relief. "There's one more thing." She paused to shore up her courage in order to say what she needed to next. "I shouldn't have brought up what happened four years ago. That wasn't fair."

"You have every right to still be angry with me," Jess said, his voice dipping low. He ran his hand over his bristled jaw. "I know I hurt you back then, Tava, and for that I'm truly sorry. If you only knew—"

A shout from nearby interrupted them. The sound was followed by a frightened whimper. Tava spun around to see the gray-and-white husky from earlier dodge a kick from its owner.

Instant fury over the animal's mistreatment pulsed through her. Their family had always had dogs on the ranch, but each was treated with kindness. Had her pa witnessed this sort of ill behavior on his journey? If so, Tava had no doubt such actions broke his heart. He might have even intervened.

But as much as she wanted to order the man to stop, she'd learned the importance of checking herself before barreling forward to right some injustice alone. With effort, she returned her focus on Jess.

"That's hard to witness," he said, looking past her toward the dog. His frown revealed his own frustration at the owner's unkindness. After a moment, he returned his gaze to hers. "Are you all right?"

Tava managed a nod. "I think I'll head to bed now."

"See you in the morning, songbird." His sincere smile felt like a balm to what had proven to be a strange and exhausting day.

"Good night, Jess."

It wasn't until later—after Carolyn and Felix were asleep

and Tava had marked another tally on the back of her pa's letter—that she remembered Jess had started to say something before they'd witnessed the incident with the dog. Something about if she only knew.

Too bad she hadn't thought to ask him before coming inside the tent. Then again, perhaps it was best to leave well enough alone. They'd both apologized, and Jess had acknowledged for the first time that he'd hurt her in the past. Yet right before drifting off, Tava couldn't help wondering if his next words would have resurrected her long-buried hopes or painfully laid them to rest once and for all.

7

ROBUST SINGING NUDGED Jess awake. He hadn't meant to doze while waiting for Archie to return, but exhaustion had claimed him at some point. Sitting up, he scrubbed his hands down his face and rubbed his tired eyes. The singing moved closer. Was it coming from Archie? Jess stood and peered out the tent flap. A figure stumbled toward him, moving as much from side to side as forward.

"Archie?" Jess whispered loudly.

The person halted. "Jess! What're you doin' here?"

"Hoping to keep you from waking everyone." He walked over to Archie and took hold of his arm. The smell of alcohol wafted off the young man's clothes, causing Jess's stomach to turn with remembrance. "Let's you get inside the tent."

Archie allowed himself to be led as he broke into boisterous song again. After lifting the tent flap, Jess guided Archie inside, then helped him sit on one of the two pallets they'd placed on the ground.

"You shoulda come with me." Archie leaned forward as Jess settled on his own pallet. "I found me some new friends. Nice friends. First round was on them."

Jess loosened the laces of his boots. "Who paid for the rest?"

"Um . . . Brown bought one, and I bought one. Or maybe it was two."

Judging by his drunken state, the young man hadn't stopped at just two or three rounds. "Do you have any money left?" Jess set his shoes aside.

"Course I do," Archie retorted with a smug sniff. The sound of him rustling through his pockets was followed by a sudden cry of dismay. "Where'd it all go?"

Jess had expected such an outcome, but he still felt grief on Archie's behalf. "You have nothing left from what you took with you?"

"No." Archie collapsed onto his side, as though his discovery had sapped him of any remaining strength. "Where's my money, Jess?"

"My guess is your new friends took it."

The young man moaned. "But they seemed so nice."

Jess cringed at Archie's rationalization. It was like conversing with his younger self after he'd left home. His supposed *friends* had seemed nice at first too. However, when they'd finally parted ways, Jess had been left penniless, injured, and staring up into the barrel of a rifle. Thankfully Quinn Rutherford hadn't shot him on sight.

"What am I gonna do?" Archie lamented with a sob. "If I tell my father, he'll never let me live this down. And my mother..."

If Archie had only listened to his advice earlier ... Still, Jess couldn't judge him too harshly. He'd been in a similar position, and he knew full well the power of compassion over condemnation—particularly when it came to escaping a father's expectations.

"Do you have any other money tucked away somewhere?"

"I ... I might." The young man sniffled. "I didn't take everything with me." The desperate edge was fading from his voice.

Jess glanced at the piles of canvas bags. "Do you remember where you stashed the rest?"

"Where, where, where?" Archie mused in a singsong voice as he sat up. "I think I put more inside my stove? Yes, my travel stove."

Standing, Jess located the small stove. He opened the door, half-fearing he'd find nothing. But his hand brushed stacks of crisp bills.

"You can double-check in the morning, but there's definitely money in there."

Archie let out a whoop. "I'm going to be all right."

"Yes, you are. But right now, you need to get some sleep."

The young man lay back down on his pallet before popping up again a few seconds later. "You won't tell Tava about this, will you?"

"She's going to suspect something when you aren't able to hike to Sheep Camp tomorrow."

"I can't make the hike?" Archie echoed. "Does that mean you're gonna leave without me? Please don't leave without me."

Jess returned to his side of the tent, unsure what to do. He didn't want to wait an entire day before moving on from Dyea, and Tava wouldn't either. However, he didn't like the idea of leaving Archie behind either. There was a definite advantage to having another man traveling with them, and for good or ill, Archie was a part of their group.

His hesitation clearly frightened the young man. "If you help me make the hike," Archie pleaded, "I'll pay for the natives to carry everyone's things. Yours and Tava's and Carolyn's . . . you won't have to spend a dime. Just help me make it, Jess."

The poor kid had no understanding of the consequences that followed a night of being drunk. "I'm not going to let you pay for the rest of us. Besides, you aren't likely to want to do much of anything when you wake up tomorrow." Jess exhaled heavily, then added in a show of empathy, "I've been where you are, Archie, and the last thing you're going to feel up to doing is hiking. Trust me."

"No." Archie's volume rose again. "I can do it with your help."

Did Jess want to help him? "All right," he finally concurred. "I know a few tricks that used to help me ease the effects from a night's worth of drinking."

With him assisting Archie, their group could hopefully still make it to Sheep Camp by evening. Jess might have to hire a wagon or packhorse to convey the young man, but he'd do it if it meant keeping all of them together and moving forward.

"That's good," Archie murmured. "And I'll pay for all the help then. All the help . . ." He was clearly losing his fight against staying awake.

"I'll have talk to Tava and Carolyn in the morning about you paying for the natives' help yourself." Jess wanted to be sure the women were on board with the plan. "But if they agree, I'll see that you're able to make the hike tomorrow."

"Ah . . . thanks . . ." The statement of gratitude came out as little more than a whisper, and a snore soon accompanied it.

After spreading out on his pallet, Jess situated his blanket across his legs and torso. Archie might not feel as grateful tomorrow once the repercussions of his adventurous night hit him in full force. But at least Jess knew what to do to help.

Would Tava find that odd or concerning? On the ranch, there'd been a firm no-alcohol rule for all of the employees and ranch hands, and Jess had always abided by that tenet. It wasn't until he'd left the ranch that he had fallen back into his old habit of drinking, but he'd wised up real quick that time.

He would forever be in Quinn's debt for allowing him to return home once he had fully changed.

He rolled onto his side and shut his eyes, knowing he ought to sleep. They would all need their strength tomorrow, especially Archie, as they hiked to Sheep Camp at the bottom of the mountain pass. He just hoped his offer to help the young man wouldn't stir up new problems later on.

◆◆◆

Exiting the tent the next morning, Tava shivered in the brisk air and tucked her coat closer around her. If their group left as early as they'd planned, they would be to Sheep Camp by tonight, and she would be that much closer to her pa. Of course, Carolyn had insisted they needed a good breakfast first and had asked Tava to see if either of the men was awake and willing to help set up the stove.

She took a step toward the other tent and found Jess and Archie already standing outside, their profiles to her. She opened her mouth to say hello, but the greeting froze on her tongue when Jess upended a bucket of water over Archie's bare head. The young man spluttered, but he didn't seem shocked at being soaked.

"Wh—what's going on?" she asked, baffled.

Jess whirled around. "Tava." Guilt peppered his expression as he lowered the bucket to his side. "Archie needed help waking up . . ."

"So you doused him with water?" She glanced between the two men. Neither seemed angry. If anything, Archie acted embarrassed as he wiped his dripping face. His shoulders began to shake as his shivered.

"Good morning, Tava." He inclined his head toward her as if he weren't wet and cold. "Apparently the water was needful after my rather disastrous night." Archie touched his forehead and winced.

Tava peered more closely at him. "Are you sick?" His eyes were bloodshot, yet she didn't think that was the result of being drenched.

A flurry of panic filled her empty stomach. She didn't want to leave Archie behind, specifically if he was ill, but she also didn't wish to sit around Dyea when she could be moving steadily closer to her pa. "Will you be able to make it to Sheep Camp today?"

"Of course. I'll be right enough before too long." His gaze flicked to Jess. "At least, that's what Jess says. He knows—"

"Will you buy some coffee?" Jess's question overrode the rest of the young man's words. He withdrew several bills from his pocket and extended them toward Tava.

Nothing about this situation made sense, but if coffee would help Archie feel better, she would get it. She curled her fingers around the money. "Carolyn is wondering if one of you can help her with the stove, so she can start making breakfast."

"What if we eat at a hotel instead, after you bring the coffee back? I'll pay for it this time," Jess offered. "That way as soon as the tents are down, we can start for Sheep Camp, without having to wait for the stove to cool."

Tava was in full agreement about starting their hike sooner. "All right. Is the coffee for all of us?"

"No, it's for Archie . . . and me." Jess wouldn't quite meet her eyes when he added, "Ask them to make it as strong as they can."

She frowned. "But you don't like your coffee that way."

"I know, but that's what we need." He raked a hand through his hair, making it stand on end. "Please, Tava."

She couldn't resist the pleading in his voice. "Let me tell

Carolyn about breakfast, then I'll head to the hotel where we ate last night."

"Thank you." Jess faced Archie, who hadn't moved. "You'd better change into dry clothes. I'll get another bucket of water so we can all fill our canteens."

Tava ducked back inside her own tent. Felix sat on his pallet, pulling on his shoes while his mother rummaged through the bags of supplies.

"The men are awake."

Carolyn turned. "Oh, good. Once we set up the stove and procure some water, I can start on breakfast."

"Actually, Jess wants to pay for everyone to eat breakfast at a hotel. That way we don't have to wait for the stove to cool." Tava lifted the bills in her hand. "First I've been tasked to bring him and Archie a kettle of strong coffee."

Her friend's eyebrows rose. "That seems a bit odd. I don't recall either of them requesting strong coffee in the morning on the steamer."

"It's no less odd than Jess dumping a bucket of water over Archie's head as he did a few minutes ago."

Carolyn laughed, then stopped when Tava didn't join in. "Did they have a fight?"

"I don't think so. They weren't acting upset." She shrugged. "Who knows? Jess said Archie needed help waking up, and Archie mentioned that his night hadn't gone well." Tava slipped Jess's money into her pocket. "I'm assuming he meant after he went off exploring."

"Ah." Carolyn gave a slow nod. "I think I understand."

"You do? What's going on?" Apparently everyone else could make sense of the bizarre morning.

Her friend shot a look at Felix, who had finished with his shoes and was now playing with his wooden soldiers. "I believe our friend Archie," she explained in a hushed tone, "may have had too much to drink last night."

Tava dropped her mouth open in alarm. "You mean he's . . . drunk?"

"Less so this morning, I'd imagine, especially after a good soaking."

She wanted to ask how Carolyn had knowledge of such things, but she felt too embarrassed at her own naivety to inquire.

Clearly sensing the unspoken question, her friend said, "My brother struggles with staying away from alcohol and has for a long time."

"I'm sorry." Tava wished she could think of something more to say. "A cold dousing with water and some strong coffee helps?"

"It does." Carolyn set about packing her and her son's blankets. "It'll minimize the effects, though Archie will likely have a rather odious headache today."

"I should hurry and procure the coffee then." Tava stepped toward the tent door. "I'll be back."

She slipped outside a second time, thinking over what Carolyn had told her. Glancing at the men's tent as she walked past, she wondered how Jess had known what to do to help Archie. Did he also have a family member who struggled with drinking? She should know the answer. After all, she and Jess had been best friends for seven years. Yet again, some of the specifics about his life remained unknown to her.

The town's noise hadn't diminished in volume throughout the night, and even at this early hour, people and animals still moved about the streets. One day in Dyea, and Tava was already missing the peaceful solitude of riding the borders of the ranch with only a horse and her own thoughts for company. Had the disquiet bothered her father too?

When she reached the hotel, she found the dining room full. However, the cook agreed to part with a pot of strong coffee in exchange for money. Kettle in hand, Tava carefully retraced her steps, keeping her pace slow enough to avoid running into anything or anyone. The men's tent had already been taken down by the time she reached camp.

Archie sat, dressed and dry, on a nearby stump, holding his head in his hands. Jess and Carolyn were taking down the other tent, while Felix made another attempt to befriend the mistreated dog. The poor animal kept glancing between its owner's tent and the boy as if conflicted.

"Here's the coffee." Tava brought it to Jess.

He smiled, his earlier agitation gone. "Thank you. Would you mind pouring a mug for Archie?"

"Will he be able to hike? Or should he wait and try to make it to Sheep Camp tomorrow?"

"He doesn't want to wait or be left behind." Jess followed her gaze in Archie's direction. "In fact, he volunteered to hire the natives himself, if we'll allow him to stay with us."

Carolyn's eyes widened. "He's willing to pay for all of the help?"

Nodding, Jess helped her fold the canvas.

"That's a very generous offer." One Tava didn't really want to turn down. Then she and Jess could save the money they'd planned to use to hire packers. But she still worried that Archie would slow them down.

Judging from the way Carolyn chewed her lower lip, Tava's friend had been contemplating the same thing. "What do you think, Jess?" Carolyn asked.

"I think we ought to accept. I'll make sure Archie doesn't lag too far behind."

"I've worried about Felix keeping up as well." Carolyn turned to observe her son.

Tava did the same. Watching the boy's interest in the husky gave her a sudden idea. But first she needed to give

Archie his coffee. "I'll pour this for Archie," she said, hefting the kettle, "while it's still hot."

She found a mug and filled it to the brim with the strong brew, then she carried it over to the young man. "For you." She knelt in front of the stump and presented Archie with the cup.

"Thanks." He sampled a swallow before coughing. "It's strong, isn't it?" he choked out.

"Are you feeling any better than before?"

He tried to nod, but it ended in a wince. "Jess reassured me the splitting headache fades at some point."

"Are you sure you don't mind paying for all the help?" Before she put her plan in place, Tava had to be certain Archie intended to go through with his.

He downed more of the coffee. "Jess told you about that, huh?" Archie lowered the mug to his lap. "I was a fool last night, but I'm hoping you can all forgive me. I figure paying for the help is a way to keep myself from being a further nuisance."

"You're not a nuisance." She might not agree with the young man's choices, but his regret was more than evident. "We don't want to leave you behind."

"Truly? You still think well of me?"

She sensed he meant more than his misguided adventure from the night before. But Tava couldn't offer him anything more than friendship and compassion.

Was that how Jess had felt toward her when he'd come back to the ranch? The likelihood elicited a physical pang inside her heart. Yet if he hadn't been able to offer more in their relationship, wasn't it kind to let her know and not string her along? The question was probably worth pondering over later.

Setting down the kettle, Tava stood. "We're grateful to

have you along. Now finish the coffee, and we'll all head to the hotel for breakfast."

She left him and joined Felix. "Any luck?" Tava asked, stooping next to the boy. The husky had hazarded a few inches forward, but that was all.

Felix pushed out a heavy sigh. "He seems too scared to do anything."

Given what Tava had observed last night, she knew the boy spoke the truth. "I think he is scared." She just hoped she could change that.

"Why don't you go help your ma?" Tava suggested as she straightened. She didn't want Felix witnessing the potential failure of her idea.

He glanced between his mother and the dog, obviously debating what to do. Thankfully, Carolyn called him over right then, and Felix obeyed.

Inhaling a calming breath, Tava approached the tent that belonged to the dog's owner. A peek over her shoulder proved that the husky was the only one paying any attention to her.

"I'm hoping this works, boy," she muttered to the dog.

She tapped her knuckle against the tent pole and waited. Silence echoed from the other side of the canvas, and she knocked again.

"I'm comin'," a voice snarled.

At the sound, the dog lowered its head onto its paws. The tent flap was thrown back a moment later, and the middle-aged man from the night before glowered at Tava with eyes as red rimmed as Archie's earlier. "Who are you, and why are you knockin' at my door?" His build was nowhere near as large as that of the man she'd confronted yesterday, but Tava had firsthand knowledge of the way he treated a helpless animal.

She attempted a smile, in spite of the increased pounding

of her heart. "Good morning. I'm sorry to bother you, but we're pulling out soon." She swallowed the dryness in her throat. "Before we go, I'd like to buy your dog."

"My dog?" The man glared at the creature. "Whadaya want with a worthless thing like him?"

Tava ignored his question in favor of her own. "How much did you pay for him?"

"Ten lousy dollars, but he ain't worth half that."

She removed ten dollars from her pocket. "I'd be willing to take the dog off your hands for what you paid for him."

"After all the trouble I've gone through to care for him, I wouldn't take less than twenty-five." He kicked his leg in the direction of the husky, who scuttled out of the way just in time.

Tava pressed her lips over an angry remark, both at the man's idea of caring and at the exorbitant amount of money he wanted for a dog he didn't even like. "What about twenty? That's twice as much as you paid for him."

The man scratched his chin. "Twenty, huh? I can maybe get me a decent dog with that."

"Done. Twenty it is." She fished out another bill and placed the money in the man's open palm. "What do you call the dog?"

The money disappeared into the stranger's soiled shirt. "Never got around to givin' him a name."

Someone in their group could surely come up with a name for the animal. "Come, dog," Tava called as she moved back from the man's tent. The husky sat up, but it turned to look at its previous master.

"Go on, you mutt. Go with her."

The dog exchanged a long look with the man before climbing to its feet and trotting over to Tava. She let him sniff her. With that introduction completed, she held out her hands so that he could explore those next. Then she scratched him behind the ears.

"Thank you, sir."

He didn't respond as he stomped into his tent.

A swell of triumph drew a smile from Tava. She'd done it—she had saved the dog. "Let's go meet the others," she told the husky, taking several more steps in that direction. The dog cocked its head, then followed after her. She could hardly wait to introduce the rest of the group to their newest addition.

8

NAVIGATING THE FIRST stretch of the trail toward the distant mountains didn't require too much exertion, despite the sixty-pound pack on his back. That didn't mean Jess wanted to jog along in single file, as the two native families were doing farther ahead. The men carried one hundred pounds of supplies each. Jess shook his head at the prospect and felt gratitude all over again for the help Archie had hired.

The path they treaded passed through meadows and forests, crossing the river here and there. Spruce trees mingled with birch, cottonwood, and willows. And other than the presence of their fellow hikers and some leading packhorses, the setting felt downright tranquil after the noise of Dyea.

Jess splashed through the river, the chill of the water seeping into his pant legs before he strode up the opposite side. He'd decided to remain at the rear of the group, to look after anyone who started to lag behind. Tava hiked several yards in front of him, while the Halls and Archie maintained the lead—thanks in part to the husky Tava had bought. The dog kept darting forward, then racing back to urge the others to follow.

He'd witnessed the husky's ill treatment the night before and felt as angry as Tava had over it. Yet he'd been just as stunned as the others when she had announced that the dog would be joining their group. Felix had recovered first and excitedly asked the animal's name.

"He doesn't have one yet," Tava had informed the boy.

They'd all thrown out ideas. But it wasn't until Carolyn had suggested Dusty Gray that the dog had responded with a bark. Archie had recommended shortening the name to Dusty, and the rest of them agreed. Within minutes of meeting everyone, Dusty had acted as if he'd been traveling with them from the beginning.

Jess paused to readjust his pack. Something sticking up from the brush caught his notice. It didn't appear to be a tree root or a rock. Curious, he stepped toward it. The object turned out to be a clothes trunk. Someone had obviously dumped it here on the side of the trail, and Jess couldn't blame them. Carting such a thing would be heavy and cumbersome. Still, he couldn't help wondering if the person had felt relief as they walked away or remorse at having to leave their belongings behind.

Up the trail a little farther, a smaller trunk also sat forgotten. A framed picture had been propped against it, as if the owner had taken one final look before placing it carefully on the ground and moving on.

Jess picked up the frame. Judging by the lack of water damage to the wood, the item hadn't been languishing here for long. He used his coat sleeve to wipe away the dirt from the glass. A husband and wife and their seven children stared up at him. Jess swallowed. It was like looking at his parents and six siblings, back before he'd left home.

How had his family fared since then? The question had never been far from his thoughts the last seven years.

He'd been too afraid to write them letters at first, terrified his pa would find him and drag him back to the farm. Later, when Jess had more confidence in himself, he'd accepted

Quinn's offer to inquire after the family. Tava's father had done as promised and discovered that the Lawmens had lost the farm where Jess had grown up. None of their former neighbors knew where the family had gone after that. Their whereabouts remained a mystery to him.

Jess often wondered if any of his brothers or sisters had also struck out on their own. For their sakes, he hoped so. He prayed every night for them, and had since he'd walked away from the farm. But that didn't mean he didn't feel guilt over leaving his younger siblings behind.

Would he ever find a place of belonging, where regret over his relationships didn't plague him in quiet moments? He'd been unable to protect his family back then, but his choice to protect Tava four years ago had inescapably hurt her.

Even though he hadn't returned to being the man he'd once been, Jess still didn't know if it would be enough—for Tava or her father. Would Tava even want him if she knew about his past or that his feelings for her ran much deeper than friendship? Or was it time, once they got back to the ranch, for him to consider moving on for good?

"What are you looking at there?"

Tava's voice startled him, and Jess fumbled to keep from dropping the picture. "It's something left behind by one of the gold seekers who came this way." He lifted the frame for her to see.

"They just left it here?" Her brown eyes filled with dismay as she glanced from the picture to the lonely trunk.

Jess placed the frame back in its spot of reverence. "Sometimes that's necessary, when you can't shoulder the weight any longer." He straightened and gripped the straps of his pack. "Then you wonder if you should've walked away sooner."

She seemed to grasp that his words hinted at something deeper, because her brow furrowed with confusion as she shifted her valise from one hand to the other. The books inside had to be weighing her down, but she hadn't complained yet.

"Do you need to rest?" he asked, noting the tired line of her shoulders beneath her pack.

Tava shook her head. "I'm fine."

"Let's catch up to the others." He offered her an encouraging smile that she returned after a few seconds.

There was plenty for Jess to think about and decide before they reached Dawson, but he also knew the importance—and necessity—of simply putting one foot in front of the other. And for now, that was what he'd do.

The farther Tava hiked, the heavier the books in her grip became. She wrapped her hands around her valise and tried carrying it in front of her, but that increased the ache in her arms. Perhaps she ought to place the books inside her pack. But doing so would mean dropping back even farther from the rest of the group. Already Jess outpaced her by a few yards, though he'd pause whenever he noticed her lagging behind him.

Tava returned to hefting the bag in one hand and trading it to the other every few minutes. How much longer could she endure carting the extra weight? The valise had nothing else in it, save for the books. All of her clothes and toiletries she'd placed inside her pack. Jess might be willing to carry the books if she asked, except he was shouldering more weight on his back than anyone else in the group. She didn't want to slow him down by adding to his burden.

Her thoughts went to the picture frame he'd discovered beside the abandoned trunk. How forlorn the items had looked sitting neglected to the side of the trail. Tava couldn't imagine leaving behind such significant mementos of home and family.

The muscles in her left arm complained, signaling that it was time for the books to change hands again. But this time her fingers wouldn't fully grip the heavy bag. It slipped from her grasp and landed with a dull thunk in the dirt. Maybe she ought to try adding it to her pack after all.

She cut a glance at Jess up ahead. He hadn't yet noticed her stopping. Tava slipped off her pack. The release of weight from her shoulders pulled a small cry of relief from her mouth. Some of the people hiking past her, who were stooped beneath their own packs, would be making this same trip over and over again. Just as her father had done. She shook her head in disbelief, unable to imagine it.

Tava opened her pack, added the books, and shouldered her burden once more. Her knees sagged with the additional weight, but eventually she got her legs beneath her. She used the tips of her fingers to pick up the empty valise, and she resumed hiking. However, her pace didn't improve. If anything, her steps slowed. Up ahead, Jess had stopped to wait for her. Blinking back tears of frustration, Tava forced her tired limbs to keep moving.

"Where are your books?" he asked, looking at the limp bag in her hand.

She tried to appear at ease, but the added pressure on her back increased as she stood still. "I put them in my pack." Tava motioned to the canvas bundle he held in his hands. "What are you carrying now?"

"Felix's pack." Jess hoisted it in the air. "He was getting tired and starting to slow down. I volunteered to carry his bag for a while."

"That was nice of you." And while she meant it, his

chivalry also ended the possibility of him carting her books for a stretch.

Jess strode forward, and Tava fought a protest as she followed. A short rest would have been nice, but she understood his drive to keep moving. She felt it too. If they didn't maintain a steady gait, they might not make it to Sheep Camp by evening. Which would put them a day behind in tackling the pass.

She managed to stay next to Jess for several hundred feet. But her breathing sped up more the longer she tried to match his pace. After another minute or two, Tava had to stop.

Stepping off to the side, she removed her pack a second time and bent over her knees, trying to catch her breath. From the corner of her eye, she saw Jess turn around.

"What's wrong?"

Tava waved a hand at him. "I just need a moment. You can keep going."

"I'm not going to leave you behind." He glanced over his shoulder up the trail. "We are going to have to move faster to catch up with everyone."

She managed a quick nod. The Halls, Archie, and the native families were no longer in sight. Embarrassment added to the flush of exertion on her face. Tava hadn't even managed to keep pace with Archie, who despite being drunk the night before was maintaining more speed than her.

"I'm coming," she reassured Jess.

Tava replaced the pack on her shoulders, but this time, her legs refused to hold her upright. She dropped to her knees with a soft cry.

Jess hurried to her side and knelt down. "It's the books, isn't it?"

She didn't bother to answer as she stared at the dirt through a sheen of tears.

"Tava?" He waited for her to look at him. "You can leave them behind."

"No." She shook her head. "They're for my father. He'll be happy to have more books."

"He'll be happiest to have *you* there."

"But . . ."

She pressed her lips together over another argument. Jess was right. Yet how could she part with the books? Her pa loved reading, and she'd imagined his face lighting up with gratitude when she presented them to him.

"I would carry them myself if I could," Jess said, his tone earnest. "But we'd be in the same predicament, with someone still lagging behind the rest."

Tava squeezed her wet eyes shut for a moment. She knew what she had to do. After sliding her pack off her back, she removed the books from inside.

She ran her finger across the cover of the first one. Memories of her father flitted through her mind—times when she'd found him asleep in his reading chair and times when he'd read out loud to her, his deep voice rising and falling with inflection.

Would she experience those moments again? Or like the books she held, would those times become faded recollections?

Exhaling her worry in the form of a sigh, Tava set the stack of books in the grass. This would be their final resting place. Sorrow still clogged her throat, forcing her to cough so that she could speak.

"He'd want us to keep going, wouldn't he?" She turned to look at Jess.

He nodded. "That doesn't mean it's easy to let go of something that belonged to your pa."

"It's like saying goodbye to him all over again." The truth of her own confession resounded painfully inside her.

Until Jess's hand rose to cup her cheek. "I'm still praying every night that's the only goodbye you'll have to make."

"Me too," Tava whispered.

His featherlight touch and intent gaze had the same effect on her breathing as hiking had minutes ago. But Jess was attempting to offer comfort, nothing else.

Tava broke his gentle hold by reaching for her valise. She set the empty bag atop the books, knowing it would give them a little shelter. Then she climbed to her feet. "The others are going to wonder what's keeping us."

"True."

Jess helped her put on her pack, and they started up the trail once more. When they reached a bend, Tava paused to peer back at the spot where she'd left her father's books. The stack was barely visible. A pang of grief had her clutching the straps of her bag more tightly. She would do her best to hold to Jess's words and hope that there would be no more goodbyes in her future.

9

THEY CAUGHT UP to the others right before the trail entered a canyon. To Jess's relief, Tava had kept pace with him the whole way without staggering or becoming winded again. Traces of sadness still clung to her like cobwebs, and he understood why. Giving up her father's books hadn't been easy.

"There you two are." Archie straightened from the rock he'd been leaning against. "We figured we'd better wait for you instead of continuing on."

A tinge of pink rose into Tava's cheeks. "Sorry we ended up lagging so far behind."

Carolyn waved away her apology. "It was nice to have a rest." She glanced between Tava and Jess. "Everything all right?" The hopeful glint in the woman's green eyes made Jess instantly suspicious. Did Carolyn think they'd orchestrated being left alone at the back of the group?

"It was my fault," Tava said. "Jess was helping me readjust my pack." She didn't elaborate, and Jess respected that it wasn't his place to mention her having to leave the books behind.

He turned to where Felix was attempting to wrestle a stick from Dusty's teeth. "How are you doing, Felix?"

"Me and Dusty are doing good. Aren't we, Ma?"

The boy's mother smiled at him. "You're both doing splendidly. I do think it's time to carry your pack yourself again."

Felix made a face. "I guess."

"What do you say to Jess for helping you?"

The boy grabbed ahold of his bag. "Thank you, Jess."

"You're welcome." Jess helped Felix arrange the pack on his shoulders. He would've carried it a little longer, but he appreciated Carolyn's desire for her son to do his part. And in truth, Jess didn't mind giving his arms a rest.

"Want to hike with me and Felix at the front, Tava?" Archie asked as the group prepared to set off again. According to the young man, the native families had already entered the canyon.

Tava didn't answer right away, making Jess hope that she'd choose to remain near the back with him as she'd done so far. Except then she nodded. "I can join you two."

"Wonderful." Archie's grin set Jess's teeth on edge. Annoyance mingled with his disappointment. He attempted to hide both by pretending interest in the nearby trees. After removing his hat, he relished the way the breeze cooled his sweat dampened hair. He still wasn't sure whether he'd made a mistake or not by touching Tava's face earlier. He had enjoyed hiking alongside his best friend without everyone else around for once.

By the time he replaced his hat and motioned for Carolyn to proceed him, the other three and Dusty were already pulling ahead. Traversing the trail through the canyon wouldn't be an easy—or quick—undertaking. Particularly for Carolyn, who had to navigate the boulders, roots, and toppled trees in a dress.

Jess's decision to remain at the rear of the group, whether Tava did or not, proved fortuitous when Carolyn encountered a large felled tree. Stopping, she eyed the giant obstacle with a frown.

"If you hold my hand," he said as he came up alongside her, "you can step onto the log and then down—just like you would stairs."

"Right." She threw him a wry smile. "It's no different than going up and down a staircase."

He chuckled as he helped her over the tree. "See? You did it."

"Thank you." She bunched part of her skirt in her hands and sidestepped a bulky tree root. "I appreciate the help, especially since I imagine you wish you were up ahead with someone else right now."

Jess didn't have to ask who she meant, but he wasn't going to divulge anything either. "Yep, Dusty sure is a good traveling companion."

It was Carolyn's turn to laugh. "Very well. I know when not to press."

They continued hiking, Jess offering her aid whenever they faced a particularly rough patch of ground. "I'm seeing the wisdom of Tava wearing pants," Carolyn remarked when they paused to rest. "Maybe then I wouldn't be slowing us down so much. Even Felix has stayed in front."

"We've made it this far." Jess fanned his face with his hat as he looked back the way they'd come. "Now, if it were a competition, I might feel sorer about being left behind."

She followed his example by waving her hand in front of her flushed cheeks. "Sort of like you felt before we started up the canyon?"

Jess cut her a glance. He wasn't sure he understood what Carolyn was trying to say, but he guessed she'd somehow noticed his earlier disappointment. "Not sure I know what you mean."

"I was talking about your reaction when Archie invited Tava to hike with him."

Warmth crept up Jess's neck. "You ready to keep hiking?"

He expected Carolyn to be amused at his obvious discomfort, but she wasn't. When she spoke again, her tone had gentled. "I understand your position more than you think." She moved past him. "I know how hard it is to see someone interested in something you've convinced yourself you maybe didn't need anymore."

With her hiking ahead of him, Jess didn't bother to mask the shock that leaked onto his face. While Carolyn didn't know the extent of his feelings for Tava—and how they hadn't changed with time—her compassionate words still rang with truth.

"I liked my Noah the first time we met," she continued, clearly not bothered by Jess's silence, "but I wasn't sure I was ready to settle down. I'd been living independently for nearly two years, and I didn't want to give that up. Then some other young lady at church started paying attention to Noah and he to her." Carolyn shook her head. "It didn't take me long after that to realize I felt more for him than I'd been willing to admit. So I mustered up the courage to tell him, and we were married a month later."

Her gumption was admirable, and Jess appreciated her willingness to share her story, even if his and Tava's situation didn't completely mirror hers. "I imagine it was real tough losing him."

"It was. I miss him every day." She brushed at her eyes with the back of her hand. "I don't know all of the obstacles between you and Tava, but I'm confident that Archie isn't one of them."

With his help, she tackled climbing around a large

boulder. When Jess released her hand, Carolyn didn't move forward. Instead she studied him with an earnest look. "May I ask what's really preventing you from making your feelings known?"

Familiar regret squeezed him. "It's complicated."

She raised an eyebrow, clearly unimpressed by such a vague answer. And it was little wonder. She'd been honest in relaying her story. Perhaps Jess could impart more than he otherwise would have.

"Even if I did say something, Tava likely wouldn't believe me." He waved Carolyn forward, knowing it would be easier to keep sharing if she wasn't watching him. She complied. "A few years ago, I insisted Tava and I stay friends. It's only been on this trip that I realized how much that hurt her. I don't know that she can forgive me." Of that or his other mistakes.

"You're like my Noah. A good, kind man," Carolyn said over her shoulder before she faced the trail again.

The significance of that comparison wasn't lost on Jess. Things might not be as straightforward for him and Tava as it had been for Carolyn and her late husband, but even the little he'd shared helped ease his sorrow over the past.

"We all do things we regret, Jess, and we affect the people we love. However, if Tava returns your feelings, then I imagine she—"

A sudden cry pierced the air somewhere in front of them. "That sounds like Tava."

"Oh no." Carolyn met his gaze with a worried one of her own. "I hope nothing's wrong."

Jess took her elbow in hand, and together they rushed forward. He didn't know what had happened, but the growing dread inside him was clue enough that it couldn't be good.

She'd been talking with Archie when Dusty suddenly darted between them and knocked them both off-balance. Tava tripped over something and landed in the dirt, her right foot twisting beneath her. The pain that shot up from her ankle tore a sharp yelp from her mouth. Pulling herself to a seated position, she brushed the debris from her pant legs and hands.

Across from her, Archie had regained his feet, but he stared in horror at his torn sleeve. A line of blood had formed on the exposed skin of his arm.

"Are you all right, Archie?"

He seemed to collect himself. "I think I cut myself on a tree branch." He glanced down at Tava. "What about you?"

"I tripped, but I should be fine."

To prove the point, she attempted to stand. But the instant that Tava placed her weight on her right foot, the ache intensified. Panic mingled with her pain as she sank back down. She couldn't be injured. Not when she needed to walk, and hike, and scale the mountain tomorrow. Reaching her pa sooner than later depended on her ability to move. Yet if she couldn't even put pressure on her ankle . . .

Archie extended his uninjured arm toward her. "Let me help you up."

She let him assist her onto her feet. However, the moment Archie released her, she braced herself on a nearby boulder to avoid stepping on her ankle.

By then, Felix had raced back to join them, Dusty at his heels. Tava didn't blame the husky—the dog hadn't known there wasn't enough room to easily squeeze past.

"What happened?" The boy looked them over, his gaze widening at the cut on Archie's arm.

Before either of them could answer, Jess and Carolyn hurried up the trail toward them. "Are you hurt?" Jess asked.

"Dusty accidentally bumped us off the trail," Tava explained, "and Archie was cut on the arm." She hoped mentioning the young man and his injury would draw the focus away from herself. Hurt ankle or not, she had to keep going.

Her plan temporarily worked as Jess and Carolyn looked over Archie's arm. "It's not deep," Carolyn said after examining the wound.

"I found the rest of your sleeve." Felix waved the piece of cloth in the air.

His mother took it and tied the fabric around the gap in Archie's sleeve. "When we reach Sheep Camp, we'll see if someone has some salve that we can put on that cut."

Archie nodded. "Thank you."

"What about you, Tava?" Jess looked toward her. "I heard you cry out."

"That's because I tripped over a root or a rock." She spread her arms out. "But no broken bones or blood, see?"

Jess's frown conveyed his blatant disbelief. "You're fine?"

"We should keep going," she hedged. "The canyon probably comes to an end not too far ahead."

"Dusty and I saw the end before we ran back," Felix said.

The dog barked and licked Tava's hand as if seeking an apology. "I forgive you, boy." She petted Dusty's ears and lifted her head to find Jess watching her. When he motioned for her to go ahead of him, she swallowed a frustrated groan. If she preceded him up the trail, he would notice her limping.

"Why don't you and Carolyn take the lead this time?" she suggested in a casual tone.

Jess narrowed his eyes. She could practically see him turning over her proposal in his mind and trying to reason out its motive.

Her rescue came in the form of Felix. "Come on, Ma." The boy grinned at Carolyn. "You can see how fast me and Dusty can be."

"Not too fast. We don't need anyone else getting tripped or cut today." She turned to Jess. "Do you mind helping me a little longer?"

He finally looked away from Tava. "I don't mind."

She breathed a sigh of relief as he and the Halls moved up the trail. Avoiding Jess's scrutiny would be far easier at the back of the group.

"You coming?" Archie waved after the others, then winced at the movement.

"I'm right behind you."

Tava lowered her hand from the boulder and took a step on her uninjured foot. Apparently satisfied she was coming, the young man followed after the rest of the group, his good hand cupping his bandaged arm.

Her ankle protested when she attempted to step on it next. Tava cringed and hastily traded her weight to her other leg. Then she tried the process again. Each time she used her injured foot, it aggravated it more. Soon her foot began throbbing inside her boot. Yet she had no other choice but to keep shuffling forward and reminding herself to take full breaths, rather than the shallow ones the pain dictated.

How would she possibly make it all the way to Sheep Camp today, let alone up to the pass tomorrow? Discouragement burned in the form of tears that dangerously blurred the trail in front of her.

Please, God, she pleaded silently. *Help me keep going. I have to find Pa. I have to know for myself what happened to him. Don't let me fail him too.*

The canyon finally ended, though Tava felt as if an eternity had passed before she arrived at that point. Her mind felt hazy from the anguish of walking on her ankle, and she'd fallen behind—again. The others had stopped and were drinking from their canteens. Not surprisingly, the native families were nowhere in sight. By now, they'd likely reached the evening's destination with all of the supplies.

All the more reason to push onward, Tava told herself.

A nearby tree stump seemed as heavenly a gift to her as the water from the rock to the thirsty Israelites. She limped toward it and sat, stretching her right leg forward. With shaky hands, she removed the cap of her canteen. Tava drank several swallows, wishing the liquid could purge her pain as effectively as it quenched her dry throat.

Several minutes later, Jess rose from where he'd been resting on the ground. "It's not much farther to Sheep Camp, but Eugene told me the trail gets steeper."

The latter news nearly yanked a cry of dismay from Tava's lips. Of course the trail would rise to meet the base of the mountain, but she hadn't counted on hiking it with a twisted ankle.

Knowing her ankle needed every second of rest, she lingered on the stump as the rest of the group climbed to their feet and resumed hiking. At last Tava stood. Maybe the short reprieve had somewhat improved the condition of her injury. She tried to reassure herself further with the reminder that a break or a sprain would take longer to recover from than twisting her foot.

Tava pulled in a deep breath and exhaled slowly. Ahead, Jess had turned to wait for her once more. If she didn't hurry, he'd question her reason for dillydallying.

Anxious to conceal her hurt ankle a little longer, she moved forward more rapidly than she had yet. Unfortunately, the quickened pace proved too much. As she took another step, her leg buckled beneath her, and she crumbled to the ground.

"Tava!" Jess sprinted toward her, his earlier suspicions confirmed. She had been injured when she'd tripped. What he didn't know was how badly and why she'd refused to tell anyone.

She held her right boot between her hands as Jess knelt beside her. "Is it your foot?"

"Yes," she hissed, her voice clogged with pain. He hated to see her hurting.

Archie and the Halls followed in his wake as Jess reached for the laces of her boot. "How bad is it?"

Her fingers immediately pushed his aside. "I twisted my ankle. But if I rest it a little longer, I can keep going."

"You can't hike like that." He sat back on his heels. "It'll worsen your injury and increase the time it takes for it heal."

Tava's eyes sought his, their brown depths full of pleading. "I'm not going to let a sore ankle stop me. We have to reach Sheep Camp tonight if we want to make it over the pass tomorrow."

"Is something wrong?" Carolyn asked as she, Felix, and Archie formed a semicircle around them.

Tava tucked her leg to the side of the stump. "I twisted my ankle when I stumbled, but it'll be fine."

"You sure?" Archie looked as skeptical as Jess felt.

Still, Tava answered with a decisive nod. "We don't have much farther to go."

Jess bit back his arguments as he stood. The remaining distance was far enough, and then there was the mountain to tackle tomorrow. Concern yawned inside him. Waiting for Tava's foot to heal would cost precious time they didn't have, yet she'd hurt herself more if she didn't stay off that ankle.

He blew out his breath, trying to tame his worry. All he could tackle right now was the present. "We'll get you to Sheep Camp tonight."

Relief eased the strained lines on her face. "Thank you. I just need a few minutes more to rest."

"It'll take me longer than that to procure a wagon."

Tava visibly stiffened. "A wagon? No."

"I think it's a good idea," Carolyn said.

Felix hopped up and down. "Can I ride in the wagon too?"

Tava's scowl burned in Jess's direction. "I don't need a wagon."

"That may be true." Carolyn rested her hand on Tava's shoulder. "But you do need to reach your father. And that means accepting help to get there."

The breath she expelled spoke of resignation. "All right."

Jess threw Carolyn a grateful smile. "If all of you will wait here, I'll be back as soon as I can."

As he hurried back up the trail, he wondered why Carolyn's words had softened Tava's stance when his hadn't. The woman had appealed to Tava's urgency to reach her father, but so had Jess when Tava had struggled with leaving the books behind earlier in the day. That couldn't be the reason then. If he didn't know any better, he would think she associated a ride in a wagon with accepting help from him personally.

Jess nearly faltered in his pace as the truth of his own conclusion struck him. He couldn't recall the last time Tava had asked him for help. While she did seem to appreciate his opinions and openly listened to his responses, it had been ages since she'd petitioned him for assistance with a need of her own.

It was another painful reminder of the chasm that hadn't fully closed between them. One Jess had been the first to dig that fateful night.

Would their friendship ever return to its former depth?

Jess wanted to believe so. Would that be more likely if he continued to do all in his power to help them reach Quinn in time? If so, he needed to find a wagon or a packhorse for the man's injured daughter, whether she welcomed it or not.

He had made a promise to her pa—and to Tava, too, by coming on this trip—that he would look out for her and help her, and Jess was as determined as ever to keep his word.

10

THE WAGON JOLTED to a stop in front of one of the shacks jammed among the tents on Sheep Camp's single road. The building hardly resembled a hotel. Still, primitive or not, Tava was grateful for the chance to be free of the jolting, bumpy conveyance.

She hadn't ridden the wagon alone either. Carolyn, Felix, and even Dusty had joined her, and Tava had appreciated the company. The intermittent conversation with the Halls had helped keep her mind off the pain in her ankle.

As much as Tava didn't want to admit it, Jess had been right. She wouldn't have made it so far without a ride—not without seriously delaying their arrival at the base of the mountain and possibly reinjuring herself as well.

When he'd returned to the group with a wagon and driver, Tava had asked Jess how much he had paid for the help. "It was worth every dime," he'd answered.

Tava hadn't pressed him for details. She'd still felt irritated with him over his insistence that she couldn't keep hiking. She didn't enjoy feeling helpless or being treated as if she were an invalid. Or, maybe, it was feeling beholden to Jess that she didn't like. Yet sometime during the rough ride, humility—and regret—had finally caught up with her.

Jess had been determined to see that she kept going. Only not on her twisted ankle. And despite spurning his help in the

117

past, Tava could see that he hadn't let such a thing stop him from being a good friend—her best friend. So much so that he would use his own money to pay for a wagon to carry her.

It was true he'd hurt her deeply in the past, and because of it, Tava had convinced herself that to protect her heart she had to be seen as independent and above needing his help. That way Jess couldn't get close enough to wound her again.

Yet despite all of that, his friendship had remained consistent. It hadn't ebbed and flowed as hers had. Such a realization pained her more acutely than her foot. She'd held on to what she thought was hurt, when instead it had actually been her pride she'd been clinging to so tightly.

"Need a hand to climb down?" Jess asked, tugging Tava's attention to their present surroundings.

She hadn't accepted his aid getting in or out of a wagon in four years. And that was about to change. Gathering her courage, she placed her palm against his.

Surprise riddled Jess's features, prompting a tiny smile from Tava, before his hand closed over hers. The warmth that flowed up her arm at his touch erased her amusement—changing it to something unsettling yet not unpleasant.

As she had earlier when Jess had cupped her face, she reminded herself that his offer of assistance stemmed from friendship. Even if friendliness wasn't the cause of the flutters inside her stomach.

Jess clasped her elbow in his other hand and helped her descend from the wagon bed. "There you go."

"Thanks." She gingerly set the toe of her right boot on the ground, while keeping the majority of her weight on her left.

"You're welcome." He tipped his hat toward the hotel. "I can help you inside."

The rest of the group was already moving toward the door. If Tava wanted a moment alone with Jess, it had to be now.

"I appreciate that you got the wagon." She studied the front of the building to avoid looking at him directly. "I was upset earlier about being too injured to walk, but I'm sorry I placed most of that frustration on you."

She lifted her eyes to the towering peaks and glaciers that surrounded them. Their wagon driver had pointed out the small dent in the mountain that was the Chilkoot Pass. From down below, it appeared impossibly out of reach. Would she even be able to hike to it tomorrow?

Reaching the summit apparently involved a grueling upward climb. There was even a point where the path's angle stood at almost thirty-five degrees. Just the idea of scaling something that steep renewed the ache in Tava's foot.

"What if I can't make it, Jess?" The words slipped from her mouth. "I can't stand the thought of waiting here for several days, when we could be over the pass and on our way toward my father by then."

He gently squeezed her elbow, prompting her focus back to him. "You're not alone, songbird. I'm just as determined as you to reach Quinn. If that requires carrying you on my back the entire way up the mountain, I'll do it."

The firmness of his resolve momentarily calmed her fears. Somehow she would make it over the mountain tomorrow—she had to. And when she penned her nightly tally mark on the back of her pa's letter, it would be from the opposite side of the pass.

"Ready to head inside?" Jess asked. "If there's a chance I'm carrying you tomorrow, I'm going to need all the sustenance I can get."

Tava jabbed him playfully in the ribs, relieved and grateful to return to their old camaraderie. She'd missed this familiar easiness between them since leaving the ranch. "What are you implying, Mr. Lawmen?"

"Nothing at all, Miss Rutherford." He chuckled, his gaze shining with hidden delight. "Nothing at all."

Jess had never tasted anything as good as the meal served at the hotel that evening. The fare was simple enough—hams, eggs, bread, and hot coffee. But after a day of hiking, his exhaustion and hunger transformed the meal into something akin to perfection.

The sleeping accommodations, however, were less than ideal. Given the early start they wanted to make on the pass the next day, their group had decided to forego camping and join the throng inside the hotel.

Patrons occupied all the available floor space, making it difficult to walk without stepping on somebody. After searching, Jess and Archie located a section of unoccupied ground on the second floor for the women and Felix.

Jess assisted Tava up the rickety steps. She'd soaked her ankle in the nearby stream after supper and bound her foot with a strip of cloth. According to her, the swelling had gone down some, but she still couldn't put much weight on it.

Upstairs Carolyn withdrew a blanket from her pack and spread it over the floorboards. "Sorry I only have the one," she said to Jess and Archie.

Jess shook his head, dismissing her apology. "I've slept on worse than a hard floor and a roof overhead."

"Not me." The candlelight emphasized the excitement in Archie's light-blue eyes as he studied the sleeping masses. "This is truly roughing it, isn't it?"

Swallowing a retort, Jess offered a simple nod instead. The effects of the young man's inebriation had long since worn off. With his arm properly bandaged now, Archie was apparently eager for adventure again. For his part, Jess considered their day adventurous enough with two sustained injuries—and they still had so far to go.

Tava looked about the room as Jess helped her sit on the blanket. "Where will you two sleep?"

"There's another vacant spot in the far corner." He pointed in the direction. "How's your ankle feeling?"

She grimaced as she slipped her unlaced boot from her right foot. "It was doing better before I attempted those stairs." Worry cut across her brow. "What if my ankle isn't better by morning? If the stairs aggravate it, tomorrow's climb certainly will."

He didn't wish to tell her that the same thought had crossed his mind. The pass wasn't something to be tackled halfheartedly. If Tava wasn't up to hiking all the way up the mountain, they would have to wait at Sheep Camp another day, until she felt ready. But that wasn't what she needed to hear tonight.

Jess met her troubled gaze. "Let's see how your ankle is in the morning. I'll be praying tonight that it feels better."

"I will too," Carolyn said, taking Tava's hand into her own.

Some of the anxiousness slid from Tava's expression. "I guess we'll see in the morning."

After bidding her and the Halls good night, Jess led Archie to their selected spot. He didn't bother to remove his boots this time. Instead he plumped up his coat as a makeshift pillow and lay down.

Jess shut his eyes and did his best to tune out the snores and snuffles in the room as he offered his nightly prayer. He thanked the Lord for helping them make it through another day toward Dawson and Quinn. As was his habit, he listed out the names of his family next.

Watch over Ma, Clive, Rowena, Pete, Mary Jane, Susan,

and Oscar. He inhaled a slow breath and added on the exhale, *And Pa too.*

Then he asked that if possible Tava's ankle would be able to endure the strain of climbing tomorrow. The mountain would surely test their resolves to reach the Klondike, so Jess ended his prayer with a petition that they would each be able to meet the challenge.

Every one of her muscles protested the night on the hard floor when Tava awoke the next morning. She sat up slowly, then stretched her arms and back. Carolyn and Felix were still asleep. A glance at the far corner confirmed Archie hadn't risen yet either, but Tava couldn't see Jess. She wasn't sure where he would have gone, unless he'd left the hotel to speak with the native families about the trek up to the pass.

Thoughts of making the day's climb with her injury worried Tava's lips into a tight line. She studied her right foot, attempting to assess which of her aches and pains radiated from there. But other than a general feeling of stiffness, her ankle no longer hurt.

She allowed herself a moment of cautious relief before offering a prayer of gratitude and a plea for additional help. After putting on her boots, she tied the laces, making sure the ones on her right shoe remained loose.

Carolyn and Felix woke as she finished. Her friend put away the blanket and helped Tava stand. The stiffness in her ankle became more pronounced as she put weight on it, but the stabbing pain from yesterday hadn't yet returned.

With Carolyn's assistance, Tava carefully maneuvered her way downstairs. Felix followed, dragging their packs behind him. In spite of the earliness of the hour, the tables were filled with hungry patrons once more. The smell of eggs, bacon, and coffee drew a gurgle of hunger from Tava's stomach.

"Do you see Jess?" she asked as Carolyn guided her to a seat at the end of one of the benches.

Her friend's gaze swept the crowded room. "Is he still upstairs?"

"I don't think so."

Felix set the packs beside the table. "Can I get Dusty now?" The hotel owner had allowed the dog to sleep in the kitchen and had even fed Dusty some of the supper leftovers.

Carolyn shook her head. "You need breakfast first, then you can find Dusty and give him some of your bacon."

"All right," the boy said with a sigh. Tava didn't blame him for wanting to see his friend as soon as he could.

Archie joined them, lowering his bag next to theirs on the floor. "Anyone know where Jess went? He was gone when I woke up."

"I'm not sure," Tava answered. "Hopefully he'll be—"

"Morning." Jess strode up to the table, looking as sleep tousled as the rest of them. "I found something for you, songbird." He held a tall branch in his hand. At her questioning look, he added, "It's a walking stick, to help you climb. I figured you might need one, and with no trees on the mountain, this was the place and time to find one."

That had been his reason for leaving the hotel? Tava wrapped her fingers around the stick, its width perfect for gripping. The thoughtfulness of his gift touched her.

"It's perfect. Thank you, Jess."

Giving her a smile, he set down his pack and stooped beside her foot. "How does your ankle feel?" He touched the toe of her boot.

"It's stiff, but the pain is gone." She carefully placed her stick against the pile of canvas bags.

"Let's hope that means it's a little better." He stood. "Do you still want to try for the pass today?"

Tava glanced at the others. They were ready, and she didn't want to hold them back another day. Besides, she hadn't parted with her father's beloved books to sit around here until tomorrow.

She met Jess's gaze and nodded. "I want to try."

For one brief second, Tava thought she caught a glimmer of admiration in his eyes, but it was gone just as quickly. "We'd best eat then," he said. "From what I saw outside, the native families are nearly ready to go."

She scooted over to make room for him on the end of the bench, but Archie dropped into the vacated spot. "You don't have to tell me twice to eat." Tava bit back her disappointment as Jess found another empty seat.

The meal absorbed everyone's attention. When they'd finished eating, Jess handed Tava her walking stick, and she climbed to her feet. The five of them moved to a corner of the room to put on their warmer coats. With that complete, they shouldered their packs. The added weight on Tava's back increased the burden on her ankle, but she hoped using her stick would help counter the effect of carrying her bag.

When the Halls left to collect Dusty from the kitchen, Tava followed Jess and Archie outside. The frigid air drew a shudder from her, and she ducked her nose as best she could into the collar of her coat. As she watched the natives depart for the mountain, she envied their ease of movement, in spite of the heavy burdens on their backs.

Carolyn and Felix reappeared with the husky in tow, and Dusty eagerly greeted Tava and the men. It was time to move, and not a moment too soon. The cold had begun to penetrate Tava's layered clothes, and she hoped hiking would keep it at bay.

Their group started forward. Tava's foot felt sore inside her boot, though using the stick as an aid lessened the pain. Her slow progress meant the others soon outpaced her by several yards.

At the base of the mountain trail, Tava stopped to stare up at the vertical expanse. Her father had been required to climb this path over and over again, in order to carry all of his things to the summit. Had that been the beginning of his ill health?

"You ready?" Jess asked. Once again, he'd waited for her.

Tava pulled in a deep breath that instantly chilled her lungs. *I'm coming, Pa. Just hold on a little longer.* Pressing her stick firmly against the incline, she took her first step up the mountain.

11

HOUR AFTER HOUR they climbed, always treading upward. Tava's legs burned from the effort, and her heavy pack rose and fell with her labored breaths. Occasionally she would pass the carcass of some unfortunate horse at the side of the trail, which filled her nose with the awful scent of rotting flesh. Pulling air through her mouth reduced the smell but not by much.

Fatigue had long ago settled into every one of her bones and muscles. Yet the summit remained tantalizingly out of reach no matter how many times she forced her feet to keep moving, her stick anchoring her to the mountainside. Her ankle throbbed, but Tava feared that if she paused to rest for more than a minute or two, she'd be too tired to move again.

Every now and then, she would glance at the tramway moving along its metal cable high above her head, carrying goods to the summit. She almost wished she could hitch a ride among the piles of supplies, regardless of the terrifying height.

Felix and Dusty had led the group at first. But their own pace had slowed as the day wore on. Now just a few feet separated them from Archie and Carolyn. Other hikers filled in the gap between the three of them and Tava, while Jess maintained his place behind her. At some point they'd passed the natives, who had slowed under the extra weight they carried and the steepness of the trail.

Neither Tava nor Jess spoke—it required too much energy. Yet his silent presence provided a measure of comfort to her and inspired her to continue trudging forward.

They had to navigate the worst parts of the trail on hands and knees. And while crawling relieved the strain on her ankle, Tava didn't want to lose her walking stick in the process. Which required her free hand and her knees to shoulder most of the work.

By late afternoon, she could hardly feel her limbs at all. Her determination to reach the top had dwindled to a sputtering spark. Lifting her gaze, in hopes that the summit would appear much closer, Tava discovered a series of large rocks and boulders barring the way ahead. Tears of weariness smarted in her eyes. Their morning start felt like a vague memory from another lifetime. Surely she'd been climbing this mountain for years.

She approached the first boulder and stopped. It would be difficult to scramble up the rocky surface with only one good foot. She'd need both hands free as well.

"Something wrong?" Jess's voice sounded slightly muted in her ears.

She didn't know whether to nod or shake her head as she stared at the impenetrable obstacle before her. Jess touched her coat sleeve, and the numbness clinging to her cracked.

"I don't think I can climb this with my hurt ankle." She twisted to face him. "Even if I can get a toehold with my other foot, I'd have to drag myself up the rock. And that requires two hands." She clutched her stick more tightly.

Jess studied the rock. "I have an idea. Let me see your stick."

After she handed it over, he turned her around so her back was to him. Tava felt him fiddling with the straps of her pack. "What are you doing?"

"The stick will stay tucked through the bag's straps." He stepped back, his hands empty.

She twisted to see the stick poking out from the side of her pack. "That helps. But how do I scale these rocks with an injured foot?"

"I'll give your other foot a push from behind."

Tava frowned. "That just means more work for you."

The enormity of what still lay ahead of them crashed over her with such force that Tava lowered her chin to her chest, too exhausted to hold her head up any longer. "I don't know if I can keep going, Jess."

He clasped her shoulders between his hands. "Look at me, songbird." When she did, the resolve in his blue-green eyes had never shone brighter. "Do you want to reach Dawson?"

"Yes," she whispered.

"Do you want to find your pa?"

Something flickered to life inside her. "Yes," she repeated more loudly.

"Then you have to keep climbing, and I'm going to help you. All right?"

She couldn't physically press on alone. But did she dare rely on Jess, placing her trust in him, in order to continue forward?

Tava searched his face. Unsurprisingly, there wasn't a hint of guile there. Jess had been a true friend to her and her father for years. She needed no further proof of that than his being here on this mountain trail, far from the ranch.

What she wanted more than anything in the world was to reach her father. And she couldn't do it by herself—she needed Jess's help.

"All right," she echoed with a nod.

Facing the rock once more, Tava placed her hands

against its rough exterior and gingerly placed the toe of her right foot into a notch in the rock. Jess then pushed up on her left foot. The momentum propelled her far enough forward to make climbing the rest of the boulder a little easier.

She kept moving until she cleared the rock. Without the grounding of her walking stick, the ache in her ankle increased, but she didn't slow. Her earlier tears broke free of her lashes, and she let them fall unchecked, willing all of her burgeoning energy into ascending the next boulder and the next. Each time, Jess would give her foot a push until Tava could scramble forward on her own.

At one point she noticed Carolyn, Archie, and Felix aiding each other over a particularly large rock. Dusty waited for them above, his tongue lolling to the side in a pant.

A feeling of solidarity washed through Tava at the sight of the others inching their way forward too. She wasn't facing this grueling hike alone, and she would have been if Jess hadn't come on this trip with her.

Gratitude nudged at her exhaustion. She peered over her shoulder at Jess, but he wasn't a few feet behind her as she'd expected. Instead he stood unmoving beside the boulder she'd almost finished scaling.

"Jess?"

He didn't lift his head.

Alarm shot through Tava, and she twisted fully to face him. "Jess?" she repeated with greater volume.

His hat finally rose to reveal the haggardness etched across his every feature. She'd never seen him so defeated before, and that frightened Tava more than anything else she'd experienced since stepping foot on the mountain.

Mindless of her injured foot, she scooted down the rock until she reached its edge. "Are you hurt?"

"He was right," Jess murmured.

"Who was right?"

He shook his head as if he hadn't heard her. "I'm so tired. Just . . . so . . . tired."

The words sent a shard of guilt through Tava. Was it little wonder that he was tired? He'd assisted each of them the day before, and now he was helping her again. Assisting her up the rocks and climbing them himself meant twice the work for Jess. Yet he'd been more than willing to do it.

He hadn't given up on her, and she wouldn't give up on him either. Jess wanted as much as she did to reach her father. Now it was up to Tava to see that he did.

"Take my hand, Jess."

The firmness of her tone seemed to pierce his despair. "Why?"

"I'm going to pull you up," she explained, leaving her hand outstretched toward him.

His mouth turned down. "You can't. You might hurt your ankle again."

"Maybe, but I can still help you." At his hesitation, she added, "You've done so much for the rest of us. It's your turn now."

His frown didn't completely disappear, but he did grasp her hand. Tava held on and rose to her knees to pull him forward. Jess used his free hand to grip the rock, then hoisted himself up. The tug of his weight pressed her legs and feet into the rock face. Her ankle thudded with pain too, but Tava pressed her lips against it.

Once Jess reached her side, he assisted her onto her feet. "Thank you . . . songbird." His voice broke on her nickname, and he swallowed. Tears glistened in his own eyes. "What do you say we keep working together? I'll push, and you pull."

Nodding, Tava limped forward. She waited for Jess to drop hold of her hand, yet to her surprise, he didn't. His fingers remained securely tucked around hers. Whether the gesture meant anything more than kindness and friendship no longer mattered to her in this moment.

Somewhere on the mountain, she'd set down her burden of heartache from that night four years ago. Doing so had allowed forgiveness to finally heal her hurt. And that, Tava thought with a slight tip of her lips, made her feel as victorious as surmounting the pass surely would be.

◆◆◆

Removing his hat to cool the dampness of his forehead, Jess gulped in air and surveyed the scenery. They'd made it to the summit! Never before had he seen anything so majestic. Mountains capped with snowy peaks, pristine glaciers, and deep valleys spread out around them. On the opposite side of the pass, the blue of Crater Lake looked like a splash of paint on some giant canvas, with darker smudges along its edge in the form of stubby trees and shrubs.

Jess glanced down at the line of humanity moving slowly toward the pass. Off to his left, a pair of hikers deposited their things on the ground, then headed back the way they'd come—just so they could make the trek all over again with the next pack of supplies. Immense gratitude washed over him that their group wouldn't have to do the same.

"We did it," Tava said in a reverential tone. "We climbed all that way."

He turned toward her. She held her walking stick again as she gazed at the landscape. The wind blew strands of her dark-brown hair across her face, and Tava reached up to brush them away, her expression elated. She'd not only accepted Jess's assistance on the climb, but she'd willingly helped him in return, despite her injured ankle.

"Jess? Did you hear me?" She cocked her head in amused confusion. "We made it over the pass!"

He grinned. "We did, didn't we?"

Before he could second-guess himself, he scooped her into a hug and lifted her off the ground. Her walking stick clattered to the ground as her laughter rang in his ears.

"We're that much closer to reaching your pa." He set her carefully back on her feet.

Her genuine smile warmed him thoroughly, despite the crisp air. "Only two lakes and five hundred miles of river left," she teased. But he could tell she felt every bit as grateful as he did to have surmounted the pass.

As Tava stepped back, the others crowded around to join the celebration. Even Dusty gave a tired yip of excitement.

Jess put on his hat and ducked down in front of Felix. "Your pa would be real proud of you."

"Yes, he would," Carolyn agreed, her voice catching with emotion.

The boy's chest visibly swelled with pride. "Don't forget Dusty. He made it too." Hearing his name, the husky came to sit beside Felix.

"Great job, Dusty." Jess scratched the dog behind the ears, then he stood.

"I wish my father could see me." Archie shoved his hands into his pockets. Somewhere along the ascent, the cut on his arm had reopened, leaving dried blood on the bandage. The young man appeared to be as physically weary as the rest, yet he'd led the pack for a good portion of the punishing hike. Whatever lack of stamina he believed himself to have, Archie had proven his own strength on the mountain today.

Jess held out his hand to him. "It's a shame your father can't see you. You climbed harder and faster than any of us."

"Thanks, Jess." The young man clasped his hand, the dismay fleeing his countenance. When Jess released his grasp, Archie spoke to Tava. "I can't believe I hiked all that way."

With what they'd accomplished today, Jess wished they could linger here a little longer, basking in their success. But they still needed to confirm with the North-West Mounted Police who were posted at the summit that each member of their group had their year's supply of food. Night was also fast approaching, and Jess preferred to reach their destination before then.

The hike down to Crater Lake would be short but steep. Lake Lindemann stood a few more miles beyond. That would be their stopping place for the night and for the next few weeks, while they built themselves a boat to carry them to Lake Bennett and on to the Yukon River.

Once their business at the summit was concluded, it was time to move on. Felix and Dusty led out, followed by Carolyn and Archie. Jess motioned for Tava to go next. But after a handful of steps, she froze, a small gasp escaping her mouth.

"Your ankle?" he asked.

Tava gave a curt nod. "It hurts too much to walk on it, even with my stick."

If she couldn't use the walking stick anymore, was there another way to help her move without further aggravating her injury? Jess studied the terrain and the others picking their way down the trail. A possible solution began to form in his head.

"Archie?" he called out.

The young man spun around. The Halls did the same. "What?"

"We need your help." Jess motioned for him to come back, then returned his focus to Tava. "Let me carry your stick." She handed it to him after a second. "I've thought of something that might work better."

Once Archie had retraced his steps, Jess instructed him to stand on Tava's left side. He positioned himself on her right.

"Put your arms around each of our necks as best you can," he explained to her. It wouldn't be easy to hold on with all three of them carrying packs, but he hoped his idea would work nonetheless.

Tava did as he suggested.

"Now, you'll want to step when we do. My hope is that with us bearing most of your weight, you shouldn't have to use your ankle much."

"It's worth a try." A recognizable spark of grit lit her eyes.

Jess and Archie linked arms over her pack. "Ready?" Jess said as he glanced at each of them in turn. They nodded in answer. "All right. Here we go."

They attempted to step forward in unison, but their gait didn't match, resulting in a jerky shuffle. Tava cringed, making Jess wince as well.

He stopped their movement with a tug on Archie's bag. "This time we step on three." They looked at him as he counted. "One . . . two . . . three." Like one person, the three of them moved in tandem. Jess's breath whooshed out in relief.

He offered an encouraging smile and counted again. After a few minutes, he no longer had to count. Stillness blanketed their trio. Jess figured Tava and Archie must be concentrating as hard as he was to avoid a misstep. While their pace wasn't fast, they did make good progress.

Eventually they reached the shore of Crater Lake, where the Halls and Dusty had stopped to wait. Jess and Archie helped Tava over to a rock so that she could sit for a moment. Jess set her walking stick next to her.

"Thank you both," she said.

They couldn't rest for long. Already they were racing the daylight to reach Lake Lindemann. "Can you keep walking?"

In answer, Tava got to her feet with the help of her stick. "I'm coming, slowly but surely." He appreciated her attempt at levity. But from the way her lips drooped, Jess knew she wanted to be able to move as freely and steadily as the rest of them.

"We're getting close," he reassured. "Once we make camp, you can stay off that ankle as long as you need. I'll even do the cooking."

She sniffed in disbelief. "Would that be a blessing or a curse for the rest of us?"

"Ouch. That hurts, songbird." He clapped a hand against his chest. "You told me my flapjacks weren't half bad."

Tava shrugged as she cautiously maneuvered her way over the uneven ground. "Nothing's half bad when you eat it once or twice a year. But every day for weeks on end?"

He chuckled, grateful they could still joke after the agonizing day. "You'd better teach me how to make your beans and cornbread then."

"I guess I should."

Her half smile succeeded in easing some of his weariness. Teasing and bantering with Tava had always rejuvenated him. And this trip was proving no different.

A few paces ahead of him, Carolyn walked side by side with her son, while Dusty plodded along beside them. The familial scene filled Jess with the familiar yearning to belong to someone himself. He wanted a family of his own someday. Was such a thing possible for one like him, who'd made so many mistakes?

Tava called his name, and he spun around to find her standing in place. Jess didn't have to ask the reason. She sagged over her stick, her face pale with pain and fatigue.

He looked for some place for her to sit as he hurried to her side. A fallen tree provided a seat for her while they figured out what to do next. "Let me help you to that log."

She eyed the object as if she wasn't certain she could manage one more step.

"Allow me." After slipping the bag off her back, he hoisted Tava into his arms and carried her to the log. He set her down carefully before sitting beside her.

"What can I do? Do you want Archie and me to help you walk again?" They'd have to assist her much farther than they had earlier, but he would try in order for her to reach camp.

Her shoulders slumped lower at his suggestion. "My foot can't support any weight at all."

"Then I'll carry you on my back."

Jess recognized the futility of that idea as soon as he voiced it. Even if the others helped with their packs, they wouldn't make it to Lake Lindemann by dark with him carrying Tava. They would all have to stop and rest over and over again.

She shook her head. "It won't work."

Camping right here wasn't an option either. They'd pulled ahead of the native families earlier in the day, so they had nothing in the way of food or shelter at present.

The rest of the group had stopped as well, but they waited where they stood. Jess didn't blame them for not having the energy to retrace their steps to see what the delay was about now.

"What about a horse?" he suggested. "One of us could go ahead to find one and bring it back."

Tava appeared to consider the idea. "Do you think they'd be back before dark?"

"It'll be close. But you won't be alone. I'll wait with you."

Her mouth tightened. "You need to be the one to go." She waved toward the others. "You seem the least tuckered of all of us, and you know your way around horses. If anyone can find a decent mount and return by dark, it's you."

He hated the thought of leaving her behind, but her reasons for him going made sense.

The other three trailed slowly toward them. "Are you all right, Tava?" Carolyn asked.

"No." Her voice held the unmistakable threat of tears. "My ankle is going to give out altogether if I keep walking on it."

It was up to Jess to ensure that didn't happen. "I'm going to head as quick as I can to Lake Lindemann and see if I can find a horse to bring back for Tava to ride. But she shouldn't stay here alone."

"I can stay with her." Archie tossed a smile at Tava.

Jess kept back an irritated grunt. The young man's eagerness irked him, but he appreciated the knowledge that Tava wouldn't be by herself.

He shifted his attention from Archie to Carolyn. "Do you and Felix want to stay or come with me?"

Carolyn looked down at her son, then back up at Jess. "We'll join you. It will save you time on your return to not have as many people in tow."

Jess acknowledged her wisdom with a nod. "Hopefully by then the natives will be to Lake Lindemann too. If so, would you mind starting supper for the rest of us? I can help you set up the tent and the stove."

"Of course." Carolyn embraced Tava. "I'll be praying for you." She eased back as she added, "God willing, Felix and I will be waiting for you with hot food and a bed to rest on."

Tava's lips lifted slightly. "That sounds wonderful."

"I'll be back as soon as I can." He locked gazes with Tava. "If it gets dark before I return, you and Archie stay right here so I can find you."

She nodded. "I will."

"Keep her safe," he said to Archie.

"You can count on me, Jess."

Only the conviction in Archie's voice and Jess's certainty

that the young man would follow through could compel him to walk away. Still, he threw a glance over his shoulder. Archie had settled onto the log next to Tava.

Jess faced forward again, knowing he wouldn't soon forget the image of them seated side by side. It called to mind the other admonition in Quinn's note, for Jess to see that the right man won Tava's heart. But Jess didn't want her being courted by anyone other than himself. Did Tava's father feel the same, or had his words hinted at the need for someone else to enter his daughter's life? Without talking to the man, Jess couldn't say for sure.

One thing he did know. If Quinn didn't approve, Jess would have to get used to the idea of Tava having other beaus. Because at some point she would. Then he'd have to get accustomed to walking away and allowing someone else to be at her side—just as he had tonight.

Was that something he wanted to experience day in and day out? He inwardly shook his head. For the first time since leaving the ranch, he wondered if returning was still what he wanted to do.

12

WATCHING JESS STRIDE off, Tava had to bite her lip to keep from calling him back. She didn't want to wait without him, while night advanced closer and wild animals began prowling about the lake. With Jess nearby, she felt braver and more optimistic, in spite of the circumstances. Yet if she hoped to save her ankle from permanent injury, she had to stay put.

What would Pa say to me right now?

Tava searched her memory for something he'd told her that would help things feel less bleak. A recollection tripped forward in her mind. Before her father had departed for the Klondike, he'd told her not to forget that the low notes in a tune were every bit as necessary as the high ones.

"Every song needs both," her pa had reminded her.

The memory drew a hymn to Tava's lips. She hummed it to herself, grateful that the music lent her something else to think about besides her throbbing foot and their present situation.

"That's a nice one," Archie said when Tava finished humming the chorus.

She'd nearly forgotten his presence. "Do you like to sing?"

He shrugged. "I suppose. Mostly I do it at my mother's insistence."

"Will you sing with me"—she bumped her shoulder

against his—"if I insist?" It would help pass the time and keep her feeling calmer.

Archie's expression brightened. "It would be my pleasure." Leaning closer, he added, "I'm honored to be of help."

Forcing a smile, Tava scooted away a few inches. "I appreciate it." And she did. Just not in the way Archie hoped. "What songs do you enjoy best?"

"You pick, and I'll join in if I know it."

She thought through the songs she liked best, some lively, others slower. Given the difficulty of their day, a cheery number seemed in order. Tava sang the first two lines of one of her mother's favorite toe-tapping songs—"While Strolling through the Park One Day." Archie quickly added his voice to hers.

His rich tenor sound surprised her, and she stumbled over the next few notes. Archie apparently noticed, because his smile turned smug. Tava corrected herself, and together they sang the rest of the tune without mistake, their voices blending in harmony.

When the song ended, she twisted to face Archie. "I didn't know you could sing so well."

"It's not something I do often, mostly in church," he said, surprising her with his modesty. "The singing we did on the steamer was the first time in ages I've sung for the enjoyment of it."

"That was true for me as well."

Tava thought back to that day on the boat. Her mind had been too consumed with other things to notice the young man's talent.

She picked a few songs, and Archie suggested some that he liked. It was fun singing with him, given how well matched their voices were. At one point, he attempted to sing bass, and the result left them laughing.

For a while, Tava forgot about her injury and the fading light. However, when their singing faded to quiet again, she eyed the growing darkness with concern. The native families had passed by their spot some time ago, along with a number of other hikers. But surely an hour or more had passed since the last person had walked past. Her stomach rumbled, reminding her that it had been hours since she'd eaten anything.

Had Jess found a horse? Was he riding back right now?

"You and Jess have been friends for a long time, right?" Archie asked, disrupting the stillness between them.

Tava nodded. "He's worked on my family's ranch for seven years."

"And the two of you have never been . . . sweethearts?"

Thankfully the shadows hid Tava's blush. How was she supposed to answer? She decided to reply with her own question. "Why do you ask?"

"No particular reason." She sensed more than saw his shrug. "Sometimes the two of you act like longtime friends, and other times you don't."

Tava shifted on the hard log. What exactly had Archie observed? "I'm not sure what you mean."

His doubtful sniff added to the heat on her face. "Your embrace on the summit, for instance. Was that you and Jess simply being friendly?"

"Yes," she said in a decisive tone as she pulled her coat tighter. The temperature was descending the longer they remained here.

There had been nothing more than friendship between them during that moment on the pass, at least when it came to Jess and his view of her. That hadn't stopped Tava from wondering the exact same thing as Archie—whether Jess's hug had been motivated by something more. She didn't appreciate the way the young man's misguided perceptions stirred her vain hopes to life again.

"Jess and I *are* good friends, but we're here to find my father. That's our sole purpose for coming here together."

Archie startled her by setting his hand on top of hers. "I'm sorry I jumped to conclusions."

"It's all right." Tava slid her fingers out from under his and tucked them in her lap. While she was grateful for his apology, she didn't welcome his touch. "I'm glad I've made new friends on this trip."

Before Archie could respond, a rustle sounded from the brush. "What do you think that was?" Tava said, her pulse kicking up when the noise repeated itself.

"I don't know." She thought she heard him gulp nervously. "Do you still have that stick?"

She picked it up and extended it toward him. "Here."

After taking the walking stick from her, Archie stood. "What do we do if it's a bear?"

"You want to make as much sound as you can." Tava willed her pounding heart to slow. "You'll need to appear larger too."

"How do you know that?" he asked, his tone incredulous.

Tava kept her gaze trained on the gloom in front of the log. "I've encountered a bear or two back home."

"What? Really?" She could imagine his pale face growing whiter.

The sound drew closer, followed by a scraping noise. Could the animal be dragging its dinner behind it? They didn't need the creature fearing they might rob it of its next meal. Tava tensed, her hand gripping the log. If only she could stand and defend herself as Archie could.

A sudden pierce of light temporarily blinded her. Tava squinted against the brightness. When her vision cleared, she saw Jess moving toward her, holding a lantern aloft. He wasn't alone, either. Dusty walked beside him, pulling a sled that scraped along the ground.

"Jess!" Relieved at his return, Tava didn't mind that she'd be riding to Lake Lindemann on a sled rather than a horse. "You made it."

He came to a stop before them. "I couldn't find a horse, but an old-timer agreed to let me rent his harness and sled." He glanced at Archie and the stick the young man held. "Everything all right here?"

"We weren't sure if you were a bear or not," the young man said, passing the stick back to Tava. "But I knew what to do."

Tava chose not to correct him. "We're fine." She pulled herself to her feet. Her ankle ached, but staying off it had greatly reduced the pain. "Just ready to leave."

"Let me help you onto the sled." Archie offered her his hand.

She'd already accepted a great deal of help today, and this was one task she could perform on her own. "Thanks, but I can do it." Tava hobbled forward and lowered herself onto the sled.

"The ride back won't be smooth," Jess said as he shouldered her bag, "but Dusty will get you to camp in one piece."

Tava smiled. "Rough or not, I'm glad we didn't have to sit out here all night."

"Agreed." Archie put on his pack. "But it would have made a great story."

"With no food to eat or matches to start a fire?" Tava shook her head. His idea of adventure differed greatly from hers.

Jess knelt next to Dusty and adjusted something on the harness. "I wouldn't have left you out here to fend for yourselves—I would have come back for you, songbird."

His murmured words disappeared beneath the noise of the sled as the husky walked forward. But Tava had heard him, and the assurance and care behind his statement filled her with gratitude.

It had been such a difficult day, hiking with her twisted ankle and accepting help again and again from others, including Jess. Yet, in spite of her bone-weary fatigue, her thankfulness expanded as she bumped along on the sled. She'd scaled the mountain and made it to the other side, and in doing so, she'd come one momentous step closer to reaching her father.

Standing above Jess on the platform known as the sawpit, Archie tugged the whipsaw upward. Then Jess, mindful of the marked chalk line on the peeled log, pulled the saw down to cut the wood. Sawdust sprinkled his face, and he blinked to free his eyes of the flecks.

In the past week and a half, he and Archie had repeated this same laborious process over and over again, switching places at the sawpit every other day—all in an effort to produce enough crude planks to fashion a boat. Jess's arm and back muscles had long since hardened against the soreness that had plagued him in the beginning.

During the day, the sound of dozens of saws and hammers hovered like a cloud over the camp at Lake Lindemann, mingling with the chorus of animals and the frequent puttering of rain. At night, the noise transformed as the shipbuilders returned to their tents for supper and sleep, so that they could repeat the work on the early morrow, when the land was covered over in white frost.

Every day, handfuls of gold seekers arrived from the pass, while others launched their completed vessels into the lake and left the camp behind forever. And every day, Jess felt more anxious for him and Tava and their group to move on as well. It was that desire to leave that compelled him to endure the daily rigors of the sawpit.

Once he and Archie finished cutting the log, they added it to their growing pile of wood. They would soon have enough planks to begin constructing their boat at last. It would be larger and wider than a regular rowboat and would sport a sail as well as oars and a crude rudder to help them navigate the wind, water, and rapids ahead.

The sky was weeping again as he walked beside Archie toward the tents. "I can't wait to leave this miserable place for good," the young man grumbled.

Jess agreed but chose not to comment. He'd learned it was best to wait out Archie's tide of complaints. There was plenty for him to grouse about too—the dismal weather, the monotony of the food, the damp that penetrated everything, and the mind-numbing job of working the whipsaw.

There were certainly times when Jess was sorely tempted to gripe about the miseries as well. However, since that would only make things feel twice as bad, he bit his tongue instead and reminded himself that Quinn had survived this crucial part of the journey—they could as well.

When they weren't working in tense silence and Jess wasn't getting an earful of Archie's peevish remarks, the young man would often ask questions about Tava. What her favorite things were, were there any men back home that she seemed to fancy, did Jess think she would ever want to live somewhere other than the ranch? Since Jess preferred the inquiries to the griping, he did his best to answer.

Archie's interest in Tava had only grown since their arrival at Lake Lindemann, but Jess could see how one-sided the attachment remained. Not that Tava didn't treat Archie with friendliness. She simply didn't act besotted with him.

"When do you think we can stop cutting wood?" Archie asked, the rain dripping off his blond hair and sliding down his cheeks. His paleness had been replaced by a healthier ruddiness, a result of all the hard work.

Jess wiped the drizzle from his bristled face. He'd taken to wearing a beard these days, so that he didn't have to shave in the cold morning air with freezing water from the lake. "My guess is, tomorrow or the day after that we ought to have enough planks to start building."

"Well, hallelujah for that." Archie paused. "Tava's ankle seems to be healed."

Jess threw him a sideways glance, unsure of the conversation's new direction. "She is walking on it without the aid of her stick."

Tava hadn't liked staying off her foot and being mostly confined to the tent as her ankle healed. But she'd done it without complaint. Jess hadn't heard her grumble either, about not being at the sawpit. Instead she spent her days helping Carolyn prepare meals and keeping Felix entertained. Yet, each morning at breakfast, he read in those brown eyes how much Tava wished she could wield the whipsaw herself, and he saw her growing restlessness as their time at the lake stretched longer and longer.

"Maybe I'll invite her on a walk tonight," the young man said, "if the rain lets up."

Jess nodded absently, almost wishing he'd thought of such an idea himself. Would Tava have viewed his invitation in the same friendly vein as he knew she would Archie's? Most likely.

They reached their tent a few minutes later, and both of them ducked inside to exchange their damp clothes for dry ones. The small sheet iron stove had warmed the air beneath the canvas—thanks to Tava. She lit their stove every evening in preparation for their return from the sawpit. Then he and Archie would head next door to join her and the Halls for supper.

Who wouldn't love a thoughtful, strong woman like that? Jess thought as he pulled on clean socks and slipped his feet into his boots again.

Dusty greeted them as he and Archie entered the Halls' tent. "How did it go at the sawpit?" Tava asked.

Archie beat him at answering. "We should be able to start on the boat tomorrow or the day after."

"Really?" Anticipation blossomed on her face. "That's wonderful."

Jess scratched Dusty's ears, then settled on the ground next to Felix. "See anything interesting today?"

"No." Felix knocked over one of his wooden soldiers with a flick of his finger.

Carolyn turned away from the stove. "We'd hoped to go explore those boulders at the side of the lake, but the rain started up again."

"It's always raining," Felix said with a scowl.

Jess couldn't argue with that. "We're going to need help with building the boat, rain or not." He righted the soldier. "Do you know anyone who might be interested?"

"Me!" Felix rushed to his knees and leaned forward. "I can help."

"Good. Things will go faster with three."

The boy's mother mouthed a thank-you to Jess before she placed the food onto plates.

"Make that four," Tava said as she passed around the dishes. "I know how to use a hammer."

After Jess offered the blessing on the food, each of them, including Dusty, dug into the fried eggs. Jess's earlier musings returned as he ate.

Tava was as adept at using a skillet as she was a hammer. She was also kind, beautiful, and determined. No doubt there'd be plenty of men who felt the same about her, when she did finally decide to give her heart to someone.

The latter thoughts had him recalling Quinn's note again. But tonight, the responsibility placed on him regarding Tava's future happiness felt heavier than carrying his pack up to the summit. How he could perform such a task without finding fault in her every suitor? And that was only if her father was no longer alive. If Quinn still lived, Jess would be absolved of having to help Tava with matters of the heart and could hopefully obtain permission to pursue her himself.

The urgency to act, to reach her father as soon as possible, thrummed harder inside him. However, he could do nothing until the boat was ready.

Too agitated to sit anymore, Jess rose to his feet. "I'll wash the dishes."

"That would be nice," Carolyn said, "but we haven't eaten the applesauce I made."

"I'll pass on the applesauce and get started on washing what dishes I can."

He felt Tava's gaze linger on him as he gathered up most of the dishes and a towel for drying them before exiting the tent. Outside Jess sucked in a breath of damp air. The rain had stopped, which meant Archie would probably be able to walk with Tava as he'd planned.

Frowning at the thought, Jess made his way down to the shore. He filled the skillet with a little water and some pebbles, then swirled the mixture around the dish to clean it. When he finished, he rinsed the pan and started on his plate and utensils next.

"I brought the rest," Tava said from behind.

Jess glanced over his shoulder to see her holding the remaining dishes. "Thanks. Just set them next to the others."

Tava did so, but she didn't leave. She knelt beside him instead and picked up the towel to dry the dishes. "You were pretty quiet at supper."

"Got a few things on my mind."

Thankfully she didn't press him for details. "That's great news about the wood for the boat. How long do you think it will take to build it?"

"A week? Maybe less with you and Felix helping."

Her sigh revealed her hope for a shorter timeframe. "It already feels as if we've been here for months."

"I know, but Archie and I have been cutting wood as fast as we can."

He sensed her watching him. "I wasn't saying that you haven't been working really hard or fast."

"Of course." Jess passed her a plate, but he didn't immediately let go when she gripped the edge. "I just want so badly to keep going. To reach your pa as fast as possible." He let go of the dish and studied the lake. "If there was any way we could have left sooner, I would have already made it happen."

To his surprise, she reached out and touched his sleeve. "Jess?" She waited for him to look at her. When he did, he found her expression taut with earnest resolve. "You've done everything in your control so far to help us reach my father as quickly as we can."

The warmth of her fingers seeped through the fabric of his coat. "Believe me," she continued, "remaining in one place has been hard for me too." Her grim smile coaxed one from him. "We need a boat to continue, and that's what you're working on."

"You're right." Her belief in him—and in them working together—soothed his impatience. And prompted him to rest his hand on top of hers. "Thank you, songbird."

Tava went perfectly still, but she didn't pull away. She lowered her gaze to his sleeve, and after a brief pause, she threaded her fingers with his. Jess's heart hammered in his chest, even as he told himself the simple gesture meant nothing beyond friendly consolation. Then Tava lifted her chin, revealing the tiniest flare of esteem in her brown eyes.

"These dishes won't dry themselves." Her laugh sounded strained as she released him to pick up the towel.

Yet Jess didn't feel the least bit disappointed that the moment between them had ended. Or that Tava would likely join Archie for a walk tonight.

He knew what he'd seen in her gaze. And however small, that hint of emotion renewed his energy to make the boat and head for Dawson once more. Regardless of what had happened in the past, he now had reason to hope it could be different in the future. He just needed to convince Tava and her father of that.

13

TAVA INWARDLY CRINGED at the annoyance rolling off Archie in tangible waves as they strolled silently along the lake's shore. Farther up the beach, Felix and Dusty chased each other.

She'd agreed to take a short walk with Archie, but she had purposely asked Felix to come as well. The boy had been looking forward to exploring before the rain ruined his plans, and Tava had included him so that Archie wouldn't derive false meaning from her accepting his invitation—one he seemed to regret having made, given his short answers to her questions.

Maybe it was just as well that he didn't wish to talk. Tava's own thoughts were less on making conversation and more on Jess and their interaction earlier.

Tava had welcomed the chance to reassure him—as he had so often done for her. She had even offered an encouraging touch to his arm. But when Jess had slipped his hand atop hers, all attempts at friendly consoling had disappeared. In contrast, she had let herself believe for one small instant that his gesture stemmed from something deeper. Something that had been there years before.

Too soon, she had recognized her folly and had broken free of Jess's gentle grip. But it wasn't until after Tava had finished drying the dishes, and muddled her way through talking about things she couldn't recall now, that her pulse had finally slowed to normal. Only then did her fingers stop tingling from being laced with his.

The confusion inside her was harder to calm. It was another reason she'd accepted taking a walk, seizing the opportunity to stretch her legs and channel her restlessness into movement.

Thankfully it was almost time to build their boat so that they could finally leave the lakeside camp. Tava had struggled with the relative inactivity of the past week and a half. Often when she went to collect water from the lake, she imagined spiriting herself across the expanse of water and on and on until she reached her father.

"Are you as eager to put this place behind you as the rest of us?" she asked Archie, in another attempt to draw him out.

He gave an emphatic nod. "I don't want to waste another minute than we have to here. Hopefully all the good claims on the Klondike haven't been snatched up."

"I haven't actually thought much about my pa's claim." Had he managed to find any gold before illness had overtaken him? "How long do you think you'll stay in the Klondike?"

Archie shrugged. Some of the irritation had fled his posture. "I suppose it depends on how well I do. I don't think I'd like to stay for more than a year."

"What will you do once you return home?"

His brow furrowed. "I don't know. My father wants me to take over for him at the bank one day, but I tried my hand at clerking and didn't like it." He turned to look at her. "What about you? Will you go back to your ranch?"

"It's my home."

But for how much longer? Tava thought.

Without extra money, they would have no choice but to

turn everything over to the bank. Would her father want to start over somewhere else? Would Jess? She couldn't imagine her life without either of them in it.

Up ahead, Felix and Dusty had stopped. They seemed transfixed with something in the distance.

When she and Archie reached the pair, Tava asked the boy, "What are you looking at so intently?"

"Over there." Felix pointed. "It looks like a deer, but his horns are different."

Tava followed the line of his arm. Sure enough, a large deer with thick, giant antlers stood at the edge of the water. As they watched it, the imposing creature bent to take a drink.

"It's a caribou, or reindeer," Archie said with as much awe as Felix. "I read about them. They're a type of deer, but they can live in much colder climates."

Dusty trotted forward a few steps and barked. Hearing the noise, the caribou lifted its head, then dashed away.

"I can't wait to tell Ma I saw a reindeer." The boy's grin was infectious. "Come on, Dusty. Let's go tell her." He took off at a run, the husky at his heels.

Archie waved at their retreating figures. "I guess this is where we turn around." He no longer appeared annoyed with her for inviting Felix along.

With a nod, Tava fell into step beside him, shivering at the dropping temperature. "Thank you for suggesting a walk."

"My pleasure."

She resisted a groan when he directed a full smile her way. Maybe it would take more time for Archie to realize her feelings for him wouldn't change. She did appreciate his friendship and help, and that of Carolyn's. As difficult as waiting had been the last while, Tava knew that she and Jess would have remained here even longer if they had been on their own. The presence of the others was another blessing she thanked the Lord for each day and night—along with the continual plea that her pa would hold on until she made it to his side.

◆◆◆

Five days later, their boat stood ready to launch. Along with Felix, Tava had assisted the men with building the craft, and she'd relished the chance to finally do something toward moving forward in their journey.

The next morning they all helped carry their supplies to the water, where they were stowed inside the boat. Up the beach, several smaller groups were doing the same with their handcrafted vessels. Even the mundane task of loading the boat felt purposeful. Finally they would be able to cross the lake.

Since coming to the camp, Tava had learned about the tricky gorge that stood between Lake Lindemann and Lake Bennett. Their group could either risk fording it or carry the boat and all of their things overland. The latter choice was the safest, but it required time to complete. Probably several days. And time wasn't a commodity Tava could afford to squander.

Archie wanted to brave the gorge, while Carolyn wished to avoid it. Tava had sided with Jess that the best option would be to wait and see how they felt when they reached that point.

Once everything had been loaded, a member of the Mounted Police wrote down the serial number that Jess had been required to paint on the bow of the boat. The policeman then took down their names and the addresses for their next of kin. Tava wasn't surprised when Jess gave the man the ranch's address, just as she had. All of their information would be sent to police posts ahead, and their group would need to check in at each one. This ensured that no boat or its occupants would become lost or forgotten on the journey northward.

With that completed, Jess helped her and the Halls into the boat. Dusty required some cajoling, but at last, the husky hopped inside as well.

"On to Dawson!" Archie hollered in a boisterous voice as he clambered aboard.

The boat rocked with the movement, and Tava gripped the side. Carolyn's face didn't look as ruddy as usual. Being on the water this time would be much different than their last voyage, aboard the well-crafted, sturdy steamer. Would the boat they'd fashioned with their own hands endure the trek across the lake, let alone the hundreds of miles of waterways that stood between them and the Klondike?

Jess pushed the vessel the rest of the way into the water and climbed inside. "I'll steer first, if you want to manage the oars," he said to Archie.

The young man agreed to the plan, and the two men took up their respective places. Within minutes, the boat had left the shore behind. A stiff breeze pushed at the vessel, but Jess and Archie managed to keep them mostly on course. The other would-be sailors soon overtook them and pulled ahead, their boats riding higher in the choppy water.

Tava gripped her hands together and fought down a wave of panic. The boat hadn't tipped over yet, and it hadn't instantly sunk either. She had to have faith that they would be able to reach the opposite side of the lake—that somehow their vessel would withstand the elements and the large expanse of water around them.

Sometime later, Archie proclaimed between labored breaths, "I don't know how much longer I can row into the wind. My arms are starting to burn."

"Let's switch, then," Jess said.

The two traded places, and Jess maneuvered the oars through the water. Now that he sat facing Tava rather than behind her, she noticed the tightness of his jaw. He was worried too, and that knowledge frightened her more than anything.

"Are we going to tip over?" Felix asked in a small voice. Dusty whined as if echoing the question and laid his head on his front paws.

Carolyn dutifully shook her head, but her green eyes hadn't lost their concern since they'd set off. "I'm sure we'll be fine."

"Why don't we sing?" Tava suggested, as much for herself as for Felix.

The boy shook his head. "I don't want to." He burrowed into his mother's side, his eyes wide as he stared at the waves.

Tava searched for something else to do to take their minds off their nerves. "How about a story?"

"What kind of story?"

What kind, indeed? She'd never been one for storytelling, preferring songs to tales. But there had to be some memory she could share that would keep Felix's attention centered on her and not on the boat's rough progress.

"How about a funny one?" she said with a sudden burst of inspiration.

The boy's gaze lit with interest. Tava took that as permission to begin. "This is a story about Jess." She threw a meaningful glance in his direction, and he played along by feigning a groan. "It was the first time he'd participated in a roundup after coming to the ranch."

"What's a roundup?" Felix asked.

She leaned toward him and Carolyn as if imparting a secret. "We round up the cattle each spring and fall—first to brand the new calves and then to take the cattle to market.

That fall, Jess was our newest ranch hand, but he'd never been around cattle before."

"Not true, songbird," he protested, his breathing sounding as strenuous as Archie's had earlier. The powerful thrust of his arms and shoulders attested to the herculean effort needed to pull the oars through the water.

"I'd been around cows before, at least milk cows. I did grow up on a farm."

Tava blinked in surprise. She hadn't known this detail about his life before coming to the ranch. "You're ruining the story." She kept her tone light so that he would know she was teasing.

"Don't let me stop you from telling it." His blue-green eyes twinkled. "I'll set Felix straight later with the *real* story."

She pretended to scowl for the sake of her audience and was rewarded with a giggle from Felix. "As I was saying, Jess and I rode out with everyone else."

"You got to ride in the roundup too?" The boy looked impressed.

Tava nodded. "Ever since I was eleven." It wasn't hard to recall her excitement at finally being included and the joy she'd felt riding alongside her father. One day she hoped to do the same with her own children.

"Wow," Felix murmured. "I want to ride in a roundup."

Carolyn smiled down at him. "You still have three years to go until you turn eleven."

"What if you and your ma came to visit the ranch?" Tava said. "We could take you out riding."

"You and Jess?"

She realized she'd spoken without thinking. Jess might be there in a year or two, but he might not. Tava felt his gaze on her, but she didn't dare lift her eyes to his, afraid of the answer she would see there.

"Are you going to share what happened next?" The question came from Archie.

"Yes." Tava cleared her throat. "Jess was assigned to help manage the strays. So when one of the cows broke loose from the group, he went after her. Only, he stopped his horse about ten yards from the cow, took off his hat, and began speaking to the creature like you would an acquaintance on the street."

The boy twisted around to look at Jess. "Why'd do you that?"

"I was trying to talk the ornery thing into moving."

Tava couldn't help a laugh at the memory. "The cow started moving, all right, but in the wrong direction. Jess followed and kept talking to the animal. That's when I came up and asked him why he wasn't driving the cow back toward the herd."

"I insisted that was exactly what I was doing. Except the cow was the one doing it wrong."

Carolyn's giggles mingled with her son's. "I wish I could have seen that."

"Oh, it was a sight none of us ever forgot," Tava smiled at Jess. "I finally took pity on him and showed him how to properly drive the cow back to the others."

"Is that really what happened?" Felix looked to Jess for confirmation.

He gave a nod. "Tava told it right." His focus moved from the boy to her. "It was a day I haven't forgotten either."

What other days did he remember? The two of them had shared a myriad of experiences in seven years—funny, sad, joyful, strained. Tava wanted to go on making memories together. And if she were truly honest with herself, she wanted to experience them as more than friends.

Would Jess ever feel that way again? Did he recognize their undeniable pull toward one another, which time and circumstance hadn't fully erased?

As she stared back at him, she saw his demeanor change from nostalgic to hopeful to something bordering on tenderness. Tava's heart tripped faster in response, just as it had from Jess's touch by the lake the other day.

She broke eye contact first. But Tava had studied his expression long enough to realize something important.

Her and Jess's hopes for the future might not be the same. Yet she understood one thing unequivocally now. Jess was every bit as aware as she of the invisible thread that still stretched between them.

14

TAVA WATCHED THE approaching shoreline with immense relief. Just a few more feet and their ship's maiden voyage would be at an end. Dusty couldn't wait any longer. The dog jumped from the boat and swam the rest of the way. Felix would have likely followed had Carolyn not held him back with a firm hand.

Once the boat neared the beach, Tava joined Jess in the knee-high water to pull the vessel onto the shore. He nodded silent appreciation, then swiped his coat sleeve across his face. She could only imagine the stamina exacted from both men to keep the boat moving, while wrestling against the wind and waves.

Archie and the Halls joined them on the beach. Immediately Felix raced after Dusty. "Don't go far," Carolyn said. "Stay close enough that you can see me."

The boy waved in acknowledgement.

Hands on her hips, Tava surveyed the area. It was relatively flat, and there were no other boats in close proximity. "This looks like a good place to camp."

Jess ran his hand through his hair, leaving the light-brown strands to stick up every which way. "We'll get a fire going, then Archie and I can unload the boat."

"Unload the boat?" the young man echoed. "Why would we do that when we're leaving tomorrow?"

A frown etched new lines of fatigue on Jess's face. "That's only if we go by way of the gorge. And after the struggle we had today, I think it's best if we go overland."

"What? No." Archie's brows dipped in a scowl. "That'll take us several days. Going through the gorge is faster."

"And more dangerous," Jess added.

Carolyn thoughtfully regarded the two men. "I agree with Jess. I don't want to risk losing some or all of our things by taking the boat through the gorge."

"What about you, Tava?" Archie jerked his hand in her direction. "You're anxious to reach your father. If we go through the gorge, we'll be to Lake Bennett that much sooner."

Each choice presented disadvantages. Tava didn't want to cart all of their supplies and the boat across the neck of land between the two lakes. On the other hand, she'd found traveling across the wide-open lake more frightening than she'd expected. Navigating a dangerous gorge would likely be much harder, especially for inexperienced sailors such as Jess and Archie.

She did wish to reach her pa as soon as possible, but she also recognized the greater setback they'd incur if they lost their belongings. As with other difficult decisions she'd made in her father's absence, she understood which course would ultimately be best.

"I'm in agreement with Carolyn and Jess," she finally answered. "It will take longer to go overland, but it's worth the extra few days to reach Lake Bennett in one piece."

Archie's expression darkened. "So that's it, then? My opinion no longer matters." He pulled off his hat and slapped it against his leg. "May I remind you that it was me who paid for the natives to carry our things to Lake Lindemann?"

Tava had to choke back the reminder that his offer of

help had come after his own poor choices. "We certainly appreciate—"

He didn't let Tava finish. "I should have as much say in these matters as *him*. . ." He gestured with his hat toward Jess.

"Your opinion does matter." Jess's jawline seemed made of granite in that moment, though he kept his tone calm. "However, there's more than your preferences to consider. We're a group, and we need to make decisions as a group."

The young man glared at him. "You mean you get to make decisions for the group."

"That's not fair, Archie." Tava shook her head, frustrated and bewildered at his behavior. Why was he acting so obstinate and upset all of the sudden? She glanced at Carolyn, who appeared just as confused.

Ignoring Tava once more, Archie continued to direct his remarks to Jess. "What if I refuse to unload my things?"

"Then we'll leave yours in the boat," Jess replied evenly as he crossed his arms, "and wish you the best of luck heading through the gorge."

The young man clapped his hat back on his head. "You know I can't handle the boat by myself."

Jess offered a slow nod, his posture still firm. "I do, and that's why I hope you'll still throw your lot in with ours."

"But I have to reach the goldfields as soon as I can." The fight drained from Archie with the honest admission, and he slumped his shoulders. "What if all the good claims are gone? I'll never be able to prove myself to my father then."

Carolyn stepped forward and placed her arm around his shoulders. "If you can't find a suitable claim of your own, I'd consider selling my husband's share to you. Or perhaps you could buy the entire thing, since his partner is ready to be done."

"You'd do that?" Archie shot a glance at Carolyn, then at the ground. "I don't know why."

"Why?" Carolyn repeated. "Because you, Tava, and Jess have become like family to me and Felix." Lowering her arm, she stepped back to look Archie in the face. "It wouldn't be the same without you."

Tava moved to stand beside them. "She's right. I hope you'll remain with your friends, Archie."

His countenance had begun to brighten until she mentioned friendship. Tava hoped that someday he would find someone he truly cared for and who cared for him in return. In the meantime, a few more years of life experiences would help the young man prepare for that future event.

She turned to include Jess in the conversation, but he no longer stood on the beach. Tava caught sight of him striding away toward some brush. "Jess?" She took a few steps after him.

He twisted to face her. "I'm going to find firewood," he called back.

Even at a distance, she sensed the tension rolling off him as he spun around and continued walking. Tava glanced over her shoulder to see Archie and Carolyn trailing after Felix.

Which way to go? She looked again in the direction Jess had gone. Did he want company? The memory of what she'd seen on his face during their boat ride cinched her decision. She headed after the retreating figure.

Jess couldn't escape the group fast enough. Gathering firewood had served as the ideal excuse to walk away.

It had taken all of his strength to respond calmly to Archie's belligerence rather than ending the kid's petulant arguments with a well-planted fist. However, the fact that he'd even considered throwing a punch had left him more upset at himself than at Archie. Four years had passed since Jess had been in a fistfight, and he didn't need anyone, particularly Tava, discovering how close he had come to starting one just now.

Thoughts of her led him to recall the charged moment they'd shared on the boat. Just as he had the day they had washed dishes together, Jess had seen more than friendship in her eyes today. What he didn't know was if it signified anything or if he was simply seeing what he wanted.

"I figured you could use some help."

He whirled around at hearing Tava's voice behind him. "Help?"

"With the firewood," she said, giving him a funny look.

"Right." That's what he'd planned to do. Jess bent to pick up a few sticks, while Tava did the same.

"You handled things well with Archie back there."

The sincerity of her tone both pleased and pained him. She had no idea how close he'd come to handling things badly.

He found a thicker piece of wood and added it to the pile in his arms. "It took a great deal of effort," he found himself admitting.

"I can imagine. Archie was being rude, with little regard to what the rest of us were saying."

Jess nodded. "That kind of behavior sets my ire off like nothing else."

To his surprise, Tava responded with a laugh.

"What's so humorous about that?"

She must have seen his frown, because her expression changed at once from amusement to remorse. "I didn't mean it like that. I was only thinking that if you were really angry, I couldn't tell. You acted incredibly calm."

"The result of years of practice."

He sensed her watching him as he added another branch to his armload. "Are you saying you used to struggle with your temper?" The way she voiced the question exposed her disbelief. "I can't remember you ever lashing out in anger at anyone."

How had their conversation led here? Would saying more just incriminate him?

Again, the personal revelations fell unbidden from his mouth. "It was a habit I had to work hard to overcome." Rather than fear, Jess felt liberated at finally sharing a tiny portion of the burden he'd shouldered without her knowledge. "I had some incentive that made it easier."

"Oh? And what was that?"

Jess stopped gathering wood to peer directly at her. "You mean *who* was that."

Her gaze widened with understanding, and her hands stilled in their work. He saw her visibly swallow. "Who was that?" she restated in a whisper.

"Well, you see, there was this beautiful, smart, strong young lady on the ranch where I came to work." The sudden rapidity of his heartbeat thudded in his chest. "For reasons I couldn't fathom, she wanted to be my friend, and she treated me and everyone else with kindness." He feigned interest in adjusting the wood within his grip. "That was a powerful motivator to rein in my temper and do what I could to be worthy of her friendship."

Heavy silence cloaked the air between them as he finished. For several long seconds, the only sound came from the distant murmur of people talking.

Uncertainty churned inside him. Had he revealed too much? Maybe Tava preferred not knowing what he thought of her back then.

When she spoke at last, her quiet words rang with conviction. "I never saw that young man with a short temper. The one I hoped to befriend was solicitous and caring and funny.

Handsome too." He lifted his head and caught her soft smile. "And for the first time in my life, I wished so desperately I could go back and repeat my mother's lessons on being a proper young lady." She ducked her chin in self-consciousness. "Because I wasn't sure this young man would ever see me that way. As someone more than a friend or a kid sister."

Her admission knocked the air from Jess. Thankfully, Tava wasn't looking his way to notice him gaping stupidly at her. But what else could he do? She'd all but confessed to having feelings for him since the beginning of his time at the ranch.

Had those feelings disappeared four years ago, only to resurface now? Or, like Jess, had she simply concealed them?

His mind awhirl, he still managed to step toward her. "Tava . . ."

"Yes?" Her pretty features lit with unmistakable hope.

"I—"

The sound of someone coming their way interrupted the privacy and magnitude of the moment. "Jess?" Felix hollered. "Tava? Ma's wondering if you've found wood yet."

Jess cleared his throat, certain the disappointment in Tava's demeanor matched his own. "We're here," he called back.

The boy darted through the brush, Dusty behind him. "Do you have the wood?"

"Plenty of it." He hoisted his armful.

Jess cut a look at Tava and wished he could read the different emotions filling those luminous brown eyes. Would they have a chance to renew their conversation? Or would things remain unsaid, as they so often had in the past?

"I'll lead the way." Felix motioned for them to follow.

Jess indicated for Tava to go ahead. "After you."

Her answering smile held the same hint of shyness it had

the night before Jess had left the ranch for the first time. The sight of it renewed his unspoken questions regarding her feelings—and the anticipation that they matched his own.

"I'm proud to know you, Jess," she said as she walked past him.

He smiled back, her praise more precious to him than gold. "I feel the same about knowing you, songbird."

Following behind her, he felt like whistling for joy. But a warning in the back of his mind reminded him that Tava still didn't know everything about his past. Would she still be proud to know him then? Would her father approve of the subtle shift in their relationship?

Jess didn't have the answers yet. However, he would keep moving and praying and hoping that when all was said and done, the next chapter of his life would include being at Tava's side. Not as a bystander but as one with the right to claim her heart.

15

FROM HIS PLACE at the boat's rudder, Jess eyed the sky overhead with growing wariness. Dark clouds knocked against each other like boulders over Lake Bennett, and the wind had doubled in strength in the past few minutes. Navigating the lake's whirlpools and precarious currents was tricky enough; doing so in a storm would be near impossible.

He'd hoped to be much farther down the lake by now, especially since their group had needed two full days to carry their supplies and the boat overland to avoid the gorge connecting Lake Lindemann to Lake Bennett. Though it had required a great deal of time and effort, Jess didn't regret their choice.

"The water is getting rough." Tava turned in her seat to look at him, her brow creased with worry.

He dipped his chin in a grim nod. "We should look for a place to land."

"Maybe it'll blow over," Archie said loudly to be heard over the increasing noise of the wind.

Several raindrops smacked angrily against Jess's face. "I don't think so."

"But we're nowhere near the end of the lake." The young man paused in rowing and bent forward over the oars to catch his breath. "We'll have a long way to go tomorrow."

A wave smacked the side of the boat, sending spray over all of them. Felix yelped with fright, while Dusty cowered in the bottom of the boat. Archie scrambled to position the oars in the water again. One look at his wide eyes told Jess that there'd be no further argument about whether to land or not.

Carolyn held her son close. "Can we reach the shore?"

"With some effort," Jess replied.

The rain fell with greater fury, making it difficult to see. Jess blinked the moisture from his eyes and steered the boat in the direction of the shoreline. Another wave doused them with water. Cold trickles ran down his collar into his shirt, and he shivered.

"Almost there." The wind tore his words from him and tossed them toward the sky.

Jess squinted through the deluge. They were moving quickly toward the edge of the lake when he caught sight of a rock jutting up near the boat's bow.

"Watch out," he shouted, pulling on the rudder.

Archie glanced over his shoulder and rowed hard to the left. The boat tipped, causing shouts of alarm from Tava and the Halls. But after scraping against the rock, the vessel righted itself. Just ahead, Jess spied a patch of beach. They were almost there.

Dusty, however, had endured enough. The husky suddenly scrambled to his feet and dove into the rough water.

With a cry, Felix tore away from Carolyn and lunged for the dog. But the movement threw the boat slightly off-balance. One moment the boy was stretched out across the side of the boat, and the next he disappeared beneath the waves.

"Felix!" Carolyn screamed.

Jess tore off his coat. "Tava, take the rudder." He didn't wait for her to respond before he dove into the water. His feet hit the bottom sooner than he'd expected, and he shot back up to the surface.

Searching the waves, he saw Felix flailing close by. Jess swam toward him and grabbed his coat before Felix could slip back under the water. "Hang on," he cried, placing the boy in front of him. Felix obeyed by holding on around Jess's neck.

A few powerful thrusts of his arms and legs brought Jess to shallower water. He kept a tight grip on Felix and walked onto the beach. Only then did he set the boy down. Dusty hurried over to lick Felix's face. The boy grabbed a hold of the husky and sobbed.

Satisfied the pair would be all right, Jess returned his attention to the boat. He waded out waist-deep and gripped the edge of the bow. With Archie's help at the oars and Tava at the rudder, the three of them wrested the craft toward the beach.

Jess dragged the boat partway out of the water, then collapsed on the ground. His chest hurt from breathing hard, and his legs felt shaky. He watched as Archie assisted Carolyn and Tava from the vessel. Felix's mother rushed forward and dropped to her knees beside her son, throwing her arms around him and Dusty.

Tava knelt in front of Jess. "Are you all right?" she asked, her voice clogged with emotion. Despite his answering nod, she lifted her hands to grasp both sides of his face as if she needed tangible proof. "You're not hurt?"

Her touch and concern sent warmth spilling through him. "I'm very wet." He shivered. "But I'm fine, honest."

Still looking worried, she sat back on her heels. "We need to get you and Felix dry."

"We're all soaked through," Archie muttered as he stalked past, carrying the oars.

Jess recognized the feeling of not belonging when he saw it. "Thank you for rowing, Archie," he said through chattering teeth. "We wouldn't have made it to shore without you."

The young man's posture relaxed some. "Thanks. I'll set up one of the tents, so we can get out of this rain."

"Then I'll start a fire in the stove." Carolyn approached Jess, her expression weary but grateful. "Thank you for rescuing Felix." She gripped his hand and squeezed it. "If there's anything I can ever do . . ."

Jess shook his head. "I was glad . . . to do it." His shivers were making it harder to talk.

Carolyn rummaged up two blankets and placed one around her son and the other around Jess. Holding the ends together with one hand, he attempted to help with the tent. But Tava shooed him out of the way. He didn't like feeling useless, but he also couldn't deny how nice it felt to have someone looking out for his welfare.

His thoughts went to Quinn and the woman who'd been nursing him. It was a relief to know that, in the absence of family, Tava's pa had someone caring for him too until Jess and Tava could be there.

Though the rain still drizzled outside, their group of five, and Dusty, remained warm and dry within the Halls' tent. No evidence remained of their harrowing experience exiting the water two hours earlier. Still, Tava kept glancing at Jess, who was seated beside her, and at Felix to assure herself that they were both fine.

She'd watched in horror as Felix and Jess had entered the water. Not even the knowledge that she didn't know how to steer a boat had terrified her as much as being powerless to save them. She didn't know how to swim. And until Jess had resurfaced and grasped onto Felix, she'd believed he couldn't swim either.

It was another piece in the puzzle of his past life that she had discovered while on this trip. Jess knew how to swim; he'd grown up on a farm; he had once struggled with his temper; and he had apparently been as enamored with her from the start as she'd been with him.

The memory of their poignant conversation as they'd gathered firewood the other day sparked a fluttery feeling inside her. She'd never come so close to sharing her heart with him. And judging by the attractive vulnerability on his face, Jess hadn't either. Yet they'd both bravely attempted to narrow the closing gap between them.

If only they hadn't been interrupted . . . Tava still wondered what Jess had been about to tell her before Felix arrived.

They hadn't had an opportunity to speak alone since. But Tava had sensed a new depth to their relationship. Nothing outright, though there'd been moments over the past few days when she'd met Jess's eyes and felt a stir of awareness, of understanding.

What would her pa think of her and Jess's changing friendship? She'd never confided to him her true feelings for Jess, yet she found herself longing for his sage advice.

The conversation around the tent nudged into her thoughts. "You're going to have lots of stories to tell your friends when you get back home, Felix." Jess smiled at the boy.

Felix had his arms clasped about his knees in a casual pose. But it had taken him nearly until supper was ready to stop shaking from the cold and the fear over his near-drowning. Carolyn had encouraged him to talk about it, and that had seemed to calm his anxiety about being in the boat again tomorrow.

"I can show them Dusty too." Felix patted the husky, who sat next to him. Dusty licked the boy's chin.

Carolyn ran her hand over his son's mussed hair. "Actually, honey, the dog belongs to Tava. She's the one who bought him."

The boy's eyes widened with sudden dismay. "You mean I have to say goodbye to him when we get to Dawson?"

"You could probably find a dog there to buy," Archie suggested.

Felix shook his head. "No other dog is as good as Dusty."

"He is remarkable," Jess said. "Reminds me a little of the dog my family owned named Blue Belly."

The boy smirked, temporarily forgetting his sadness. "Blue Belly? That was his name?"

"It was." Jess leaned back on his hands. "We chose him from a litter of new pups. But since the dog couldn't come home with us right then, the owner dabbed a bit of blue paint on the pup's white belly so we'd know which one was ours. When we did bring him home, my little brother insisted we call the dog Blue Belly."

Tava smiled at the funny name—and the realization that Jess had at least one brother.

Felix chuckled too, then sobered. "You're lucky you got to bring the dog home."

The plaintive note in his voice squeezed at Tava's heart. When she'd purchased the husky, she hadn't thought much beyond rescuing him from his harsh owner and giving all of them, especially Felix, a furry companion.

Since that morning in Dyea, he and Dusty had been inseparable. The dog even slept at the boy's feet each night. Felix had also risked his life earlier trying to go after Dusty. Tava hated the idea of separating them—and that made her decision of what to do about the dog's future come easily.

"If you owned Dusty, would you promise to always take care of him and treat him kindly?" She already knew the answer, but she wanted to give Felix a chance to voice his commitment out loud.

The boy's whole body trembled with his vigorous nod. "I will. I promise."

"Is your mother all right with having a dog at home?"

Felix swiveled to face Carolyn. "Are you, Ma?"

She gazed fondly at her son. "I do like Dusty very much. He's a good dog, isn't he?"

"He sure is." The boy scratched the dog behind the ears.

His mother exchanged a long look with Tava. "We would love to take him home with us. But are you certain that's what you want to do?"

Nodding, Tava leaned forward, catching Felix's eyes. "If you and Dusty will come visit the ranch as soon as you can, you can keep the dog."

"Woohoo!" Felix jumped to his feet. The husky scrambled up as well and let out an excited bark.

Tava laughed along with Carolyn and the men. "What do you say to Tava, Felix?" his mother prompted.

"Thank you, thank you, thank you, Tava."

He rushed forward and wrapped his small arms around her neck. The unexpected embrace startled her, but after a moment, Tava hugged him back.

She'd never had much interaction with children. Yet she had come to truly appreciate Felix's presence in the group. He brought a child's innocence and enthusiasm to the otherwise difficult trip. Perhaps one day she would have a son of her own and she would gift him with a dog too.

Felix released her and embraced Dusty next, burying his face in the dog's gray and white fur. "We don't have to say goodbye, boy."

"Thank you," Carolyn whispered to Tava.

She answered with a smile, knowing she'd done the right thing—both in buying Dusty and in giving him to Felix.

Something settled on her knee. Looking down, Tava saw it was Jess's hand. She lifted her chin to meet his gaze. The admiration there left her mouth dry, and her cheeks flushed from more than the stove's heat. Feeling emboldened, she covered his hand with her own and twined her fingers with his, as she had that day by the lakeshore.

Tava sensed someone else watching her. A glance at Archie, seated on her right, proved her suspicions correct. The tight lines around the young man's mouth hinted at his displeasure at seeing her and Jess holding hands.

Archie looked away first, but his blatant disapproval stirred uneasiness in Tava. She squeezed Jess's hand, then returned hers to her lap. Yet try as she might, she couldn't shake a prickle of premonition that their troubles were far from over.

16

TO TAVA'S GREAT relief, they crossed the rest of Lake Bennett and the bay known as Windy Arm with little difficulty, save for trying to land on the bay's swampy shore. Now their next obstacle lay just ahead—Miles Canyon and its subsequent rapids—and Jess and Archie would be navigating it alone while Tava and the Halls walked the five miles overland to its end.

Tava didn't like the thought of the men battling the rapids by themselves, even if the torrent of water posed more of a threat to their supplies than to life or limb. But the Mounted Police wouldn't allow women or children to ride through the canyon on the boats.

"Just wait for us at the end of the rapids," Jess said. He and Archie had landed the vessel along the shore to let Tava and the others disembark.

Carolyn nodded. "We'll be praying for you." She gave each of the men a quick hug, and Felix offered them a goodbye wave.

Then it was Tava's turn for farewell. Concern dried her throat as she met Jess's gaze. In her mind, she kept seeing the image of him disappearing beneath the water during the storm.

She coughed to speak. But what should she say? She couldn't ride with them, but she hated the idea of not knowing what might be happening to them at any given moment. Much like she felt about her father.

"You'll be careful?" she finally said.

The look in Jess's blue-green eyes suggested he understood what she couldn't put into words. "I promise we'll meet you at the end, songbird."

"You'd better." She wrapped her arms around him and hugged him tight. Jess held her in return, and for one brief moment, she no longer felt afraid.

He released her all too soon, but Tava had the memory of his embrace to carry with her. "Good luck, Archie." She offered the young man a hug as well. "We'll be waiting for you both." With a wave, she followed after Dusty and the Halls. She looked back once. Archie had climbed back inside the boat, and Jess was preparing to launch the craft into the water. But he paused as well and peered over his shoulder in her direction. When he saw her watching, he offered an encouraging smile.

How many times through the years had she received this exact smile from Jess and felt better? Hundreds, maybe. The quiet gesture of reassurance didn't fail to calm her in this instance either. Squaring her shoulders, she smiled bravely in return, then hurried after the others, a prayer on her lips.

Watch over them, and keep them safe.

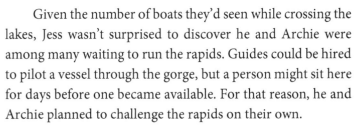

Given the number of boats they'd seen while crossing the lakes, Jess wasn't surprised to discover he and Archie were among many waiting to run the rapids. Guides could be hired to pilot a vessel through the gorge, but a person might sit here for days before one became available. For that reason, he and Archie planned to challenge the rapids on their own.

As had become their routine, Jess would man the rudder

and Archie would row. Doing so had served them well during the lake storm. However, now that spot of bad weather felt like child's play compared to what they would face up ahead. Only his desire to reach Quinn as quickly as possible could induce Jess to attempt something as precarious as taking their handmade craft through the series of rapids.

If they could just make it through unscathed—that's what Jess had been praying for all day. Not for the first time, he felt relief that Tava and the Halls wouldn't be riding in the boat this time.

Jess hadn't expected Tava to give him a farewell embrace, though he'd welcomed it all the same. Holding her in his arms, however briefly, had shored up his courage and his resolve to tackle the rapids. It was another step toward helping all of them make it to Dawson.

Neither he nor Archie said much as their boat was inspected by the Mounted Police and they were declared competent to forge the rapids. Jess figured the young man's thoughts were also centered on the monumental task before them.

At last, their turn came. Jess tightened his grip on the rudder, his eyes trained straight ahead. "Here we go," he muttered as he steered the vessel into the roiling water.

Immediately the strong current fought him for mastery over the boat, throwing wave after wave into their path and dousing everything with cold spray. Jess ignored the soaking as he struggled to guide the craft through the gauntlet of rocks, eddies, and timber. His ears rang from the roar of the water, and he had to shout for his instructions to Archie—to row hard or pause—to be heard above the thunderous noise. His hands began to ache from the effort it took to steer. But he couldn't risk loosening his grasp, even for a second.

Through the sheen of water on his face, Jess hazarded a glance at the young man's face. Archie's light-blue eyes were round with terror, but the teeniest bit of a smile lifted the corners of his mouth.

Though that single, small action didn't suddenly alleviate the danger they faced or increase Jess's prowess as a boatman, it did help ease some of his trepidation. Archie's smile called to mind a time when Jess had also thirsted to find adventure and prove himself. Could there be a better place to do that than racing down these rapids?

Besides, he reminded himself, Quinn had also made it through this very canyon. The remembrance comforted him, alighting a spark of confidence that he and Archie could do the same.

Without warning, the boat ricocheted off something unseen beneath the frothing waves. The vessel darted toward the canyon wall. "Row backwards to the left!" Jess yelled, the sound little more than a muted cry.

Archie did as directed, while Jess channeled all of his strength into guiding the vessel to turn left. For a moment, he feared they wouldn't succeed. But at the last second, the boat veered away from the side.

Pushing out the breath he hadn't known he'd been holding, Jess narrowed his concentration on the rapids straight ahead. The boat rocked and bounced through the water like a wagon careening over a set of hills.

Then, as quickly as they'd been swept into the gorge, they shot out of it. Jess could hardly believe it. He lifted his free hand to wipe his dripping beard and noticed his fingers were trembling. His clothes had been thoroughly doused, a fate Archie hadn't escaped either, and exhaustion cloaked him head to toe.

They piloted the boat farther down the river until Jess spied a place along the shore where they could camp for the night. "Let's land there," he said, pointing to the right bank.

Archie nodded.

When the water shallowed, the young man dropped the oars and jumped from the boat to pull it to shore. Jess pried his other hand off the rudder, his fingers and joints stiff from his viselike grip and the frigid water. His legs felt rubbery as he climbed out of the vessel.

He paused to gaze at the river. Other boats were exiting the canyon and floating past. The significance of what they'd just accomplished struck him, yanking an astonished chuckle from him. They'd done it—they'd survived the rapids.

Turning to Archie, he saw his own surprise, gratitude, and awe mirrored in the young man's expression. "That was something, wasn't it?" He stuck out his hand toward Archie. "I'm grateful I had you at the oars."

With a boyish grin, Archie clasped his hand. "I'm grateful I wasn't steering."

Jess laughed, though it, too, came out shaky. "You did real well. Not even your father could find fault with what you did just now."

"I hope so." Archie lowered his arm to his side.

"How many young men do you know who would've dared run those rapids?" Jess turned to the boat to unload what they needed to make camp. After that, he planned to start a fire so that they could both dry out before they caught cold.

Archie stepped up beside him. "If I'm honest, no one I know would've braved that canyon."

"See?" Jess hefted one of the packs. "I survived it myself, and I still think I'll have nightmares about it for weeks."

The young man's laughter rang out, bringing another smile to Jess's face. They'd challenged the rapids and won, putting him and Tava that much closer to reaching her pa.

———————◆◆◆———————

"Do you see them yet?" Tava craned her neck to look past the brush. Despite feeling calm after bidding the men goodbye, worry had crept back in little by little with each mile she and the Halls walked.

Carolyn shook her head. "I'm sure we're getting close." As if spurred on by her words, her son pulled ahead. "Wait up, Felix."

The boy whirled around. "Ah, Ma. I'm trying to stay with Dusty, and he ran ahead."

"He'll come back."

Felix obediently slowed his pace, though not so much that the two women could catch up. "Here, boy," he called. "Come, Dusty."

A bark floated back to them. Moments later the dog reappeared, jumping impatiently around Felix. "What is it, Dusty?"

"I think he's found something," Tava said, watching the husky.

Carolyn grimaced. "I hope it isn't a wild animal."

Racing forward again, the dog disappeared into the brush. Another bark reached them, only this one was followed by a shout of excitement.

"Did you hear that?" Tava glanced at Carolyn.

Her friend nodded. "Do you think it's the men?"

A hopeful thrill shot through Tava. "Maybe."

She and Carolyn quickened their steps. They caught up to Felix, and together the three of them hurried after the dog. Through a break in the vegetation, Tava spied the husky licking the face of someone crouched beside him. Her heart sped up in anticipation until she noticed the light-blond hair. It wasn't Jess; it was Archie.

"Archie!" Carolyn lifted her hand in greeting. "You made it."

The young man straightened. "I knew I was headed in the right direction when I saw Dusty."

Tava looked past him. "Is Jess with you?"

"No, he thought someone should stay with our things. So I volunteered to meet you."

Carolyn smiled as she gave him a side hug. "We're glad you did."

Reaching out, Tava clasped his dampened coat sleeve. "Other than wet, you're both all right?"

"We are." His grin hinted at exhausted happiness.

The four of them fell into step, Dusty scampering beside them. "Were the rapids as terrifying as they seemed?" Carolyn asked. "We could hear the roar of the water while we walked."

"Oh, they certainly lived up to their fame." Archie ran his hand through his drying hair. "At one point, we darted toward the side, and I thought we were goners. But we managed to get back into the current without any mishap."

Tava cringed as she pictured the frightening scene. "I'm glad you weren't hurt. And all of our supplies?"

"They're fine," Archie said, his pride in their accomplishment evident. "We didn't lose a single thing."

They passed several other groups who were making camp along the river. Finally Tava recognized the figure seated beside the fire. "Jess!"

"Hi there, songbird." He rose to his feet, a lopsided smile on his handsome face.

Tava raced forward and threw her arms around him, needing the solid proof of his presence. His heart drummed in time with hers, and little by little her anxiousness melted away.

Easing back, she touched his face. "You made it through."

185

"With a lot of prayer and a quart of luck."

Her eyes filled with tears as she smiled. "That's what my pa liked to say."

"I know," Jess murmured. "My guess is he said it after he came through the rapids himself."

Aware they weren't alone, Tava lowered her hand and stepped back. "I can't thank you enough for braving the rapids for us. You and Archie."

"Hear! Hear!" Carolyn said.

Tava turned to smile at the young man. However, the action faltered on her lips when she caught Archie's glare, leveled at her and Jess. Was he angry that she hadn't given him another hug?

Irritation threatened to overwhelm her gratitude. Tava didn't need to defend her decisions to Archie, nor did she expect him to agree with her. She did wish he'd respect her feelings, even if they weren't for him.

Carolyn clapped her hands. "Why don't we celebrate the men's success? I can make some more applesauce and use it to create a cake."

"A cake?" Felix smacked his lips and rubbed his hand over his belly, eliciting laughter from the rest of them.

"I second Felix's opinion." Jess grinned at the boy.

Archie dipped his chin in a nod. "A cake sounds wonderful."

With that, Tava felt the unvoiced tension between them break, along with her annoyance. How could she remain upset now that the rapids had been vanquished and there was the promise of cake?

Carolyn started on the dessert preparations, while Tava reheated beans for supper. As the men set up the tents, they recounted the details of their harrowing ride.

A festive attitude hung over their camp that night. Knowing the treat that awaited them afterwards, Tava thought even the normal supper fare tasted better. Carolyn's talent with a skillet showed in the delicious, moist cake she'd made. After every last crumb had been eaten and the dishes washed and put away, the five of them grouped back around the fire. Apparently everyone felt as reluctant as Tava to go to bed.

They talked about the next few weeks of travel and what it would be like navigating the river and camping along its banks each night. A short while later, Felix suggested they sing, and they all agreed.

During one lively song, Carolyn pulled her son to his feet, and linking arms, the pair spun around in time with the tune's tempo. Archie then asked Tava to dance, and she accepted. However, singing while do-si-doing in a circle proved too hard. All four of them ended up reclaiming their seats, out of breath and laughing.

They managed a few more songs before Felix started yawning. "Why don't we end with a slow number?" his mother suggested.

"How about 'It Is Well with My Soul'?" Archie glanced down at the fire. "My mother likes that one."

Tava shot Jess a knowing look. "That's my father's favorite hymn." Her pa had asked her to sing that one more than any other song. He'd once told her its words had comforted him more times than he could count after her mother had died.

As they sang the hymn, the words struck Tava in a new way. Their message felt especially poignant as she sat beside the very river that would lead her to Dawson and her father.

When peace, like a river, attendeth my way,
When sorrows like sea billows roll;
Whatever my lot, Thou hast taught me to say,
It is well, it is well with my soul.

The repeated refrain of the last line lodged inside her throat, making it impossible for her to finish the chorus. She truly believed her father still lived. Yet if she learned that wasn't true, could she still embody the words of the song? Could she say all was well with her soul? Her pa certainly had. No matter what they'd faced, he had held to the knowledge that God was aware of them and that things would be well—maybe not at first or for a long time but eventually.

A sharp sense of missing him pierced her enjoyment. "I . . . I need a moment." Tava rushed to her feet.

Without waiting for a response, she hurried toward the boat and the riverbank. She veered to the right, continuing several more yards before she stopped. Her chest felt tight with hope and fear, triumph and possible failure. She dragged in a gulp of air in an effort to ease the tension inside herself.

Other people were camped across the river. Tava watched them for a few seconds, then glanced away. Her gaze landed on a crude wooden cross that marked some person's grave. The name *Tobias* had been chiseled into the wood.

How had this man come to be buried here, after surviving so much? Did he have family who mourned him still? Maybe even a grown daughter who might not need a father in the ways she once had but who longed for that relationship to continue for many, many more years.

Tears blurred her vision, and it was just as well. She didn't want to look at the grave marker anymore or consider the possibility that in the not-so-distant future she might be mourning beside another lonely grave.

Folding her arms, Tava faced the river again and let her tears come. She didn't turn when she heard the sound of footfalls. Without looking, she knew it was Jess. Dusty had come with him. The husky reached her side and, with a whine, nudged her sleeve with his nose. Tava uncoiled her arm to scratch Dusty's head.

"I should've suggested another song." Jess came to a stop behind her and rested his hands on her shoulders.

Tava brushed at her damp cheeks. "It's all right." Leaning back against Jess, she stared at the water. The river's current would carry her where she needed to go, but it didn't care what outcome awaited her there.

"What if I'm wrong, Jess?" she whispered. "What if he's already gone?"

He gently twisted her around until she faced him. "Whatever happens, you and I both know we had to come." His earnest gaze bore into hers. "Whether we find what we want in Dawson or not, I have to believe there was still purpose to our journey."

She nodded in agreement. "I can't imagine not meeting the Halls and Archie." She glanced down at the dog sitting beside her leg. "Or Dusty."

Peering at Jess again, she couldn't fathom not making this trip with him either. Their mutual goal of reaching her father had united and connected them in a way they'd never experienced at the ranch. They had broken the silence shrouding their shared past too. The reminder gave her courage to voice a question she'd been waiting for time alone with him to ask.

"The other day when we were gathering firewood . . ." A blush bloomed on her cheeks at the memory of what she'd confided to him then, but Tava willed herself not to retreat. "What were you going to say before Felix came along?"

Jess's expression turned contemplative. "I'm not sure I remember."

"Oh." She glanced away, disappointed.

A nudge beneath her chin urged her to turn back. "I do know what I wish I'd done in that moment."

"What is that?" Tava asked, though she felt certain from

the intensity in his blue-green eyes that she already knew the answer.

Her pulse skipped faster and faster in anticipation as Jess leaned toward her. She shut her eyes, waiting, hoping. Then Jess's lips found hers. The sweetness of his slow kiss drew a soft sigh from her. She rested her hands on his shirtfront, his own racing heart thudding beneath her palms.

The last time she'd kissed him, their inevitable goodbye had loomed before them. Tonight, no worry or sadness marred the pivotal moment. She felt only optimism and happiness.

From the direction of camp, Felix called Dusty's name, and the husky dashed away. Neither she nor Jess made an attempt to follow. Instead he enfolded her in his arms and placed a kiss on her forehead. Tava tightened her grasp around his waist. She didn't want to let go—not when she recognized how deeply she still loved him.

It had always been Jess who held her heart, and it always would be.

17

HE'D KISSED TAVA—again—and the experience had felt as wondrous as the triumph with the rapids had been. Jess grinned. Unlike their first kiss, this one whispered at the promise of a future together.

With their hands clasped, they strode back to the campsite. The Halls and Dusty had already disappeared into their tent, but Archie lingered by the fire. He threw another stick on the flames as he raised his head. "Are you all right, Tava?"

"Yes." She offered him a smile, but it grew in brightness when she glanced at Jess. "I'm feeling better."

Jess tucked his lips around a chuckle at the teasing glint in her eyes. She'd clearly enjoyed their kiss as much as he had.

"I'm sure you are," Archie muttered in a sharp tone.

They both turned to look at him. "What do you mean?" Tava asked.

"You think I don't know what's going on?" The young man rose to his feet and thrust out his chin.

Jess frowned. "You're not making sense, Archie. What would you say is going on?"

"Tava's been lying to me." He motioned to her with an agitated wave of his hand before addressing her directly. "You assured me that you and Jess were just friends and nothing more."

Tava visibly flinched. "That was the truth when you asked me the question." She released Jess's hand and crossed her arms against her coat.

A ripple of anger ran through Jess. Neither he nor Tava had done anything wrong. Yet once again, Archie refused to see things beyond his own misguided perceptions.

"I wouldn't have kept trying to win your hand." His shoulders rose and fell with frustrated breaths. "You both must think I'm such a fool to have trusted you," he spat out. "Well, you're the ones who've acted foolish, thinking no one's watching you."

The young man's tirade stoked Jess's ire. "I don't know what—"

But Archie wasn't finished. "I've seen your coy touches and long looks." His upper lip curled in disgust. "Then to act sad about your pa, Tava, so you could sneak off—"

The false accusation erupted the pressure inside Jess. His fist connected with the young man's jaw, bringing a blessed end to the barbed words. Archie toppled backward onto the dirt.

Crouching beside him, Jess seized his coat collar and stuck his face next to Archie's. "You will take back that insinuation and apologize to Tava—now."

"You—you hit me!" Archie sputtered.

Jess eased back. "I'll give you to the count of three." The young man would not be allowed to treat Tava with such disrespect. "One . . ." he counted.

"I didn't mean anything by it." The pallor of Archie's face returned to white.

"Two . . ."

"Stop, Jess!" Tava appeared at his side, her expression pained. "You don't need to do this. I'm sure Archie is sorry."

Jess forced his fingers to let go, chagrin vying with his frustration. "It wasn't right for him to speak to you like that."

Archie scrambled backward as if he couldn't escape fast enough. His fear stirred greater remorse in Jess. He didn't condone the young man's behavior in the least, but he hadn't exactly helped the tense situation either by striking him.

"I'm sorry I hit you, Archie." Jess got to his feet. "That wasn't right of me to lash out like that, especially with my fists."

The young man glared up at him. "I suppose I shouldn't be surprised. A former drunk like you has probably picked up all sorts of bad habits."

"A former drunk?" Tava repeated, looking with confusion between the two men. "What are you talking about? Jess has never had a drink in his life."

His ears filled with a dull roar as he stared down at Archie. He'd told the young man what little he had as a way to show his sympathy—Jess hadn't expected Archie to recall much, if any, of the conversation.

"If that's true," Archie countered, "how did he know how to help me when I'd drunk too much?"

Tava shrugged. "I don't know. Maybe he knew someone who regularly became inebriated."

Everything inside Jess screamed at him to stay silent, but he couldn't. Archie would reveal the truth if he didn't. And Tava shouldn't learn of his past from anyone else.

Still, his gut twisted with fear, guilt, and self-loathing. He tried to call to mind Quinn's assurances, yet his mind remained blank of anything but the all-consuming regret.

Help me make it through this, Lord.

From the corner of his eye, he saw Carolyn standing outside her tent. Jess nearly groaned out loud. It would be hard enough sharing his story with Tava. However, when he turned to look straight at Carolyn, her expression radiated compassion and understanding. Somehow she'd guessed his long-guarded secrets.

She offered him a nod of encouragement, and the small gesture eased his inner storm just a fraction. But it was enough.

Jess squared his shoulders and faced Tava. "The reason I knew how to help Archie . . ." His words faded. He exhaled a shaky breath and tried again. "The reason I knew what to do is because I've been drunk plenty of times myself."

"Wh—what are you talking about?" Tava felt as if someone had ripped the question from her mouth. Or maybe it was from her heart. Surely she hadn't heard Jess correctly. He'd never been drunk before.

Exhaustion and emotional fatigue must have finally caught up with her. That would explain why she'd misheard him. Except . . . if that were true, then Jess shouldn't be regarding her like a man condemned to hang.

Carolyn approached and wrapped her arm around Tava's shoulders. She hadn't even heard her friend leave her tent. "My guess is, this is a long story. Why don't you and I sit by the fire while we listen to what Jess has to say?"

Woodenly, Tava allowed Carolyn to lead her. She sat in her earlier spot, and her friend settled next to her. The other woman's presence eased a little of her bewilderment and alarm.

Whatever Jess had to share, Tava reasoned, it had to do with his experiences before he'd come to work on the ranch. And he had obviously changed a great deal since then.

Jess joined them by the fire, but he didn't sit. A moment later, Archie walked over as well. Tava struggled not to glower at the young man. He'd purposely provoked Jess, and his behavior earlier had been unkind. He still hadn't apologized either. She sensed him observing her, but when she met his eye, he had the decency to look remorseful and ashamed as he lowered his chin.

Heavy silence smothered them, save for the occasional pop of the fire. Finally Jess cleared his throat.

"I grew up on our family farm, until I was fifteen." He peered down at the flames. Tava imagined he saw something else, something far away from their campsite. "It was a hard life, made all the harder by my pa's caustic tongue and his tendency to use his fists when he ran out of words to spew. More often than not, he directed his ill treatment at me, but my ma and six siblings weren't immune to it either." The admission held such pain that its sharp ache reverberated inside Tava. "It grew worse the older and stronger I got. I think because my father knew the day would come when I could best him if I wanted. When I couldn't endure it any longer, I decided to leave home for good."

Jess scrubbed his hands down his bearded face. "I had next to nothing to take with me, but I figured if I could find work, I could survive. Once the little food I had ran out, I nearly went back. But a storekeeper took pity on me and let me clean his establishment in exchange for a meal. He told me of a ranch nearby that needed workers, so I went there and got a job as a stable hand."

He pushed out another sigh as if reliving the memories. Tava gripped her hands together, knowing that at some point these recollections would reflect a Jess she had never known.

"I idolized the cowboys that worked there," he continued. "Some of them even took me under their wing. It felt good to have real friends at last, people who didn't find me worthless." He licked his lips as if trying to coax the next part of the story from his mouth. "Whenever they went to town to visit the saloon, they invited me to come along. That's where I first discovered that alcohol could take away the pain, that it could numb my pa's constant voice of ridicule inside my head and the bad memories of home. And despite being thin, I was also tall, and I learned to hold my own—and sometimes even win—in a fistfight."

Jess folded his arms across his chest. "I worked at that ranch for two years before things took an awful turn. My friends . . ." He spat out the word. "They convinced me to join them on a night raid to another ranch to steal some cattle. They'd been doing that for some time, but I hadn't ever joined them. For some reason, I chose to go that night, though I knew nothing about rounding up cattle.

"The job didn't go as planned, which was largely my fault. Several cows got away and wandered near the ranch house. It wasn't long before someone fired a gun in the air. We took off on our horses and met at the rendezvous point we'd picked earlier. My friends were livid that we'd failed, and seeing how I was the inexperienced one of the group, I was blamed." His Adam's apple bobbed as he swallowed. "They exacted their revenge by beating me thoroughly and stealing all of my money, then they left me lying there unconscious."

Tava covered her mouth with her fingers. Jess's vivid descriptions painted a horrible scene. No wonder he'd been hesitant and unsure on his first roundup after coming to the ranch.

Kneeling beside the fire, Jess held his hands to the warmth. "When I came to, I decided I could salvage things if I went back and stole at least one cow. But I didn't make it far before collapsing. I woke up again, only to find the end of a rifle aimed at me. The man holding the other end was your father, Tava."

How had she never heard any of this before—from him or her father? She tried to remember the moment she'd first seen Jess Lawmen. "I don't recall you showing up at the ranch black-eyed and bruised."

"I didn't. Quinn let me sleep in the barn, then he took me to town the next morning and paid for me to recover at one of the boardinghouses." Jess finally sat on the ground, his arms around his knees and his hands clasped together. "A few days later, he asked me how I'd ended up on his property. I told him everything. When I finished, Quinn offered me a job at the Double R—on the condition that I gave up drinking, brawling, and attempted cattle rustling. He also promised to send notice to the other ranch that my employment there had ended. In that moment, I'd never felt so grateful and beholden to another person in my life. I accepted his offer at once."

Tava studied his bent head. His loyalty to her father was strong, and now she knew why. Her pa had given the wayward adolescent a new life and a new home. And while she wished she'd known of his past sooner, she was grateful to know it now.

"I appreciate your telling me all of that." His confession the other day about his temper and Archie's comments this evening made sense to her now. So did Jess's knowledge of how to help the drunken young man.

But Jess didn't look relieved at unburdening his past. "That isn't all," he said, his voice quiet.

Tava shared a glance with Carolyn, then returned her attention to Jess. "What else can there be? You kept your promise to my father. You never drank or brawled at the ranch . . ."

She let her words trail off as understanding rushed in. Jess hadn't reverted to his old habits while at the Double R. But what about after he'd left? A hard rock of dread dropped into her stomach. Carolyn reached for her hand and gave it a squeeze, as if trying to bolster her with courage.

"I think the two of you two ought to finish the rest of this conversation without Archie and me listening in." Carolyn released her grasp and stood. "I'll wait up in case you need to talk, Tava."

She managed a tight smile. "Thank you." How blessed and grateful she felt that God had brought this dear friend into her life.

Archie rose to his feet as well, but he didn't meet anyone's eyes. "I'm sorry, Tava, for what I said earlier. And Jess . . . I owe you an apology as well." Tava suspected he meant for more than being rude—he felt bad for prodding a full confession from Jess. "Good night, both of you."

"Good night," Tava echoed.

The instant Archie and Carolyn disappeared into their respective tents, Jess picked up his story again. "You already know that I wanted to see the world four years ago." The reminder of how much she had missed him then washed over her anew. "I had grand plans, but they weren't all about experiencing new things and places. Once I'd had my fill of adventure, I planned to come back to the ranch and ask your father if I could court you."

Tava jerked her chin up. "I didn't know that."

He shrugged, as if he hadn't voiced anything out of the ordinary. "Things went well that first week or so. But I missed you and the ranch something fierce, and I wondered if I'd made a mistake in leaving. Then my pa's voice came back, more insistent than ever, reminding me that I still hadn't amounted to much in comparison with others. I was just a ranch hand, living on the good graces of someone else. It got harder and harder to resist the pull to numb my thoughts and homesickness. One night I gave in, and that's all it took."

In the firelight, Jess's knuckles gleamed white from gripping his hands together so tightly. "I ended up in a jail cell after inciting a brawl at a saloon. The sheriff let me go when I'd sobered. But I knew right then that you deserved to be with someone stronger and more disciplined than me."

Something wet slid down Tava's face. She reached up to brush the errant tear away.

"I started to fear that if I stayed away any longer, things would get worse. So I wrote your father, told him what I'd done, and asked if I could come back. He actually refused." Jess's chuckle held little mirth. "Looking back, I'm grateful that he did. But at the time, I was desperate. I begged to know what I could do to return. Quinn gave me the name of a preacher in another town and told me to go talk to him. He also informed me that I wasn't allowed back at the ranch until I'd remained sober and out of jail for six months."

His explanation gave context to the timeframe of his absence and his eventual return. Jess had come back to the Double R after his six months of sobriety.

"That's why I couldn't reclaim more than friendship with you." A note of pleading crept into his tone. "It wouldn't have been fair, not after all the mistakes I'd made."

Tava straightened on her makeshift chair. A few more tears followed in the wake of the first. "So your decision had nothing to do with what my pa would think of us or how young I was?"

Jess slowly shook his head. "Those were just the excuses I could share." He dropped his gaze to the fire again. "I didn't realize until this trip how much I hurt you that night. And for that, I am truly sorry."

"What made you change your mind?"

She hoped he understood what she meant without having to clarify. If not, she wasn't sure she could bring herself to ask him about the transformation in their relationship or the kiss they'd shared earlier—the memory of which now filled Tava with confusion rather than happiness.

The crackling of the fire and the distant barking of a dog occupied the tense stillness that accompanied her question. At last Jess looked her way, remorse and longing on his face.

"There was no change. My feelings for you have always been the same, if not deeper."

Tava pressed her lips together to stop herself from crying out at his revelation. Jess hadn't stopped loving her any more than she had stopped loving him, in spite of trying to do just that for years. Her tears fell in a steady rhythm down her face.

"That's all there is to say, I suppose." His shoulders were bunched forward in an outward sign of resignation. "Unless you have something?"

"No," she whispered.

Jess stood. "I suppose it's best to get some sleep. We'll want to leave right after breakfast."

With a nod, Tava forced her legs to move. She felt numb, inside and out. As she started in the direction of the tents, Jess stilled her steps with a light touch to her sleeve.

"I'm sorry again, songbird, for everything."

She choked back a sob. "I know you are. But it's like I said in Dyea. You didn't give me a choice, Jess. I had no say in what happened that night."

Sorrow drove furrows into his brow as he let his hand fall away. "What if I had told you all of it and your pa had approved of my intentions? Would you have still wished to be more than friends?"

"I—I don't know," Tava answered honestly.

Had it been less than an hour ago that she'd stood blissfully in his embrace? The recollection left her aching. She wanted so much to believe that Jess was the same person she'd always known, but there was so much he hadn't bothered to tell her. He'd kept silent and made decisions on his own.

His past was no longer a secret to her. Yet that knowledge was hardly compensation for how much her world had been upended this evening.

"Why did you kiss me?" The inquiry came out strangled.

Jess offered a weary shrug. "I guess I wanted to believe that the past could be laid to rest and wouldn't destroy our happiness now or in the future."

The unspoken hope behind his reply wasn't lost on Tava. But she couldn't reassure him anymore than she could herself. "I need some time, Jess. There's a lot I have to think about."

"I understand." When he fell back a step, a whoosh of cold air filled the widening space between them. "I'll see you in the morning."

She tried for a smile and failed. "See you in the morning."

Hurrying toward the Halls' tent to hide the renewal of her tears, she remembered doing the same thing four years ago. She'd concealed her weeping from Jess that night too. And the thought hurt her heart all the more.

18

JESS FOUND THE mood around the camp the next morning painfully somber. Nothing remained of the cheerfulness from the night before. Even Felix, who'd gone to bed before the disastrous events, spoke little at breakfast. Contours of fatigue showed on Tava's face, which surely matched Jess's own. He'd stared at the canvas ceiling of the tent for a long time before finally dozing off.

Thankfully Archie had been asleep when Jess had entered the tent after his and Tava's private conversation. He hadn't been in the mood to talk anymore. But the ensuing stillness had provided little balm to how gutted he felt at having his renewed hopes splintered into hundreds of tiny pieces.

It wasn't as if he hadn't visualized what it would be like to share his past with Tava. However, the reality of doing so had proven harder—and more devastating—than he could have imagined. And then Tava had asked him for time to think over everything. Those words had rung hauntingly through his head as Jess lay awake.

Would she eventually forgive him for withholding the truth? Or had he permanently destroyed their friendship?

He tried to reassure himself that he'd done the right thing. As his best friend and the woman he loved, Tava had a right to know about his former mistakes. Yet the consolation felt hollow since he hadn't been given a choice of when or how to share his confession. Archie had made that decision for him, with no regard to what Jess wanted.

Just as I did with Tava four years ago, he'd thought with searing remorse.

If he hadn't allowed his fear to get the better of him that night, he likely could have managed things differently, rather than disregarding Tava's feelings and making a choice without her say.

He planned to give her all the time she needed to come to terms with what he'd shared. Doing so would mean setting aside his plan to speak with her father, but Jess could wait. Whatever he could do to repair things with Tava, he would do it.

All five of them helped reload their things into the boat, then Jess pushed the vessel into the river. He opted to steer again, anxious to give his mind something more to concentrate on than the night before. Tava chose to sit facing him, which he took as a hopeful sign. Still, every time their eyes met, he read confusion and hurt in her gaze.

After gaining a feel for the current, Jess discovered the river's center ran fast. Archie's rowing combined with the use of their sail increased the vessel's speed. The women made quiet conversation, while Felix attempted to occupy himself by playing with his wooden soldiers.

Most of the boats on the river were similar in size and shape to theirs. But there were canoes and single-occupant rafts too. One resourceful young man had converted his sled into a floatable craft by attaching two logs to it.

Moss and rocks covered the riverbanks, and here and there Jess spied the camp of a native family. They often stood on the shore, crying out with eagerness to barter for goods with the people traveling past.

Their group reached Lake Laberge around noon, where they made the required check-in at the police post. After a cold lunch, they climbed aboard once more to begin the thirty-mile trek across the lake. This time Archie chose to steer, and Jess took up the oars. He welcomed the more physically demanding task. However, unlike guiding the boat, this one left his mind far less occupied with anything but his troubled thoughts.

He'd sought heaven's forgiveness for striking Archie. It was a mistake Jess would not repeat and one he deeply regretted. He tried to reassure himself that he hadn't succumbed to taking that drink at the saloon in Dyea, which surely counted for something. In many ways, he was a different person than the one he'd talked about last night. He just hoped Tava would come to see that and, if nothing else, accept his friendship once more.

After lunch, she'd selected a seat facing the boat's stern, which meant Jess could no longer see her expression. But her sloped shoulders indicated a crack in her normal strength—a crack Jess knew he couldn't fix this time, as much as he wished to. Tava hadn't acted angry with him today, nor had she ignored him. Yet his confession had disrupted the ease of their interactions.

"How long will it take us to reach the end of the lake?" Carolyn asked him.

Jess squinted up at their full sail and the sky overhead. Thankfully there were no storm clouds in sight. "The wind is blowing the right direction, so I'd say we might be able to cross the whole thing by early evening."

"That would be good," he heard Tava say.

He shifted his stance to see Archie. The young man had apologized again this morning, and his subdued demeanor made it near impossible for Jess to remain angry with him.

205

"You all right with pushing to reach the end of the lake?"

Archie appeared momentarily surprised by the question, but he recovered enough to nod. "I'm willing."

The rest of the afternoon passed uneventfully. Jess and Archie traded places after a few hours, mindful not to wake Felix, who slept with his head on his mother's knee.

By suppertime, they had reached the lake's end and ventured into the adjoining clear, blue water of the Thirty Mile. However, the current here was anything but tranquil. As he had at the rapids, Jess put all of his effort and focus into steering the boat, while Archie worked tirelessly at rowing. The scattered remnants of other boats that he saw along the way served as a sobering reminder to be alert and cautious.

Once they'd put the dangerous waters behind them, Jess searched the shore for a spot to land. His stomach grumbled with hunger, and his mind and body felt weighed down from lack of sleep and a full day of switching from rudder to oars and back again.

"Let's pull off ahead," he said to Archie.

The young man peered over his shoulder at the bank and nodded. They guided the boat toward the shore, where Tava hopped out and pulled them forward the last few yards. The rest of them climbed from the vessel. Dusty raced about, thrilled to no longer be confined, as the group unloaded their nightly supplies.

Sometime later Felix paused in helping Jess set up the tents. "Dusty isn't back."

"He's probably off exploring," Jess said as he glanced about the campsite. "I'm sure he hasn't gone far."

"Did you see which way he went, Felix?" Tava asked.

The boy frowned, then pointed farther down the riverbank. "I think that way. Is he going to get lost?"

"Nah." Jess bent down until their eyes were level.

"Dusty's a smart dog. He knows who loves him and where he can find food and a warm place to sleep."

Felix pushed the toe of his shoe into the dirt. "I guess so."

"Tell you what." Slapping his hands against his legs, Jess straightened. "Let's finish with this tent. Then you and me can head in the direction he went. That is, if your ma is all right with that."

Smiling, Carolyn nodded her approval.

Jess and Felix had the tent set up a few minutes later. Together they headed away from the camp, following the direction the dog had gone. Every few feet, one of them hollered Dusty's name.

At first, Jess heard nothing in response. But as they walked farther, he caught the faint sound of a bark. "Call him again, Felix."

The boy cupped his hands around his mouth. "Here, Dusty! Come here!"

A louder bark followed. "It's him," Felix said, his countenance lightening with relief. "He's up ahead. Let's go, Jess."

He chuckled as he followed after Felix. They found the husky sniffing about another campsite, where a miner had just finished setting up a tent. The man appeared to be about Jess's age.

Seeing the stranger, Felix slowed and threw Jess a hesitant look. Jess put a reassuring hand on the boy's shoulder and guided him forward.

"Howdy." Jess waved in greeting. "Looks like Dusty found your camp."

"That your dog?" The man glanced at the husky.

Felix nodded. "He's mine." As if to confirm the fact, the boy dropped to one knee and called Dusty's name. The dog immediately trotted over to Felix.

"You shouldn't have run off, boy," he scolded in a murmur. "I didn't know if we'd find you."

The man pushed up his hat brim. "He's a nice-looking husky. Had me one when I was younger. You named him Dusty, huh?"

"It's short for Dusty Gray," Jess explained.

The stranger sniffed. "Not too original. I called mine White Paw, cause he had one white foot."

Jess pressed his lips over a smile and resisted the urge to point out the unoriginality of that name. "Well, we'd best get—"

At that moment, a younger man walked into the camp, his arms laden with firewood. "You going on about White Paw again?" he said to his companion, though his blue-green eyes were full of mirth. He set down his load and straightened. "I keep telling Vincent that no other dog in the world is better than the one I had as a boy. Ol' Blue Belly wasn't a husky, but that may have been his only flaw."

Felix twisted on his heels to peer up at Jess. "Blue Belly? Wasn't that the name of your dog when you were a boy?"

"It was . . ." Jess mused in surprise.

The younger man's eyebrows rose. "Good name. I can't say I've ever heard of another dog being called that one."

Neither had Jess. His younger brother Pete had picked the dog's name. But this man couldn't be Pete. It was more likely that the two had chosen to call their dogs the same thing than it was for Jess to stumble onto his brother in northwestern Canada.

"We'll let you get back to business," Jess said with a nod.

He started to turn away, but he stopped when he noticed a faint scar near the younger man's mouth. Pete had a similar mark from tripping over their ma's rocking chair and cutting his chin. Jess peered more closely at the stranger's face, trying to find the little brother he remembered in the man's features.

"About time you got back with that wood, Lawmen," Vincent snapped at the other fellow.

Jess's jaw dropped. Could it really be Pete? He recovered enough to ask, "You wouldn't, by chance, be Pete Lawmen, would you?"

The stranger looked him over. "I am. And you are?"

"I'm Jess . . . your brother."

Pete's eyes widened. "Jess?"

The two shook hands, then Jess pulled his brother in for a quick hug. Pete clapped him hard on the back. "Look at you," Jess said as he stepped back. "You're all grown up."

"Unlike you," Pete teased. "You're just as I remember."

"Ha. That may be true, but I'm sure I can still spit seeds farther than you can."

His brother laughed, and the cheerful sound reminded Jess of the boy Pete had once been. "I was six years younger than you. Of course I couldn't spit as good as you and Clive."

"How is Clive?"

A shadow stole the merriment from Pete's face. "I don't know, actually. He up and left a year after you did. He only ever sent one letter after that."

"Which was more than you got from me." Guilt wound through Jess.

Pete shrugged with nonchalance, but Jess caught the flicker of pain in his brother's eyes. It had been hard for Jess to leave Pete and the others behind, but it couldn't have been easy for them either, especially with no word from him.

"I'm sorry I didn't write." He hoped Pete sensed his heartfelt sincerity. "I had my reasons at first, but I waited too long to change my mind. When I did decide to write, I learned the family had up and moved."

Nodding, his brother stared at something in the distance. "That would've been the third time in as many years." Pete stared at something in the distance, all the levity gone from his expression. "Truth is, I was angry at you for leaving. But as I got a little older, I finally understood why you'd done it." He looked at Jess again. "It was your courage that helped the rest of us to find our own way in the world."

"Is this really your brother?" Felix asked, his hand on Dusty.

Jess had forgotten the boy's presence in the shock of reuniting with Pete. "It sure is."

"I bet Ma would like to meet him."

Pete glanced between them. "Is this . . . your son?"

Jess shook his head. "This fine fellow is Felix Hall. He and his mother are traveling with me and Tava and another friend we met, named Archie."

"Tava?" his brother echoed. "Is she your sweetheart?"

A surge of grief washed over Jess at the question. "She's the daughter of the man I work for. That's why we're here." He paused. "It's a long story. I could you tell you at supper, if you and your companion want to join us."

"What do you say, Vincent?" Pete called over to the other man. "Want to have supper with my brother and his friends?"

His companion was working on starting a fire. "What I want is to get this fire going, and then I plan to stay and watch over our things. You go or stay. It don't matter to me."

His brother turned to Jess. "In that case, I'd be happy to join you." Pete didn't seem bothered at all by his companion's irritable manner.

"Let's go, Dusty." Felix stepped backward, motioning for the dog to follow. "Ma's gonna be so excited. We found you and Jess's brother." Spinning around, the boy led the dog toward their campsite.

Jess exchanged a smile with his brother as they trailed after the pair. "You and Vincent friends?"

"Hardly," Pete said with a laugh. "We met at Lake Bennett and decided to partner up to build a boat. We've talked about staking a claim together, but I'm still undecided. As you can see, the man can be downright ornery at times." He clasped Jess's shoulder. "Which makes me all the more relieved to find you out here, big brother."

Jess laughed. "Agreed."

The rather taxing day had taken a happy turn. Jess still didn't know what lay ahead in Dawson or with his and Tava's relationship, but tonight he would simply enjoy what little time he had with Pete.

Tava breathed a sigh of relief when Felix reappeared with Dusty at his side. "You found him." She stirred the beans she'd been warming and glanced past the boy and his dog, but she didn't see Jess. "Is Jess coming back?"

"Yep, him and his brother."

Carolyn chuckled as she ladled biscuit dough onto the skillet. "His brother? What do you mean, Felix?"

"Jess found his brother when we found Dusty."

Tava shared a befuddled look with Carolyn. Their mutual confusion ended when Jess and another man strode into the campsite a few moments later. The stranger's smile perfectly matched Jess's.

Astonished, Tava rose to her feet. Carolyn did the same. "Would you look at that?" her friend said, shaking her head.

"See, I told you, Ma." Felix wrestled a stick from Dusty's mouth. "This is Jess's brother Pete."

Pete removed his hat. "Howdy, folks." His hair was darker than Jess's, but they shared the same color of eyes.

"This is Carolyn Hall," Jess introduced. "Felix is her son."

Carolyn smiled. "A pleasure to meet you, Pete."

"Mine, as well, ma'am."

Jess waved to where Archie was setting up the other tent.

"Over there is Archie." The young man lifted his hammer in the air. "And . . ." Turning toward Tava, Jess hesitated, as if unsure how to proceed with her introduction. "This is Tava," he finally said, "the daughter of my employer, Quinn Rutherford."

A twinge of pain pinched her at Jess's choice of words. While true, they hardly represented all that they'd experienced together—or all that Tava had hoped to experience before last night's revelations had rocked her contentment.

Tava swallowed her hurt and greeted Jess's brother with genuine civility. "It's nice to meet you, Pete."

"You too," he said, placing his hat back on his head.

"I invited him to eat with us, if that's all right." Jess looked to Tava and Carolyn for confirmation.

Carolyn nodded. "We'd love to have you join us. Supper won't be anything fancy. Just beans and biscuits."

"I'm much obliged, ma'am. I haven't had a decent biscuit in weeks."

As the two made conversation, Tava moved closer to Jess. "Did you know he was coming to the Klondike too?"

"I had no idea." Emotions flickered across his face as he observed his brother—shock, happiness, relief. "I haven't seen any of my family in ten years. When I left the farm, Pete was just nine."

Tava shook her head, still stunned at the surprise reunion. "Is Pete your only brother?"

"No. Clive is just younger than me, and Oscar is the baby of the family."

From what he'd told her last night, he had six siblings altogether. "So you also have three sisters?" she said.

"That's right." As Jess peered at her, his expression clouded. "I think I'll help Archie." When she nodded, he walked away.

Tava folded her arms against the ache inside her, uncertain how or when the underlying uneasiness between them would end. The story of his past had shaken her. She'd never considered Jess to have been anything but the upstanding, God-fearing, honest person she had known since she was fourteen. To learn of his vices, and that he'd kept them from her, had left her troubled and confused. It also didn't help to know her father had been privy to the whole story from the beginning.

"How long have you known Jess?"

Pete's question startled her. "Oh . . . he came to work at our ranch seven years ago."

His brother gave a thoughtful nod. "Wouldn't have expected him to work with cattle. He was terrified of our milk cow growing up." Pete's mouth lifted in a conspiratorial smile.

"I didn't know that."

Her gaze went to Jess again. Could this be another reason he'd struggled during that first roundup? Yet he hadn't protested over her relaying the story to the Halls and Archie. She now knew a lot more about his life before coming to the Double R. But how much of it could Tava truly comprehend? Unlike her own father, Jess's had been vicious and unkind. She'd never had to struggle to find food or work, either, or felt any fear at home.

"He's an excellent cowboy," she found herself saying. "My father even made him ranch foreman three years ago."

Pete studied her for a moment, making Tava wonder what he saw. "I'm glad to hear he's found a place there."

"Where is home for you?"

Belatedly, she recalled the beans she'd been warming. She hurried over to the fire and crouched beside the pot. A slight burnt odor wafted past her nose as she attempted to stir the beans. Hopefully they wouldn't taste scorched.

"I've done my fair share of wandering," Pete answered, his earlier cheeriness fading. "Up until a year ago, I was never far from the gambling tables. Then I met a girl at a town picnic." A sentimental smile lifted his mouth. "I knew if I wanted to win her hand I had to change my ways."

The free admission regarding his mistakes surprised Tava. There was no embarrassment beneath his confession, either, just honest recognition. "Were you able to do it? Change your ways, I mean?"

"It wasn't easy. I had to learn how to make money the honest way." His smile deepened. "But I've always been good at numbers, so I found a job as a store clerk. I knew it would still be a long time before I could make enough to support a family. That's why I decided to come to the Klondike. I'm hoping to leave with enough gold to convince Emme's pa that I can provide for her."

Moving the beans off the flames, Tava stood. "She sounds like a lucky girl."

"I'm the lucky one," Pete said, his tone devoid of teasing. "Jess mentioned your pa came up here too."

"He did, but in his last letter, he said he was ill. I wanted to find out for myself if he's better or not. That's why Jess and I are headed to Dawson."

Carolyn declared that the biscuits were done. Once they'd all gathered around the fire, she and Tava passed out the food. Tava was relieved to find the beans didn't taste bad.

As she ate, she watched the brothers interact. They swapped stories of their childhood, their talk full of jesting and laughter. She hoped her reunion with her pa would be as happy—and extend beyond the hour or two that Jess and Pete had together before it would be time to say goodbye. The brothers might spot each other on the river as both parties traveled onward, but it wouldn't be the same as being together.

"Thank you for the meal." Pete handed over his empty plate and stood. "I probably ought to get back." He shot Jess a reluctant look.

Jess rose to his feet as well, his expression every bit as disappointed as his brother's.

"Why don't you go with him?" Tava blurted out, an idea taking shape at the same instant she voiced the question.

Five pairs of eyes regarded her in puzzled surprise. Tava moistened her lips. "What I mean is that you could travel the rest of the way to Dawson together, and we'll meet up with you there."

"That would be nice," Jess admitted, "but I'm needed here."

Tava placed her plate on the ground for Dusty to eat the leftovers. "The four of us could manage, especially since the dangerous parts of the river are behind us."

"Who would help us with the boat?" Archie asked.

Jess shook his head. "No one, because I'm staying with our group."

Tava swallowed a frustrated sigh. "Archie knows how to steer, and I can help row. What do you think, Pete?" She turned toward Jess's brother.

Pete spread his hands in a surrendering gesture, yet there was hope in his countenance. "It would be nice to have my big brother along. But it's up to Jess."

"You really want me to go?" Jess directed the question at Tava.

There was an edge to his tone that she didn't understand. Couldn't he see that she was only trying to allow him to have more time with Pete?

"I want you to do what you want. If that's going with your brother, then I'm fine with that."

His blue-green eyes filled with disappointment, as if he'd

been expecting a different answer from her. "What about the rest of you?"

"I hadn't counted on you not being there," Archie said. "But I think we can manage."

Carolyn studied Jess. "I don't mind rowing too. That is, if you want to go with your brother, Jess."

"You want to leave us?" Felix frowned.

Ducking down beside him, Jess tousled the boy's hair. "That's not it." His gaze flicked to Tava. "But it sounds like this is for the best. It'll only be until we get to Dawson." He put on his hat as he stood. "I suppose I'll start unloading my things from the boat."

His lack of excitement at the plan bothered Tava. Had she done the wrong thing in suggesting it? She mentally shook her head as she helped Carolyn gather up the dishes.

Things would be different without Jess, and Tava would miss him, even if she still felt conflicted about their relationship. His absence would also give her time to think about what he'd told her regarding his past, without worrying about the current awkwardness between them.

Besides, it had been ten years since he'd last seen Pete. Surely that warranted some sacrifice to allow the brothers a chance to bond once more.

19

"I THINK THAT'S all of it." Jess surveyed the pile of things they'd carried over to Pete and Vincent's campsite. He'd already bid farewell to the Halls. The time had come to do the same with Archie and Tava.

He extended his hand toward the young man. "Thanks for all of your help. I hope to see you in Dawson."

"I'd like that too." Archie accepted Jess's firm handshake. "You taught me a lot, and I'm grateful."

At any other time, his praise would have meant a great deal to Jess. He'd wanted, after all, to help Archie from the beginning. However, the knowledge that he had succeeded felt less fulfilling in this moment—now that Tava was sending him away.

Jess didn't doubt she was earnest in wanting him to spend more time with his brother, but he couldn't help wondering if there was another reason behind her suggestion. Hadn't she asked for time to think things over? It would seem she also wanted some physical distance from him.

As Archie stepped aside, Tava took his place. "I hope you and Pete have a nice time traveling together."

"Thank you. I'm sure we will."

Her mouth pulled tight at the stiltedness of his tone. "If we see you on the river, we could try to camp beside each other."

Jess shook his head before she'd finished. "Trying to land at the same time and in a spot large enough for two groups that isn't already occupied would be tough." He looked away at the bewilderment in her brown eyes. She didn't want him traveling with their group anymore, and knowing that, he couldn't bear the thought of possibly seeing her each night. Meeting her gaze once more, he forced out his next words. "I think it's best if we wait to find each other in Dawson."

"Oh, all right." She dipped her chin in a slow nod. "You'll come to the boardinghouse?" She voiced it as a question.

In spite of being hurt and angry, Jess would finish what he'd started. He owed that much to her and to Quinn. Once he knew what had happened to her father, then he would decide if it was time to make a new life for himself away from the ranch.

"I'll be there."

Some of the tension eased from her expression. "Then I guess this is goodbye for now."

The sentiment echoed one they'd both voiced four years ago. However, this farewell contained none of the promise that the other parting had, at least to begin with. If anything, their future had never looked more uncertain.

"Goodbye, Tava."

He had to curl his fingers into his palms to keep from reaching for her, to take hold of her hand or draw her in for an embrace. She no longer wanted those things from him.

Tava raised her hand in farewell. "See you in Dawson."

"See you in Dawson . . . songbird."

The next few days merged into one another as Tava and the others navigated the river.

Every morning, they ate breakfast, loaded the boat, and

pushed off into the water. Each evening, they maneuvered their way out of the current and set up camp. Archie steered, while the women traded turns rowing. When Tava wasn't at the oars, she helped entertain Felix with stories and songs.

Other than Five Finger Rapids, their time on the river remained uneventful. Yet even the treacherous-looking rapids had been easily surmounted with the help of the Mounted Police, who directed everyone to take the channel to the right. Tava had come to appreciate the exertion it took to row. It gave her something purposeful to do, knowing that each rotation of the oars brought her ever closer to her father. But the physical task left her thoughts too free to wander. More often than not, they centered on Jess.

He'd been frustrated with her when they had said goodbye, but Tava still didn't know the reason. Was he angry now? Did he think of her at all?

She often looked for his face among those they passed by. The night after Jess had left, Archie had caught sight of the three men floating past their campsite. Since then, the young man had been determined to beat the other group to Dawson. Tava didn't mind. More hours spent on the river lessened the time she had left before reaching her pa.

Still, their group felt incomplete without Jess. Tava missed him deeply. His smile, his teasing, his willingness to listen, his nickname for her—every little thing about him that she'd taken for granted for so long had vanished from her life. If she'd ever wondered what her days on the ranch would be like without him around, she'd been given a bitter taste of it now.

One night after supper, just two days away from Dawson, Felix did a show for them by presenting the tricks he'd been teaching Dusty in the evenings.

"Sit, Dusty," Felix directed.

The dog complied. Tava joined Carolyn and Archie in applauding.

"Now, roll over."

Dusty performed the roll, then scampered back up into a seated position. The three of them clapped again.

"Shake hands."

The dog placed his paw inside Felix's hand, and the boy shook it up and down.

A smile prodded Tava's mouth as she clapped once more. She had seen the duo practicing and had been impressed with their skill.

Felix faced his audience. "Let's take our bows now, Dusty." He bent in half, his eyes on the dog. Dusty dropped his front legs to the ground and dipped his head.

Tava laughed out loud at the amusing picture they made. She cheered loudly as Felix straightened and Dusty rose to all fours.

Archie clapped Felix on the shoulder. "That was splendid."

"Well done, both of you," Carolyn exclaimed. She gave her son a hug and offered Dusty a pat on the head.

Tava embraced Felix, too, before scratching Dusty's ears. "You were both terrific."

"I wish Jess could have seen the show." Felix peered up at Tava. "Do you think he'll find us in Dawson?"

She managed a nod, in spite of the sharp ache that rose inside her at the mention of Jess. "I know he will, and I'm sure he would love to see your tricks then."

Her words satisfied the boy, who found a stick and threw it for Dusty. Archie soon joined in their game. Tava searched the campsite for something to do that would take her mind off Jess's absence.

"I think I'll go for a short walk," she said to Carolyn.

Her friend glanced at Felix and Archie. "Would you mind some company?"

"No, you're welcome to join me."

Carolyn fell into step beside her as they walked along the riverbank. Neither of them spoke. A short distance from their camp, Tava heard the sounds of another group. She was about to turn back when Carolyn pointed to a fallen log.

"Want to sit a spell before we head back?"

Tava agreed and settled next to Carolyn on the log. Stretching out her legs, she noted the worn quality of her pants and boots. Her hands had grown more tan from the sun's reflection off the water, and she imagined the number of her freckles had tripled. What would her mother think of her current appearance?

Carolyn extended her legs as well. The fabric of her dress showed weeks of travel, and her face was still pink from sunburn. Yet Tava wouldn't describe her friend as anything less than a lady, despite all they'd been through. Perhaps being a lady went far beyond one's attire. The possibility inspired a spark of hope inside her—that maybe she hadn't completely failed her mother, as she'd always feared.

"It was nice to hear you laugh tonight," Carolyn said, throwing Tava a glance.

She smiled at the memory. "Felix put on a good show."

"He did, didn't he?" Carolyn clasped her hands in her lap. "The news of his father's death was very hard on him, and he withdrew into himself. But since coming on this trip, I've seen more and more of the exuberant boy he used to be."

"I'm so glad." Tava studied her friend's profile. "How did you keep going? After losing your husband?" She knew her friend well enough by now to know the personal question wouldn't offend.

Carolyn pushed out a soft sigh. "Truthfully? Right now, I

have to take things one day at a time. It's a decision I make every morning when I wake up."

"What do you mean?"

Her friend tucked a strand of auburn hair behind her ear. "Each day, I have to decide all over again if I trust God enough to know that He hasn't forgotten me, that He has a plan for me and my son, and that He understands every moment of my grief and joy." She shrugged. "If I can do that, I can move forward through another day."

The conviction behind her words felt like a salve to Tava's fears. She hadn't stopped praying to find her pa alive. But as devastated and grief-stricken as she would be if he wasn't, she could make it through—one day at a time, with God's help.

"You're a wonderful example to me." She placed her arm around Carolyn's shoulders and squeezed her tight. If Tava had been able to have a sister, she couldn't think of a better one than the woman seated next to her.

Carolyn rested her head against Tava's. "Thank you. Were you thinking of your father just now . . . or Jess?"

"Both," she admitted with a mirthless chuckle as she lowered her arm.

"May I ask you a question?" At her nod, her friend continued. "Was learning about Jess's past the reason you encouraged him to go with his brother?"

Tava shook her head. "No, I really did want him to have more time with Pete."

"Has your view of him changed?"

The same query had plagued Tava since she'd heard Jess's confession. "It did a little, at first. But the more I've thought on it, the more I've realized that, other than striking Archie, Jess has acted as the man I've always believed him to be."

She chipped at the log's wood with her fingernail until

she wrested a piece free. "When I think of all he's been through, I feel sad. Yet there are still moments when I feel upset with him for not telling me any of it sooner."

Carolyn patted her hand. "I think that's understandable." Her friend shifted on the log, her shoes tapping against each other. "Do you still wish to be friends with him?"

"Very much so." She didn't want their friendship to end. "Jess is my oldest and dearest friend. However, can I trust him to be honest with me? To tell me things in the future and not forge ahead on his own?"

"Those are fair questions."

The light laugh that dropped from Tava's lips felt like a breath of fresh air after all her inner turmoil. "You aren't going to help me answer it, are you?"

Carolyn offered her own chuckle before her demeanor grew serious again. "I can't. I think Jess can, but only if you're willing to talk to him."

"I suppose you're right." Tava bent her legs and leaned her arms against her knees.

"Maybe the most important thing to ask yourself is if you still love him."

It came as no surprise that her friend had already surmised Tava's feelings for Jess. After all, Carolyn had noticed them much sooner than Tava herself had.

Did she love Jess even now? The keen loneliness inside her had to be some kind of answer. Tava didn't miss him as a friend, either. She had only to picture Jess courting some other girl and leaving the ranch for good to know she wasn't content with mere friendship from him.

"Yes." Her answer came out quiet, but it clamored loudly inside her. "I do still love him."

Carolyn twisted around to face her. "Then he deserves to know that. Especially after sharing what he did and then having you send him away."

"I didn't send him away."

"Do you think Jess might have seen it that way?" her friend gently chided.

Tava considered the possibility, her gaze on the ground. Did Jess think she'd sent him away because she was ashamed of him and his past? The realization made her jolt upright. No wonder he'd acted angry with her. Deep regret stole her breath.

"What have I done, Carolyn?" She covered her mouth with her hand, but it didn't stay her tears. As sobs shook her shoulders, her friend held her free hand through the tide of grief.

Jess had told her that his feelings for her hadn't changed. Was that still true? Or had Tava unknowingly driven away the man she loved with all of her heart?

She needed to find out, and that meant she had to speak with him. The idea of doing so sent prickles of anxiety shooting through her. She'd been rejected by him before, and it had taken her time to move past it. Did she dare risk a second rejection by revealing her true feelings to him?

Tava knew the answer at once. As terrified as she was to be hurt again, she had to try. Jess needed to know she didn't hold his past against him. If anything, she'd come to see how his experiences had shaped him into the amazing man he was today. And that man deserved to know how she really felt—whether he returned her feelings or not.

Brushing the salty moisture from her cheeks, she lifted her chin. "As soon as we learn what's happened to my father, I'll talk to Jess. I have to tell him how much I love him."

Carolyn nodded her approval as she released Tava's hand. "I find that wise and very brave."

"We probably ought to get back to camp." Tava stood, new energy coursing through her. "I'd love to get an especially early start on the river tomorrow."

Her friend climbed to her feet, her mouth tipping upward. "Sounds good to me."

"Who would have thought when we started from Seattle that I'd finally realize what I feel for Jess?" Tava mused as they walked back the way they'd come.

Carolyn laughed. "Oh, I could have told you that from the moment I met you two."

"You're probably right." Smiling, Tava linked arms with her friend.

Whatever awaited her in Dawson, whether painful or joyous, she wouldn't discount God's merciful blessings in her life right now. She had the company of good friends and had experienced protection, clarity, and growth on her journey to the Klondike. For each of these, she would express gratitude, while also praying for the ability to say, in all matters, that it was well with her soul.

20

IN A FEW hours, they would reach Dawson, but it would only be Jess and his brother arriving together. Vincent hadn't believed Jess's claim that he wasn't there to be mining partners with Pete. The man had insisted they stop over at Split-Up City so that he could unload his supplies and find a new partner among the dozens of others who'd landed here for the exact same purpose of forging new alliances. The delay had set the brothers back by hours, and now Jess was desperate to make up the time to reach their final destination.

His anger at Tava for asking him to go had disappeared. How could he remain upset when he considered all the time that he'd been able to spend with Pete by traveling together?

In spite of their differing yet equally trying years at home, Jess had been relieved to discover that his younger brother still possessed the same cheery precociousness he had as a kid. Pete was also optimistic and easy to talk with.

He'd listened without judgment as Jess had shared everything that had happened since leaving the family farm. Jess had also confided his feelings for Tava. In turn, Pete had shared his troubles with gambling, his work to overcome those, and the girl waiting for him back in the States. They'd also discussed their other family members and what Pete knew about each one.

Jess had been surprised at the genuine grief he'd felt when

Pete told him their pa had passed away a few years earlier. He mourned for the man, who, according to his brother, still hadn't made peace with himself.

After his pa's death, Jess's ma and youngest siblings had gone to live with his sister Rowena and her husband. He'd been relieved to hear that his brother-in-law treated his sister and the rest of the family with genuine kindness and respect. Jess had also promised to write them the first chance he got.

While grateful for his reunion with his brother, Jess still wished he knew how Tava and the others were faring. Had they been able to pilot the boat without trouble? Did Tava miss him as much as he did her? Would their friendship ever be the same, now that she knew about his past? The same endless circle of questions had pestered him since leaving her and the group.

As if he'd been privy to Jess's thoughts, Pete asked, "You excited to see Tava tomorrow?" He was manning the rudder today.

"I am. But she may not be excited to see me."

"Why not?"

He threw his brother a pointed look without pausing in his rowing. "She sent me away, Pete. I find that rather telling."

"So is the fact that you didn't say no."

Shaking his head, Jess frowned. "I wanted to spend time with you, remember? Besides, Tava made it clear that having me gone was what she wanted."

"Or maybe she meant what she said about you and me getting to spend time together."

With some difficulty, Jess resisted rolling his eyes. Pete hadn't witnessed Tava's shock when he'd revealed his past to her. "Either way, she asked for time and I helped give that to her."

"Perhaps that's your problem, big brother."

Jess fought a scowl. "What are you talking about?"

"Have you ever asked yourself if you're being too helpful?" Before Jess could answer, his brother continued. "It's not wrong to help people, but things can get sticky if you try to impose *your* idea of what's helpful on someone else. More often than not, that leaves a person thinking you don't fully believe in them." Pete shot him a grim smile. "We have to fail or succeed on our own merits, while knowing the people we love are right there to weep or cheer with us."

Turning away, Jess stared at the other boats moving near theirs, his arms rotating in rhythm with the oars. Had his eagerness to help Tava in the past caused her to believe that he didn't think she could handle those things on her own? Nothing could be further from the truth. Tava was strong and capable. If anything, Jess just wanted her to see that she didn't need to be strong alone. He wanted to be there with her, to weep or cheer, as his brother had described.

He returned his gaze to Pete. "You make some fair points. But they might have come too late. Tava probably thinks the worst of me after everything I told her."

"Have you stopped loving her?"

"No." She might have sent him away, but that hadn't changed the depth of Jess's feelings.

Pete's eyebrows shot up in obvious doubt. "If that's true, then you need to fight for her. That's what women want."

"What do you mean fight?" That was the last thing he needed to do after his altercation with Archie.

His brother had no qualms about rolling his eyes at what he clearly viewed as a dumb question. "I mean, if you still love her, you don't give up on her. You fight for her by showing her in word and action that you're the changed man you've been these last few years."

Jess considered the advice. He had enough regrets

already—he didn't want to add losing Tava to the number. Maybe the time had come for him to prove how much he believed he'd changed. He swallowed hard at the thought. Was he brave enough to hold to the truths about himself, regardless of what happened between him and Tava?

He'd been terrified that he would return to his old habits on this trip. And while he'd certainly made mistakes, he hadn't picked up those former vices. Jess had remained true to the changes inside. He was a man who trusted God, who worked hard, who loved Tava, and who strove to be honest and respectful in all of his dealings.

A new question rose into his mind. Could he convince Tava—and her father—that he might be the right man to claim her heart after all?

"I'm going to fight for her." Jess punctuated the words with a firm nod.

His brother feigned a look of confusion and cupped his hand around his ear. "I'm sorry. Did you say something?"

"Yes," Jess said louder, "I'm going to fight to win Tava back."

Pete grinned. "That's better, big brother. Now put your back into rowing. We got ourselves another reason to reach Dawson as quick as we can."

The city appeared before them as Tava and the others rounded a bluff in the river. Here the waters of the Klondike met those of the Yukon, while a bare-faced mountain reigned nearby. Thousands of structures and tents and people met their wide-eyed gazes.

After they found a place to dock among the myriad of other boats, Archie volunteered to stay with Dusty and their supplies while the Halls accompanied Tava to the boardinghouse. There were no street addresses to speak of, so Tava had to duck into several different shops to figure out which way to go. At last, the three of them stood before a two-story wooden building.

Tava's heart thrashed hard and fast as she stared up at the sign. How many times since leaving the ranch had she envisioned this moment? She clutched her letter in her hand, the back filled with dozens of tally marks. In a few minutes, she would know her pa's fate, and she both yearned for and dreaded that knowledge.

Blowing out her breath, she squared her trembling shoulders. "I won't learn anything standing here."

"You can do this," Carolyn reassured as Tava moved toward the door.

She threw her friend a grateful smile and entered the boardinghouse. Occupants filled the main area, which adjoined with a dining room. The murmur of conversation filled her ears as Tava moved through the throng, searching for Nelly.

"Afternoon," a tired but kind voice said.

Tava spun around. A woman with silver hair wiped her hands on an apron. "Hello," Tava answered.

The woman's dark eyes glanced past her, at Carolyn and Felix. "I'm sorry, but I am completely full at present. You may be able to find room at one of the hotels."

"We aren't looking for a room." Tava moistened her dry lips. This had to be Nelly. "I've come to inquire about my father. His name is Quinn Rutherford."

Nelly lifted her hand to her mouth. "Are you Tava?" she asked after a moment.

Was the woman's shock a good sign or a bad one? Tava's pulse pounded harder with uncertainty. "You must be Nelly."

"I am, and I can't believe you're here. Didn't you receive my letter?"

Tava had to remind herself to breathe, but the prolonged suspense robbed her lungs of air. "We got the note you penned on behalf of my father. The one that said . . ." She cleared her throat to expel the rest of the words. "That said he wasn't long for this world."

"Oh dear." Nelly shook her head. "You poor thing. I'm so sorry."

Was this it? Tava braced herself, her fingernails digging into her palms. Would she learn in the next moment that Nelly had written the truth regarding her pa's mortality?

"I shouldn't have sent that note," Nelly said, her words coming out in a rush. "Your father was half out of his mind with fever that night, and I misunderstood what he asked me to do. The minute I realized my mistake I sent you a letter, but it clearly didn't reach you in time." Her expression conveyed deep sorrow. "I am profoundly sorry for causing you such distress."

Tava stared at the woman in confusion. "Are you saying—he's . . ."

A smile blossomed on Nelly's face. "Your father is very much alive. He's upstairs, second door on the right."

Carolyn nudged Tava in the back. "Go on. We'll wait for you."

Without a word, Tava headed to the stairs. She nearly tripped in her haste to reach the top. She hurried past the first doorway to the second. The door stood ajar. After grabbing the handle, she pushed into the room. A bed dominated the tiny space, with a table and two chairs jammed into the corner.

Her father sat at the table, reading. He was thinner than Tava remembered, his hair and beard much grayer. But his face was as familiar as her own.

She stepped into the room, the floorboards creaking beneath her feet. Her father lifted his head at the sound. As his gaze met hers, his jaw slackened.

"Hello, Pa," she managed in a wobbly voice.

"Tava?"

That single word unleashed the torrent inside her. With a sob, she crossed the room and sank to her knees beside his chair.

Jess pushed his way inside the boardinghouse. From what he could see, he'd come too late for supper. Not that he cared. Food would need to wait until he'd learned what had happened to Quinn. He searched the room for Tava. Had she come and gone already? If so, he would have no idea where to find her.

"May I help you?" an older woman asked.

He nodded in reply, guessing this had to be Nelly. "I'm looking for Quinn Rutherford."

"Ah, you must be Tava's friend."

"Is she still here?" Jess looked around the room, but he couldn't see Tava.

"She and her father are eating upstairs, but you're welcome to join them."

Jess needed several moments to ponder her words and their import. "You mean Quinn isn't . . ."

"He's alive and well," Nelly said, her gaze full of compassion and regret. "I wrote to tell you both, but apparently, my letter didn't reach you in time." She fiddled with the tie of her apron. "The long and short of it is, I shouldn't have sent that note when I did. It was a misunderstanding. Nevertheless, I'm so sorry for causing you and Tava alarm."

If anyone could relate to the consequences and remorse that came with making a mistake, it was Jess. "I, for one, am glad you sent it when you did. And I imagine Tava is too." He glanced toward the stairs. "May I go up?"

"Please." Nelly offered a smile. "They're in the second room on the right. I can bring you up a supper tray, too, if you'd like."

"Yes, thank you, ma'am."

Jess took the stairs two at a time. Outside the second door, he stopped. The enormity of all that he and Tava had experienced to get here—and the discovery that Quinn had survived his illness—caused him to sag with relief against the doorframe. Tears pooled beneath his eyelids as he ducked his chin and offered a prayer of gratitude. When he'd finished, he blinked hard and knocked on the door.

"Come in," Quinn called out.

Removing his hat, Jess entered the room. His gaze went first to Tava, seated cross-legged on the end of the bed. Her neutral expression made it difficult to tell if she was happy to see him or not. He hoped for the former, now that he intended to win her back.

Next he studied the man at the table. Jess coughed to dislodge the lump in his throat. "I have to say, you're a sight for sore eyes, Quinn."

"You too, Jess." The older man rose to his feet. "Tava mentioned you found one of your brothers on the way to Dawson. She half expected you to get here before her."

He shot a glance at Tava, wondering if she'd told Quinn about his confession too. "We had to make a stop at Split-Up City, but I came as soon as Pete and I arrived." He crossed the room, then shook hands with Quinn.

"I don't doubt it." The man pulled him forward into a tight hug. "It's good to see you."

Again Jess found it difficult to speak. When Quinn released him, he stepped back and cleared his throat. "It's good to see you too, old man."

The lines around Quinn's eyes wrinkled as he chuckled

at the familiar nickname. "I'm just sorry Nelly's letter and the one I wrote you after that didn't reach you before you both came all this way."

"Even if it had, my guess is we still would have come." From the corner of his eye, he caught Tava's nod.

"Sit down." Quinn indicated the chairs. A tray with empty supper dishes rested on the table. "I imagine Nelly might be willing to bring you something to eat if you're hungry."

Jess took a seat. "She kindly offered to do just that."

"Tava was telling me about the ranch and the changes that had to be made." Quinn sat back down.

Had that been difficult for Tava to share? Jess wondered. He'd been privy to her worry over what her father would think of those decisions. But when Jess looked her way, he was surprised—and pleased—to find confidence shining in her brown eyes.

"No one could have run things any better in your absence," Jess said, "than Tava did."

Her gaze widened at his compliment, and her cheeks flushed pink. "I tried my best."

Quinn watched Jess closely for a moment, then smiled at Tava. "I don't doubt it for a second, sweetheart. Now tell me all about your trip."

Setting his hat on his upturned knee, Jess listened as Tava described their journey. Quinn asked questions or offered comments regarding his own time on the pass and the lakes. The closeness the two of them had always shared was as strong as ever—it hadn't been diminished by time and absence. But rather than feeling like an outsider, as Jess often had at the ranch, today he felt a part of the familial scene. He had divulged his past to Tava and, in doing so, had freed a part of himself that he'd held back for so long.

A knock sounded at the door before Nelly entered, carrying a tray. "I see Jess found you." Her eyes went straight to Quinn's as she approached the table.

Smiling, Quinn shot to his feet. "Thank you for bringing him some food. Let me help you." After taking the tray from Nelly, he placed it next to the other on the tabletop.

"My pleasure." She motioned to Jess's supper. "I expect you to eat every bite, young man. You've likely had little in the way of actual food for weeks."

Jess laughed at the accuracy of her statement. "Thank you, Nelly. I promise to polish it off."

"Oh, you will," Quinn reassured him with confidence. "Nelly is the best cook in North America."

The woman blushed. "He's only saying that so I won't make him go back to eating nothing but broth."

"Maybe." Quinn's eyes sparkled with humor. "Doesn't mean it isn't true when it comes to your cooking." He walked with her toward the door.

As he lifted his fork, Jess tossed a look in Tava's direction. Had she noticed the camaraderie between her pa and Nelly?

"Where are Archie and the Halls?" he asked.

Tava wrapped her arms around her upturned knees. "They're staying at one of the hotels for now. How about Pete?"

"He's not far. He pitched his tent over in Louse Town. He'll be there until he can stake a claim."

Nodding, she stared down at her socks. "Are you glad you had more time with Pete?"

Without knowing where they stood, he considered the best way to answer. "It was good to be with my brother, and I'm grateful you made that possible." He swallowed, reminding himself it was time to be bold—to fight for her. "That being said, I wish I could have remained with our group . . . and with you."

"Tava, honey?" Quinn said, startling Jess. He hadn't realized the man had been listening. "Would you mind taking our supper dishes down to Nelly? I forgot to give them to her just now."

"Of course." Tava slipped on her discarded boots, then stood and picked up the other tray. "I'll be right back."

"No need to rush." Her father leveled his gaze on Jess. "It'll give Jess and me a chance to catch up."

Jess gulped, feeling uneasy. Would Quinn want to know why Jess hadn't insisted on staying with Tava for the final part of their trip? Or would he wish to know what progress Jess had made on seeing that the right man won her heart?

Tava shrugged. "All right. I won't hurry."

As she disappeared from the room, her father returned to his chair. Jess set down his fork and met Quinn's pointed gaze across the table. It was time to be honest about his feelings and intentions when it came to the man's daughter.

"I have something I need to discuss with you, Quinn."

He hoped the man would approve of him as a potential suitor and son-in-law. But even if Quinn didn't, Jess wouldn't give up. He would keep proving himself to Tava—and her father—every day, for another seven more years if he had to.

Quinn's posture relaxed a little. "Are you going to tell me you're finally ready to ask for Tava's hand?"

"What?" Jess choked out. Had he heard the man correctly? "H-how long have you known that I love her?"

The man arched his eyebrows. "The way you feel about my daughter is as plain as that beard on your face. It has been for years. Why do you think, when I thought I was dying, that I asked you to see that the right man claimed her heart?"

"Wait." Jess shook his head in confusion. "You meant *me*?"

Leaning back against the wall, Quinn pinned him with

another probing stare. "Do you really think I'd want Tava to marry anyone else?"

"I . . ." Shock and hope vied for dominance inside him. "You need to know, I told her about my past—all of it. It was after that when she encouraged me to travel the rest of the way with Pete."

"And you think that's because she can't accept your past?"

Jess lifted his shoulders in a shrug. "I don't know for sure."

"Tell me this." Quinn dropped the chair legs to the floor and leaned forward. "Do you believe that even with your mistakes you're worthy of notice and love?"

Did he? Jess thought back over his life, before and after coming to the Double R. For so long, he'd told himself he was unworthy because of his past. Yet when he searched his heart, that belief was no longer there. "I do believe that," he said in a clear, firm voice.

"Then that, son"—Quinn smiled at him—"is all that matters to me. And my guess is, that's all that matters to my daughter too."

The words settled like a balm inside him. "Thank you, Quinn."

The man propped his elbow on the table and wagged a finger at Jess. "If you really want to thank me, then quit pining over my daughter and ask her to be your wife."

Jess laughed. "I've got to speak with her first, old man. But I take it I have your blessing?"

"You have more than that." Quinn's expression sobered as he reached out to clasp Jess's arm. "You have my faith and confidence that you'll both love and honor each other in the way you both deserve."

21

SHE HADN'T MEANT to be gone nearly half an hour. But, after thanking Nelly for caring for her father, Tava had volunteered to help wash the large stack of dishes. Nelly had looked visibly pleased at the offer. As they worked, the two of them had traded questions and stories.

Tava had been surprised to learn that Nelly had once been a wealthy society lady in Seattle, before she and her husband had lost most of their money in the Panic of '93. Not long after that, their only son had died. Nelly's husband followed a few months later.

Heartbroken, Nelly had decided she needed a fresh start. She'd worked in her youth in her parents' boardinghouse, so she decided to run her own. After hearing of the gold rush, she had sold everything she could and used what little remained of her husband's fortune to make her way to Dawson. She opened a tent restaurant first, then eventually built the wooden boardinghouse.

Despite the tragedies of the past—or maybe because of them—the older woman still exuded kindness and optimism. She hadn't allowed her losses and hardships to harden her heart.

Tava could say the same of Jess. The years before coming to the ranch had been difficult for him. Yet despite his experiences and mistakes, he'd kept trying to improve and change. Like Nelly, he also exemplified compassion and hope—and that only increased Tava's love for him.

However, Jess wouldn't know that unless she told him.

"I'm going to head back upstairs." Tava set the towel she'd been using on the sideboard.

Nelly's smile carried warmth and gratitude. "Thanks for the help. I already feel as if I know you, with all of the stories your father has told me. He prayed every day for you, even when he was too sick to sit up or hold a spoon. I know he was worried about you losing another parent."

Blinking back tears, Tava glanced at the doorway. "Did you ever think he wouldn't make it?"

"Numerous times," Nelly admitted with a sigh. "While he was praying for you, I was praying just as hard for him." She brushed a strand of her silver hair away from her forehead. "He's a good man, your father. Most of the miners who traipse through here have treated me with respect, but Quinn took the time to get to know me as a person."

The woman's dark eyes softened, as they had each time that she'd mentioned Quinn. The way the pair had interacted upstairs hadn't escaped Tava's notice either. Had her pa and Nelly developed feelings for each other? It was a question Tava hoped to have answered. But first, before she lost her nerve, she had to speak with Jess.

She felt relieved that he no longer seemed angry with her. His words of praise about running the ranch in her father's absence hadn't been the necessity she'd once believed they would be, but the heartfelt compliment had meant a great deal to her. His admission about not wanting to leave her had renewed her hopes too.

Did it mean he wouldn't reject her again? Her lingering fear over that possibility had been the reason for schooling her reaction to seeing him in person again. However, afraid or not, she didn't want to wait any longer to share her feelings with him.

Resolved, Tava returned to her father's door. She knocked lightly, then stepped inside. Her father stood up from the table, a smile on his weathered face. Tava glanced at Jess, but she couldn't riddle out what he was thinking from his stoic demeanor.

"Would you mind if I spoke to Jess in private, Pa?" She prided herself on sounding confident.

His smile deepened. "Not at all. I believe Jess has a few things to say as well."

Tava shot Jess a look of surprise. He flushed and rubbed the back of his neck.

Quinn rested his hands on Tava's shoulders. "I know what you risked to come here." His own brown eyes welled with tears. "And I'm grateful that you did. I've missed you a great deal."

"I've missed you too."

He wrapped her up in a hug. "I'm proud of you, Tava, and I know your mother would be too. You've grown into an amazing woman."

No tribute could have filled her more thoroughly. "Thank you," she whispered when he released her.

"You don't need to worry about what's going to happen to the ranch. My claim is small, but it's produced enough gold that we ought to be able to pay the bank in full and buy some more cattle."

Gratitude coursed through Tava as she grasped his hand. "Oh, Pa. That's great news."

"The three of us can talk more later." He kissed her cheek. "I'll be downstairs." Leaving the door slightly ajar, he left the room.

Tava blinked away the moisture in her eyes as she turned to face Jess. He stood beside the table, watching her. Where did she begin? She ventured forward a few steps before stopping. The silence between them felt charged with expectation.

Her heartbeat quickened, and she clasped her hands together nervously. Memories of that devastating night four years ago hovered at the edges of her mind. Then she recalled her conversation with Carolyn by the river. Allowing herself another moment with the fear, Tava let it go. She'd endured so much to reach her father. Now it was time to be brave for her and Jess.

"I owe you an apology."

Jess reared back a little in surprise. "For what?"

"For not being more forthright. I should have told you what I was feeling before you left with Pete."

His expression changed from bewilderment to wariness. "How did you feel?"

She risked another step toward him, her fingers tightening their grip. "When I learned about your past, I'll admit, I was shocked and confused." Pain flashed in his blue-green eyes, and he glanced away. "I needed time," Tava hurried to explain. "But it wasn't because I thought less of you. I was upset that you hadn't told me those things before. And I was frustrated all over again that you plowed ahead with your insistence that we be friends without giving me the real reason why."

"That was wrong of me." He gripped the back of his empty chair. "I should've told you everything years ago. I see that now." His shoulders rose and fell with a shrug. "At the time, I hated the idea of you no longer caring for me. I didn't want to drive you away with my mistakes."

Tava waited for his eyes to meet hers again. "I don't think any less of you for your past mistakes, Jess."

"You don't?" The hopefulness on his handsome face renewed her tears.

"No." She shook her head as she crossed the last few feet that stood between them. "The truth is . . ." Tava swallowed hard. "I never stopped loving you, though I tried to, believe me." She gave a self-deprecating sniff that prompted a chuckle from Jess. "But I couldn't change what was in my heart."

He moved to stand in front of her, his hand rising to cup her cheek. "Now that you know everything about me, does it change anything?"

"It's knowing everything about you that has made me realize how much I still love you." A sense of freedom washed over her at saying the words she'd kept locked away for years. "I never intended for you to feel as if I was sending you away, and for that, I'm sorry. If that changes how you feel, I'll—"

His gentle kiss supplied her with the answer and bound up her fears once and for all. Joy spilled through Tava as she looped her arms about his neck and kissed him in return.

Many moments later, she eased back to look at Jess. "You'd better not insist that we return to being friends," she half teased.

"Not this time, songbird." His grin caused her breath to catch. "I'm hoping to be much more than friends."

Tava did her best to hide her smile and asked, with feigned innocence, "And that means?"

"It means I want to marry you, Octavia Rutherford, and as soon as possible too." He unwound her arms and held her hands in both of his. "I want to be your husband and honor, love, and care for you always." He lifted her fingers to his mouth, then placed a kiss against her knuckles. "Will you consent to be my wife?"

"Yes," she whispered as happy tears trickled down her cheeks. "I would love nothing more than to marry you, Jess Lawmen, and be your wife."

He offered another grin before kissing her breathless.

"I do have one condition." She smiled sweetly at him.

Jess pretended to frown. "What would that be?"

"Now that we know my father is better, we should head back to the ranch before winter sets in. But I don't want to make the journey without being married to you first."

He nodded slowly, his eyes reflecting her own happiness. "What do you say to a wedding the day after tomorrow?"

"I say, it's about time."

Jess laughed and pressed his forehead to hers. How grateful she would always be for the long journey that had brought them together at last. Then—because she could, without reservation or uncertainty—Tava kissed *him*.

EPILOGUE

Montana, October 1899

TAVA SWISHED HER dustrag across the mantel, then lifted her and Jess's wedding photo to wipe beneath it. She studied the image and smiled, remembering how handsome her husband had looked in his suit that day. He hadn't been the only one wearing new clothes either. With help from Carolyn, Tava had found a gown worthy of a wedding at one of the shops in Dawson. The dress had been simple but decidedly feminine—her mother would have loved it.

Tava set the picture back in its place of prominence. Her thoughts remained on her wedding day as she continued dusting. She and Jess had shared the church that morning with another bride and groom—her father and Nelly. The pair had announced their intentions to wed after Tava and Jess had shared their news.

Tava hadn't been entirely surprised by the announcement. The love between the older couple was as undeniable as hers and Jess's, and she was grateful her father would once again know happiness in marriage. So a double wedding had been planned.

Archie, Pete, and the Halls were all in attendance, and

after the ceremonies, both couples had their pictures taken. For supper, Tava's father had treated everyone to a delicious meal at one of the hotels. It had been a beautiful day with family and friends.

Less than a week later, Jess and Tava had departed on a steamer bound for home, via the all-water route. Her father would be staying in the Klondike for another year to work his claim. It had been hard telling him goodbye all over again, but Tava was grateful he wouldn't be alone this time.

Saying farewell to their friends hadn't been any easier, though Tava was relieved to leave them well settled. The Halls would be living at the boardinghouse, while Carolyn helped Nelly. Archie had taken an instant liking to Tava's father and the camaraderie had been mutual. The young man planned to work with Quinn to learn the ins and outs of mining. Then, as part of his arrangement with Carolyn, Archie would take over working her late husband's claim.

Tava moved to the piano, the hem of her long skirt swishing around her shoe-clad ankles. She no longer minded dresses as much as she once had.

Hearing the creak of a floorboard, she turned to see Rita entering the parlor. The older woman's smiling gaze went straight to the cradle in the corner, where two-month-old Peter Quinn lay napping.

"I can do that," Rita whispered, motioning to Tava's dustrag.

"I don't mind." Tava kept her voice equally as hushed, to not wake the baby. "It gives me something to do besides pace the floor and check the window every five seconds."

Rita chuckled. "I know just how you feel, honey."

Today Quinn and Nelly were finally coming home. Jess had driven into town earlier to pick them up at the train station, and Tava had grown restless waiting for their arrival.

A shout from the yard drew both women's attention to the window. Rushing forward, Tava peered out. Oscar stood outside, waving his hat in the air at the wagon lumbering up the lane.

"They're here!" Tava threw a grin at Rita, then hurried over to the cradle. "It's time to wake up, little man." She lifted her son carefully, then tucked his blanket more snugly around his tiny body and kissed his round cheek. Peter stirred, blinking blue eyes up at her. "Hello, sweetheart. It's time to meet your grandparents."

As Tava headed for the door with the baby in her arms, the housekeeper settled a coat around her shoulders. "Thank you, Rita." The older woman pulled on her own coat, and she and Tava stepped onto the porch.

The brisk autumn air cooled Tava's flushed cheeks. Years before, she'd waited out here with equal excitement for another reunion. How much her life had changed since that evening long ago when Jess had returned to the ranch. She'd learned to forgive him and accept his help, and he'd learned to forgive himself and talk things over with her.

Her eyes went to her husband's. Jess waved, and Tava returned the gesture. Beside him on the seat sat Nelly. But as Tava glanced at the wagon bed, she saw more than her father's familiar face.

"Hi there, Tava!" Felix called from where he stood behind the seat.

Tava hurried into the yard, her mouth gaping in delighted shock. "Felix! Carolyn! Archie! What are the three of you doing here?"

"Don't forget Dusty," her father added.

The second the wagon stopped, the husky sprang from the vehicle and ran up to Tava. She freed one hand to scratch his head. "It's so good to see you, boy."

Jess helped Nelly and Carolyn alight from the wagon. The women headed straight for Tava and the baby. "Oh, isn't he a dear?" Nelly exclaimed, giving Tava a side embrace. "Can I hold him?"

"Of course." Tava relinquished the baby into Nelly's arms.

"I see things have changed around here." Carolyn threw a meaningful glance at Tava's dress.

With a laugh, Tava hugged her friend. "I'll admit they are more comfortable than I used to think."

"Are you surprised to see us?" Carolyn's green eyes twinkled.

"Yes! I can't believe you're here." Tava waved her hand in an arc to include Felix and Archie. "All of you."

Archie jumped down the from the wagon. "When we heard Quinn and Nelly were heading outside, the three of us decided it was time for us to leave too. We traveled as a group, and when we reached Seattle, Quinn invited us to come with them to the ranch."

Tava pulled Felix and Archie in for a double hug. "I'm so glad you've come." She stepped back and pretended to study them in earnest. "You're both taller than I remember, and twice as handsome."

The young man flushed at her compliment. There was a maturity about him that hadn't been there the year before. From her father's letters, Tava knew that Archie had worked hard as a miner. And though his monetary success in the Klondike didn't compare to his father's banking fortune, he had grown in confidence during his time away.

"This is what a ranch looks like, huh?" Felix assessed the house and grounds.

Tava's father and Jess laughed out loud. "This is it," Quinn said.

"Hello, Pa."

His warm embrace engulfed her. "I've been counting down the days until we saw you again, sweetheart."

"Me too." She wiped at her damp eyes as he released her.

Quinn turned toward the porch. "Where's that grandson of mine?"

Tava waved at Nelly, Carolyn, and Rita, who were cooing over the baby. "I don't know that you're going to pry him away from his grandmother."

"She's so happy to be part of a family again," he said, his gaze full of love as he watched his wife.

Squeezing her father's hand, Tava smiled. "We're blessed to have her."

Quinn cleared his throat and gave Tava's hand an answering squeeze. "I probably ought to make some introductions." He strode forward to clap Oscar on the shoulder, and together they approached the huddle of women. Off to the side, Felix and Dusty were exploring the nearby corral.

Tava moved to where Jess and Archie were unloading the luggage. Her husband deposited several bags on the porch. On his return to the wagon, he stopped to slip his arm around her shoulders.

"What do you think, songbird?" He motioned with his hat at the happy gathering.

She encircled her arms about his waist. "I still can't believe everyone is here."

Something in his low chuckle made her ease back to see his face. There was a definite spark in those blue-green eyes.

"Did you know the others were coming with Pa and Nelly?"

Jess shrugged, but he was grinning. "Maybe."

"It was all his idea," Quinn said above the melee over his grandson.

Tava tucked her head beneath Jess's chin and tightened her grasp. "Thank you. It's a beautiful surprise."

"I was hoping you'd think so." He pressed a kiss to her brow.

Joy and affection flooded Tava as she surveyed the group. "I love the surprise, but what I still love best is this husband of mine and his heart of gold."

Jess nudged her to straighten. He brushed a few strands of hair from her face, his regard full of tenderness. "Your love for me and Little Peter makes it easier to be that kind of man."

"And do you love this wife of yours in return?" she teased, looping her arms around his neck.

He set his hands on her waist as his mouth kicked up in a grin. "I love her from here to the Klondike and back again." Jess leaned closer, his next words whispered. "But in case she forgets that now and again, I aim to remind her with surprises . . . and plenty of kisses."

Tava made a show of peering around at all their guests. "I've seen your surprise, but no kiss."

"Then I'd better rectify that right quick."

Tossing his hat into the wagon bed, her husband tipped her backward and brought his lips to hers. Tava met them ardently, amid the jubilant guffaws and cheers from their dear friends and family.

AUTHOR'S NOTE

Gold was discovered along the Klondike River in the Yukon Territory of northwestern Canada in August 1896. However, the world did not learn of the discovery until almost a year later, when a number of miners landed in San Francisco and Seattle, toting more than two tons of gold with them. For a country that had been affected by the financial panic of 1893, the promise of riches in the faraway goldfields became a siren call to thousands. People from all walks of life and occupations responded. The northwest part of the United States, which had been hit particularly hard, profited greatly from the gold rush.

Those traveling to the remote area of the Klondike were required to bring with them a year's supply of food in order to prevent widespread starvation. The two main trails to reach the goldfields led from Skagway, Alaska, to Lake Bennett via the White Pass Trail, or from Dyea, Alaska, to Lake Lindemann via the Chilkoot Pass. From there, the gold seekers had to build their own boats to navigate the five hundred miles of water from Lake Bennett to Dawson City, where the Klondike River met the Yukon River.

It's estimated that one hundred thousand people set off for the Yukon region, but only around thirty thousand succeeded in completing the journey. About four thousand miners found gold.

All of the places mentioned are real, except for the Double R Ranch. Two books were invaluable to my research and in piecing together what the journey to the Klondike would have been like—*The Klondike Fever: The Life and Death of the Last Great Gold Rush* by Pierre Berton and *Gold Rush in the Klondike: A Woman's Journey in 1898–1899* by

Josephine Knowles. Mrs. Knowles traveled to Dawson by way of the Chilkoot Pass in 1898, the same year as my characters.

Berton's book describes the ruling by the Mounted Police that women and children were not allowed to ride in the boats through the rapids at Miles Canyon and that the vessels had to be steered by men whom the police deemed as competent. However, another source I read states that the police wouldn't allow anyone through the canyon without a guide to pilot their boat. For the purposes of my story, I chose to use the rules Berton cited and interpreted the latter to mean that anyone declared competent could go through the canyon, with or without a guide.

The discovery of gold in Nome, Alaska, in 1899 brought an end to the Klondike Gold Rush. While relatively few gained great wealth off the gold from the Klondike and its tributaries, those who braved the wilds of the north to reach the goldfields there proved to themselves and the world the tenacity of humankind.

A *USA Today* bestselling author, Stacy Henrie graduated from Brigham Young University with a degree in public relations. Not long after, she switched from writing press releases and newsletters to writing inspirational historical romances. Born and raised in the West, where she currently resides with her family, she enjoys reading, road trips, interior decorating, chocolate, and most of all, laughing with her husband and kids. Her books include *Hope at Dawn*, a 2015 RITA Award finalist for excellence in romance. You can learn more about Stacy and her books by visiting her website, stacyhenrie.com.